He reached out before him, spreading the six fingers of each hand as if to stave off something that was attacking, and a gasp of breath came from his open mouth.

"Wha' is it?" the child asked, peering up from the daisy chain she had been making on the little expanse of lawn before Balam's dwelling.

Balam looked at the child with those strange, fathomless eyes, and wondered if she might recognize the fear on his face, the fear that had threatened for just a moment to overwhelm him.

The child smiled at him, chuckling a little in that strange, deep way that human children will. "Uncle Bal-bal?" she asked. "Wha' is it?"

"The Ontic Library has been breached," Balam said, his words heavy with meaning, fully aware that the child could never comprehend the gravity of them. "Pack some toys, Quav. We're going to visit some old friends."

It had been almost three years since Balam had last spoken with the Cerberus rebels, but the time had come to do so once again.

Other titles in this series:

James Axler
Outlanders®

DISTORTION
OFFENSIVE

A GOLD EAGLE BOOK FROM
W★RLDWIDE®

TORONTO • NEW YORK • LONDON
AMSTERDAM • PARIS • SYDNEY • HAMBURG
STOCKHOLM • ATHENS • TOKYO • MILAN
MADRID • WARSAW • BUDAPEST • AUCKLAND

First edition November 2010

ISBN-13: 978-0-373-63868-0

DISTORTION OFFENSIVE

Copyright © 2010 by Worldwide Library

Special thanks to Rik Hoskin for his contribution to this work.

Printed in U.S.A.

Fools are rewarded with nothing but more foolishness, but the wise are rewarded with knowledge.
—*Proverbs* 14:18

The Road to Outlands—
From Secret Government Files to the Future

Almost two hundred years after the global holocaust, Kane, a former Magistrate of Cobaltville, often thought the world had been lucky to survive at all after a nuclear device detonated in the Russian embassy in Washington, D.C. The aftermath—forever known as skydark—reshaped continents and turned civilization into ashes.

Nearly depopulated, America became the Deathlands—poisoned by radiation, home to chaos and mutated life forms. Feudal rule reappeared in the form of baronies, while remote outposts clung to a brutish existence.

What eventually helped shape this wasteland were the redoubts, the secret preholocaust military installations with stores of weapons, and the home of gateways, the locational matter-transfer facilities. Some of the redoubts hid clues that had once fed wild theories of government cover-ups and alien visitations.

Rearmed from redoubt stockpiles, the barons consolidated their power and reclaimed technology for the villes. Their power, supported by some invisible authority, extended beyond their fortified walls to what was now called the Outlands. It was here that the rootstock of humanity survived, living with hellzones and chemical storms, hounded by Magistrates.

In the villes, rigid laws were enforced—to atone for the sins of the past and prepare the way for a better future. That was the barons' public credo and their right-to-rule.

Kane, along with friend and fellow Magistrate Grant, had upheld that claim until a fateful Outlands expedition. A displaced piece of technology…a question to a keeper of the archives…a vague clue about alien masters—and their world shifted radically. Suddenly, Brigid Baptiste, the archivist, faced summary execution, and Grant a quick termination. For

Kane there was forgiveness if he pledged his unquestioning allegiance to Baron Cobalt and his unknown masters and abandoned his friends.

But that allegiance would make him support a mysterious and alien power and deny loyalty and friends. Then what else was there?

Kane had been brought up solely to serve the ville. Brigid's only link with her family was her mother's red-gold hair, green eyes and supple form. Grant's clues to his lineage were his ebony skin and powerful physique. But Domi, she of the white hair, was an Outlander pressed into sexual servitude in Cobaltville. She at least knew her roots and was a reminder to the exiles that the outcasts belonged in the human family.

Parents, friends, community—the very rootedness of humanity was denied. With no continuity, there was no forward momentum to the future. And that was the crux—when Kane began to wonder if there *was* a future.

For Kane, it wouldn't do. So the only way was out—way, way out.

After their escape, they found shelter at the forgotten Cerberus redoubt headed by Lakesh, a scientist, Cobaltville's head archivist, and secret opponent of the barons.

With their past turned into a lie, their future threatened, only one thing was left to give meaning to the outcasts. The hunger for freedom, the will to resist the hostile influences. And perhaps, by opposing, end them.

Prologue

The elderly man was solidly built, with a wispy gray beard that sprouted from his chin like the gnarled roots of a potato plant. He stood watching the waves from his hiding place in an alleyway overlooking the beachfront as the setting sun painted the Pacific Ocean in hues of red and pink and orange.

As the waves lapped against the shore, the old man pulled the glass bottle from one of the voluminous pockets of his waterproof coat. Streaks of grime and patches of sweat marred its once-pristine appearance, evidence of his long trek from his prior home in the Canadian wilds. He was there under instruction; his master had sent him to recruit, as he had sent the other graduates from Tenth City.

The sounds of crashing waves in the distance, the old man methodically broke the seal and unscrewed the cap of the bottle of home-brewed gin, then lifted the vessel to his lips. His nose wrinkled as he caught a smell of the clear brew. The fiery stench caught in the back of his nose and throat, not so much a smell as a feeling, a heat.

Closing his eyes, the old man tipped the bottle and felt the cool liquid splash past his teeth, wash against his tongue and the sides of his mouth. After a brief moment, he pulled the bottle away and spit the mouthful of gin out across the stone slabs of the sidewalk. The liquid fizzled there for a moment before running away along the incline of the alleyway and disappearing into the rudimentary opening of the local drainage system, a froth of saliva floating on its clear surface.

The elderly man stuck out his tongue, his eyes still screwed tight as he breathed out through the savage taste that now lined the inside of his mouth and stung at his lips. The raw taste of gin made him cough, and for a few moments he hacked and spluttered. Then his eyes opened and he pulled the capless bottle close once again, drawing it high until he held it over his own head. He looked up, seeing the dwindling sunlight dance across the surface of the bottle, feeling the weight of the liquid as it sloshed inside the clear glass. Then, closing his eyes once more, the old man deliberately tipped the bottle so that its contents poured over his upturned face, washing through his dirt-clotted hair and drenching his old clothes until his coat was sodden with gin.

Reeking of alcohol, the old man stepped out into the street, swaying left and right as though on the deck of a ship in a ferocious storm, and he began to heckle the nearest person, a pretty young woman rushing to the church hall with a sturdy bag over her shoulder, hoping to collect some of the newly arrived rations she had heard about. Frightened, the woman leaped back from the old man as he tottered from the alleyway and shouted nonsensically at her. Her heels clattered on the paving stones as she rushed away, but the old man had already dismissed her, moving on toward the beachfront and the next of his victims.

Prison had always been a breeding ground for recruitment, he knew. He only needed to get himself locked in a cell for utopia to begin. The utopia his master had promised for every man, woman and child on the planet Earth. The utopia he had already embraced.

Chapter 1

Every star was a different color. A thousand stars in the sky—a thousand different colors, no two the same.

It was as if the spectrum had lied to Pam all these years and that only now had she finally been allowed to open her eyes for the first time and truly see the universe around her. She wondered why the spectrum had been hiding all these marvelous hues, just out of sight, pretending to have its familiar selection of just seven bands of color when in actuality its variations were beyond comprehension.

Fifteen years old, Pam sat on the beach at the edge of the fishing ville called Hope, gazing up at the night sky as one thousand beautiful stars twinkled above her in their majestic greens and reds and blues and all those other colors that she didn't yet have names for. Beside her, Pam's boyfriend, Tony, was working at a little fire with a length of driftwood he had found washed up a ways along the coast. The driftwood stick, as well as that used for the fire itself, had once been a part of the grand pier that had jutted into the sea here, back before the earthquake had struck and a tidal wave had demolished it.

As Tony poked the fire, Pam turned her attention to the sea where the starlight twinkled across its surface like a flock of playful birds. Even in the inky darkness of night, Pam could see the breakers crashing downward as the ocean sprinted toward the shore, only to pull back at the last second, clawing at the beach with foamy fingers.

She had moved here just a few months ago, had traveled across the Outlands along with her mother and her little sister, in their hurry to escape the dreadful destruction of their home in the towering ville of Beausoleil. An aerial bombing raid had punished Beausoleil, levelling the magnificent ville in the space of a few minutes, killing the sinful and the blameless indiscriminately. Among those casualties was Pam's father, caught up in the explosion that had felled the towering Administrative Monolith where he worked. His body had never been recovered.

In less than a day, the magnificent ville of Beausoleil had been rendered uninhabitable as thick, inky smoke plumed into the skies above it, visible for miles around like a beacon signaling its fate. At that signal, brigands had rapidly descended upon the remains faster than the Magistrates could repel them. Pam's mother had not wanted to leave the ville until she found her husband, but once the brigands appeared the whole area had descended into savagery, like something from the history books, from before the Program of Unification had fixed everything in the whole world. When she saw her mom packing the few items that had survived in their shattered apartment, Pam had asked about her dad, saying that they couldn't just leave him behind.

"This is no place for little girls," Pam's mother had said, tears streaming down her face. A woman's shrill scream came from outside the ruined residential block even as she spoke—a scream that could just as well have come from Pam's mother's throat.

Pam had wanted to argue, but her sister, Rebecca, was just eight years old, and she really was a little girl.

And so together the family had exited the lurching remains of their smoldering residential block, avoiding the huge bomb craters as they hurried along the churned-up remnants of the road outside. There was a crowd on the street corner before them where two men argued loudly with a Magistrate dressed in black armor, the top half of his face hidden behind the intimidating helmet he wore. One of the men was shouting something about food, and before Pamela knew it the man threw a punch at the uniformed Mag. The solid blow connected with the official's jaw with a resounding crack, just below the extent of his protective helmet, and Pam heard herself gasp. She had never seen anyone attack a Magistrate, never in her fifteen years of life within the safe confines of Beausoleil's high walls.

As Pam watched, the black-garbed Mag staggered, doing a two-step dance to hold himself in place. As he did so, the Mag raised his right arm and the familiar form of his Sin Eater pistol appeared in his hand, propelled automatically from its wrist-mounted holster.

"Keep back!" the Magistrate ordered the crowd as he took a step toward the man who had struck him, his voice firm with anger.

The man who had struck out leered at the Mag, fury in his eyes. "Our families need to eat," he shouted, closing in on the Mag, his face up close to the Magistrate's. His colleague, an unshaved, tired-looking man, stepped over to join him. "Outlanders are taking everything, swarming inside the walls like vermin. And you aren't doing anything."

"Back!" the Mag ordered again, but the watching crowd was closing in on him now, the sounds of their growing dissatisfaction buzzing around them like a swarm of angry hornets.

Pam's mom had hissed at her to get a move on. "We can't stay here," she urged, pulling at little Rebecca's hand. She was crying silently, tears streaking her cheeks as if she'd been caught in a cloudburst.

Suddenly there was the sound of a gunshot, and the man who had been arguing with the Magistrate dropped to the ground like a sinking stone, a bloody stain blossoming on his shirt. Pam gasped and she heard her mom say an actual cuss word, which she had never done before, not ever.

"Come on, Pam," her mother urged, rushing into a lurching alleyway that stood between the wreckage of two buildings, the jagged masonry reaching above like clawed hands.

Pam hurried after her mother and Rebecca, but she looked back for just a moment when she heard more gunfire. Behind her at the street corner, the crowd was rushing at the Magistrate as he shot rounds indiscriminately at them. A red-haired woman fell to the ground, her head erupting with blood as a bullet slammed into her once-beautiful face. Beside the woman, two men, one of them quite elderly, doubled over in pain as 9 mm bullets sprayed them from the nose of the Mag's Sin Eater. And then, as Pam watched, the Mag disappeared beneath the surging group, the staccato bursts of gunfire muffled by the press of bodies.

"Come on, Pam," her mother's voice urged then, and Pam turned back to see her mother calling her from atop a little broken wall. Rebecca was clambering over it at her side, her school satchel hanging down by her hip on its leather strap. "Quickly now."

Pam had run to catch up with what remained of her

family, her shoes slipping a little on the debris that littered the ground. Within half an hour the three of them crept through the shattered ville walls and left Beausoleil forever, never once looking back at the smoking ruins that nestled amid the greenery of old Tennessee.

Tired and disheveled, Pam, her mother and sister had traveled west until they ended up at Hope, along with so many other refugees. Something was happening in their world, something bigger than any of them comprehended. The nine villes, of which Beausoleil was just one, had lost their leaders, the hybrid barons. The demarcation lines of the baronies themselves were blurring as the once-proud villes fell, one by one. The baronies had brought order to the landmass that had once been called the Deathlands and, before that, the United States of America. The gemlike villes had brought security. Now that security was disappearing, and the whole country was drifting back toward a hell state.

Hope was a fishing village on the West Coast, a small, tight-knit community of less than two hundred people. When the baronies had started to fall, a surge of refugees had found their way here, building a shantytown on its outskirts, and bringing with them overcrowding, disease and crime. What had once been an idyllic community had turned into a place where it was every man for himself. That was until the tidal wave had pummelled most of those temporary favela dwellings to the ground and, curiously, from that destruction a strange new sense of community had emerged.

Pam recalled her wonderful apartment in the residential Enclaves of Beausoleil, where life was regimented and she had had to wear a uniform to go to school. By contrast, Hope was dirty and cluttered and her classroom was a converted basement where she wasn't expected to wear a uniform. Indeed, some of her classmates didn't even wear shoes, and not through choice, either. But for all its grime and lack of sophistication, Hope was where Pam could sneak off to the beach and watch the waves, and where she and Tony could make out under the wreckage of the pier. After two months, Hope felt like home.

The ocean crashed once more against the shore and, as she chewed, Pam perceived something within those waves, the way the atoms clung together and broke apart like partners at a formal dance. And she saw, just for a moment, the way the whole dancing ocean was dragged to and fro by the pull of its bullying best friend, the moon, watching from above with its crescent sliver of cat's eye.

Smiling, Pam turned away from the crashing waves and saw Tony jab at the flames with his length of drift-wood. Sparks spit from the fire as Tony hooked at the food that he had been cooking there, submerged deep in the popping flames. She and Tony had come across a clutch of little mollusks that had been washed up by the tide as they walked along the beach earlier that evening, and Pam had suggested cooking them here while they watched the sun disappear beneath the swell of the Pacific.

"Go on," she had said. "It'll be dead romantic and that."

Tony pulled a face. He didn't go much for romance, unless it involved having a fumble under her shirt while no one was looking. "Won't your mom be worried?" he asked.

"Nah," Pamela assured him. "There's never any food

at home. She's probably out partying with someone even now."

Tony nodded. He liked Pam's mom; she was all right. But after the tidal wave had hit Hope, the whole ville had been turned upside down and everyone was scrabbling to find enough to feed themselves, even more than they had before. So when Pam said "partying," Tony knew that she really meant her mom was trading sex for food.

The weird mollusks they found washed ashore had hard shells the color of oil on water, and ranged in size from the very small to ones almost as big as Tony's clenched fist—the same fist that had knocked out Tim Brin's front tooth—but they tasted all right once you cooked them for a bit. The flesh was kind of salty, tasting like the ocean, and they could be a bit chewy, but Tony and Pam didn't mind. It was good to smell them cooking, a brackish, sharp kind of tang drifting within the charcoal smoke of the fire. After they had eaten the first few, they had just become used to the texture and the taste, and it hadn't really mattered after that.

Using his stick, Tony pulled the last of the dead creatures from the fire, licking his lips as he caught the aroma of the cooking flesh where it lay on the shale before his resting knees. Then he cast the stick aside and, wrapping his hands in the tails of his shirt to protect them, picked up the flame-hot creature and cracked open its now-brittle shell. A hunk of jellylike meat flopped about inside, its color a pink so dull that it looked almost gray, the flesh still bubbling as a smoky white trail plumed from it.

Tony offered the mollusk to his girl. "Last one," he said. "You want some?"

Pam looked at Tony and smiled. To her eyes, his face

seemed so beautiful, his fourteen-year-old skin smooth and taut, the fluffy dusting of his first beard cluttering his jaw. And she saw that the multicolored stars were reflected in his eyes, all those wonderful colors that she had never noticed before. "Half each," she told him, holding her hand out for the cooked flesh as it was cooled by the sea breeze.

Tony tore the pink-gray meat apart and handed Pam half. As he leaned close, he kissed Pam next to her lips, a slobbering touch that included his tongue licking at the side of her face like a dog. Then, gazing into each other's eyes, they brought the flesh to their mouths and, giggling, sucked the juices before chewing and swallowing.

The meat left a salty taste on their tongues, as though they were eating the ocean itself. Tony looked at Pam as he felt that delicious flesh slide down his throat, and he saw how she seemed to glow beneath the multifaceted light of the moon. Above, up in the sky, he, too, saw the multicolored display that seemed to emanate from the stars. Like gods, he thought. Gods in the sky.

KANE RUBBED THE BACK of his neck, feeling the tension there subside as he gazed out across the streets of Hope from the summit of the church steps. It was still busy out here despite day having given way to night, and a line of locals shuffled past on the steps as Kane tried to clear his whirring mind.

"Everything okay?" asked a familiar woman's voice from behind him.

Kane turned to see Brigid Baptiste pushing out of the rotting wooden doors of the old church to join him where he sat on the topmost stone step. Brigid was a beautiful woman, svelte of form with an athlete's musculature and a ballet dancer's grace. Her hair was a vibrant red-gold, the color of sunset, and she had painted her full lips to match. Her bright green eyes stared back at Kane from her pale face, like twin emeralds glinting from the snow. Where her full lips spoke of sensuality, Brigid's high forehead suggested intellect, and in reality she was both of those aspects and many more besides. Brigid had been Kane's colleague in the Cerberus operation for several years, and though their relationship was strictly platonic, their closeness was often akin to that of siblings. They shared the mystical bond of anam-charas, soul-friends destined to meet over and over through eternal reincarnation stretching along the flowing stream of time itself.

Brigid had dressed in scuffed but durable leathers over her shadow suit. The shadow suit itself was a wafer-thin bodysuit that was able to deflect knife attacks, offer protection from contaminated environments and also had other remarkable properties including the ability to regulate its wearer's body temperature.

Kane nodded at Brigid's question as she took a place beside him on the cool stone step, crouching so that her face was close to his while the refugees shuffled past them in a slow-moving line. The pair had been cooped up in the church for over fourteen hours, working nonstop as they distributed reconstituted rations to the local population. Elsewhere in the sprawling shantytown that surrounded the ville, another field team was distributing medicines where they were most needed. Theirs was a mission of mercy, and something that the Cerberus people seemed to have had very little time for over the recent months thanks to a litany of problems, both within their home base and across the globe.

Kane was a well-built man, with cropped, dark hair

and steely blue-gray eyes. Tall with a lean frame and muscular arms, Kane's physique was similar to that of a wolf, a machine built for hunting. His temperament was similar to that of a wolf, as well, both pack leader and loner as the situation demanded. Like Brigid, Kane was a member of Cerberus, an operation headquartered in Montana and dedicated to the uncovering of and resistance to a deep-rooted alien conspiracy that had threatened to overpower and subjugate humankind since the dawn of recorded time. That alien threat came from a race called the Annunaki, who had been mistaken for gods from the stars but were in fact a bored alien race who considered humans as nothing more than playthings, idle diversions along the bland, tiresome road of their millennia-long lifespans. Kane had accidentally uncovered inklings of that conspiracy when he had worked as a Magistrate in Cobaltville, learning to his disgust that the system he was tasked to uphold was in fact corrupt to its core. Kane had left Cobaltville, along with Grant, a fellow magistrate, and Brigid, an archivist with remarkable flair and the unusual ability of total memory recall. Together the three of them formed the energetic nucleus around which the sixty-strong facility of so-called Cerberus exiles based their operations.

Like Brigid, Kane had dressed in a shadow suit over which he had worn a tired-looking denim jacket, jeans and boots. Dressed as such, he could pass among Hope's locals with relative anonymity, although perhaps a perceptive individual might notice the proud way in which he carried himself, a vestige of his Magistrate training.

"Just wondering when it got so dark," Kane finally said as he gazed out toward the beach, the sound of

crashing waves carrying over the hubbub of the crowd.
He didn't really expect an answer.

Brigid scanned the dark sky, spying the pinpricks
of light where the stars twinkled between the looming
clouds. "It's never that dark," she assured Kane. "Not
if you know where to look."

In silence, Kane nodded his agreement as the line
of locals continued to snake slowly into the church to
collect the handouts the Cerberus team had brought.
They were military rations, many of them recovered
from certain storage centers and redoubts that Kane
had recalled from his time as a Magistrate. The rations
had been acquired in a series of perfunctory raids.

"Guess we should be getting back inside," Kane said,
"before Grant thinks we've deserted him."

Brigid's straight white teeth glinted in the moonlight
as she smiled. "Grant knows you'd never do that, Kane.
The pair of you are pretty near inseparable."

"He says that about you and me, you know," Kane
said as he stood.

"No, he says we're *insufferable*," Brigid corrected
him, slapping her hand against Kane's rear to brush off
the dust that clung to him from the step.

Kane laughed as he made his way past the milling
crowd, through the shadow-filled porch and back into
the church hall. Within, the hall was lit with flaming
torches held in sconces, and a line of people stood waiting for their turn to receive their allocated rations from
the crates that Kane, Grant, Brigid and what passed for
the local authorities had off-loaded from the Mantas
earlier that day. Other volunteers from the local area
helped, ladling bowls of soup and distributing bottles
of clean water that had been filtered clear of contami-
nants by a pump system operating in the back room of

the church. The pump continued to chug as volunteers added more water to its intake system.

The people of Hope seemed buoyant despite their current plight, and an all-pervading air of "getting on with it" appeared to be the order of the day.

With over five thousand starving people in the ville, the process of allocation based on need was slow but necessary. Many of the locals had arrived carrying bowls and buckets, sacks and carry-alls to obtain as much as they could for themselves and their struggling, starving families. But the two young men at the front of the line hadn't brought bowls or bags to transport the ration bars and purified water. Instead, as Kane watched from the far side of the room, a sixth sense triggering in the back of his mind, the two young men produced a pair of snub-nosed handguns and jabbed them in the face of his partner, the ex-Mag called Grant.

Chapter 2

"Gun," Kane snapped out in a harsh whisper, taking another step into the vast hall with Brigid just a pace behind him.

But before Kane and Brigid could venture farther into the busy church hall, several more people stepped from the ranks of the queuing locals and brought arms out from the hiding places within their dirty-looking clothes. People screamed and shouted, and everyone in the room dropped to the floor in unison as if struck by a massive weight. Kane stepped backward as he dropped, disguising himself within the shadows of the door. When he looked around he saw that Brigid Baptiste was just across from him, similarly lurking in the thick shadows cast by the porch of the antechamber, her body taut like a coiled spring.

"Hand over everything you've got left," the leader shouted as he waved his snub-nosed .38 at Grant's face, "or you're going to be breathing out of a third nostril."

"Oh, no, son," Grant growled, "you don't want to be pulling this shit with me."

Grant was a huge man, with broad shoulders and dark skin. Though heavy, his body was entirely muscle, with not an ounce of fat in evidence. His black hair was cropped very close to his scalp, but he wore a luxurious gunfighter's mustache. Right now, Grant wore a black

undershirt and loose combat pants, while his Kevlar
trench coat remained hanging over the back of a chair
behind him. For this rare occasion, curse the damn luck,
he had left his wrist-mounted Sin Eater automatic pistol
in the secure locker of the Manta vehicle parked around
the back of the church grounds.

The lead stick-up artist thrust the barrel of his pistol
closer to Grant's face, and he cocked the hammer with
a sadistic sneer curling his lip. He was a young man, no
older than seventeen by Grant's estimate, and already he
wore a fierce scar down the left side of his face, cutting
a white streak through the dark stubble and red acne
that covered his jaw. Grant's dark eyes flicked across
the room, noting the man's accomplices in an instant
before turning his attention back to their leader. They
were all dressed in muted, unwashed clothes, and none
of them looked to be much older than twenty, maybe
twenty-five.

"I done fucks like you for just looking at me, man,"
the leader announced through gritted teeth. "I'll
do everyone in this room if you fuck with me, you
understand?"

Grant fixed his dark eyes on the bandit leader as,
somewhere close to the door, a dog barked anxiously.
"Oh, yeah," he said softly, almost conspiratorially, "I
understand." Hands held loosely at his sides, Grant took
a step back toward the open crate of rations. "You want
me to hand them over one by one, or are you and your
boyfriends going to come here and carry a crate out?"

The gunman glared at Grant, irritation on his frantic
features as he considered his options. "You. You can
carry it," the man decided.

Grant snorted, his eyes still fixed on the nervous
young gunman. "Can't help you," he explained. "This

is a two-man job, buddy. You want to feel the weight of this bad boy if you don't believe me."

Irritated, the gunman spit a curse and strode toward the line of tables, stepping onto the nearest desk and clambering over it, his hollow boot heels echoing loudly against the wood like the clip-clopping of a horse. As he did so, Grant seized his opportunity, his leg snapping out and his foot slamming into the front of the table as the gunman climbed onto its surface.

The table's legs screeched as they dragged across the floor with the impact of Grant's powerful kick, and the gunman found himself toppling forward, losing his balance as the table disappeared from under him. The young man snapped off a shot at Grant, a bullet blasting toward the huge ex-Mag with a resounding crack, several people screaming in its wake.

Grant felt the bullet cut the air just past his ear, missing him by a quarter of an inch, but he was already rushing forward to meet his assailant. All around the church hall, the gunman's allies were beginning to react, turning their own weapons on the man who had attacked their leader.

"Bunch of amateurs," Kane muttered as he and Brigid readied themselves in their hiding place in the shadows of the porch. As the gunmen targeted Grant while he was safely protected behind the tumbling form of their leader, it gave Kane and Brigid ample opportunity to mount a surprise attack from the rear.

Over by the line of tables, Grant pumped his sledgehammer fist into the lead gunman's thorax, knocking the man back up into the air as he continued to fall, driving the breath painfully from his throat. The gunman toppled sideways, crying out in pain as he slammed against the wooden floor with bone-shaking finality.

A trained ex-Mag like Kane, Grant was working on instinct now, and his leg snapped out once more to kick the snub-nosed .38 out of the gunman's hand before he could bring it to bear. A stray bullet powered out from the pistol's barrel as it flew out of the gunman's hand and across the floor, embedding itself in the side of the water pump, water spraying everywhere.

As the gunman fell, his companions began blasting shots from their own weapons at Grant, peppering the wall behind the ex-Mag with shots as he leaped out of their path and rolled behind one of the tables. From his crouching position behind the scant protection of a desk, Grant extended the outstretched toe of his booted foot, hooking the nearby chair and scooting it across the floor toward him. His long Kevlar coat hung from the back, and Grant would need that if he was to make it through the next ten seconds alive.

Grant scanned the area to either side of him, seeing the other volunteers ducking behind the furniture as bullets drilled into the wall ahead. They looked frightened.

Abruptly the gunfire stopped. A moment later, Grant heard a voice from the other side of the desk as one of the gunmen spoke. "Richie?" the man shouted. "Richie, you okay, bro?"

Richie—the gunman whom Grant had knocked to the floor—groaned, his response something less than an actual word.

The speaker continued, issuing instructions to his people. "The guy went behind there. Ain't nowhere else for him to go. C'mon."

The man was half right. Grant was trapped behind the desk, but he didn't plan on going far. With a thought, he activated the hidden Commtact communication device that lay beneath his skin, subvocalizing his command. "Kane, back me up."

Kane's reply was a single, whispered "Copy." That one word was carried through the pintels of the subdermal communicator and straight through Grant's skull-casing as though the other man stood right beside him.

Commtacts were top-of-the-line communication devices that had been discovered among the artifacts in Redoubt Yankee some years before. The Commtacts featured sensor circuitry incorporating an analog-to-digital voice encoder that was embedded in a subject's mastoid bone. Once the pintels made contact, transmissions were picked up by the wearer's auditory canals, and dermal sensors transmitted the electronic signals directly through the skull casing, vibrating the ear canal. In theory, if a wearer went completely deaf he or she would still be able to hear, after a fashion, using the Commtact.

His brief exchange with Kane concluded, Grant was moving, leaping from cover and raising the Kevlar-weave coat out before him like a shield. The gunmen began firing instantly as Grant ran toward a nearby serving table, and he snapped the coat out at them, so that the long tails of heavy material whipped across the nearest thug's face.

The gunman howled as the heavy coat struck him, leaving a red mark like a blush across his right cheek. He blasted another shot from the .357 Colt King Cobra in his hand. The gunman was distracted by the coat and the heavy bullet flew wide, allowing Grant to reach his objective.

Grant grabbed the handle of the pot of boiling soup, lifting it from the hot plate and tossing it out before him at the lead thug. As the angry gunman took another step toward Grant, the bubbling soup splashed across his face, scalding him like raking fire across his exposed flesh. In an instant, the gunman forgot what he was doing and toppled backward, reaching for his burning face as he hollered in his pain. Grant ignored him, leaping over the desk and flipping the half-empty soup pot out before him like an extension of his arm, a bowler rolling a bowling ball.

The heavy pot clanged against the skull of the next stick-up man with a sound like the tolling of a bell. The man fell backward against the floor, his nose caved in and blood pouring down his face. Grant leaped atop his fallen foe, lashing out again with the heavy pot he held in his right hand as bullets slapped against the Kevlar shield he held in his left.

By then, Kane and Brigid had emerged from the shadows. Before the gunmen could react, they joined the fray, felling two of their number in a swift, coordinated attack. Running, Kane drove a ram's-head fist into the lower back of the nearest gunman before the man even realized he was under attack, forcing the man's legs to give way so that he fell to the floor in the grip of paralysis—whether temporary or permanent Kane didn't much care at that instant.

Next to Kane, Brigid dropped low, sweeping her outstretched leg at another gunman, connecting with his knee so hard that it popped the man's kneecap with an audible *tock* that sounded like the clucking of a person's tongue. The man tumbled to the wooden floor, crying out in a mixture of pain and astonishment as he turned to face his beautiful attacker. Brigid didn't even give the man a second to retaliate. Her flat palm lashed out and bruised his windpipe in a sharp, savage jab. The man's eyes rolled in his head as he sank into blissful unconsciousness.

As Kane disarmed a third gunman, Grant tossed aside the soup pot and slapped out at his own opponent's gun, knocking it aside as the bandit reeled off a burst of gunfire that echoed in the enclosed space of the church hall. Then Grant drove a massive fist into the man's gut, knocking the wind out of him and lifting him off his feet, such was the power of that incredible blow. As the man struggled to recover, coughing and spluttering from the savage punch to his gut, Grant drove his fist downward and into the man's head, breaking his cheek-bone and knocking him across the room. The gunman staggered until he tumbled over a serving table before flopping to the floor behind it.

Grant looked up and saw that Kane had dispatched his own opponent, but the final gunman was lifting his pistol and aiming it at the back of Kane's head.

"Get down!" Grant shouted to his partner as his left arm whipped out with the Kevlar trench coat once again.

Kane ducked and a bullet blasted overhead. At the same instant, Grant's coat wrapped around the gun-man's outstretched arm like a rope. As the bullet zipped harmlessly across the room, Grant yanked the coat back with such swiftness that the gunman found his arm dragged backward and his feet pulled from under him. He struggled to keep up with the sudden momentum.

Grant let go of the coat and the gunman staggered onward, hauled past the ex-Mag with the movement of the dragging coat. As he passed, Grant drove his knee into the gunman's side, knocking him to the floor. As the stick-up man crashed downward, Grant fell upon him, slapping away the hand holding the pistol and driving his other hand down to hit the man's face with its heel. The gunman was knocked senseless, his head slamming against the wooden floors with a loud, hollow echo.

"Everyone okay?" Grant asked as he pulled himself away from the final stick-up artist.

Around the church hall, the timid locals began to rise once more, smiling tentatively as they saw that Grant, Kane and Brigid had disabled all of their would-be robbers. And, spontaneously, a ripple of applause broke out among the people in that church as they showed their gratitude to their saviors.

However, hidden among the shadows near the church doorway, one woman didn't applaud. Instead, her tanned face betrayed no emotion as she watched the scene with flashing dark eyes from beneath the hood of her jacket, her faithful dog waiting at her side.

Despite the disguising nature of the loose, ragged clothes she wore, it was clear that she was a tall woman, with a slender build and an economic lightness of movement. Her face was tanned with an olive complexion, with eyes the color of rich chocolate. The woman reached up with the long fingers of her slender hand, brushing a few rogue wisps of her dark hair back under the hood, pulling the front of the hood itself down lower, the better to mask her face.

As the crowd continued to congratulate the three Cerberus warriors, the woman turned and pushed her way past the milling crowd and out of the church hall, the dog obediently trotting along at her heels. The dog was some strange mongrel, with coarse, wiry fur and the look of a coyote about it. Its eyes were exceptionally pale, washed out to a blue so faint as to be almost white.

The woman stopped at the bottom of the stone steps that led to the church hall, gazing back over her shoulder for a moment to ensure that the Cerberus people weren't following her. But no, they hadn't spotted her among the crowds, had no reason to suspect she might be here. She had come seeking food, like the other residents of the shattered ville of Hope, but she hadn't expected to bump into familiar faces like theirs. Her name was Rosalia, and she had met with the Cerberus rebels once before.

Rosalia had been here six weeks ago, when the earth-quake had rumbled through the ground and the towering tidal wave had pummeled the beachfront. She had been a bodyguard then, in the employ of a local brigand called Tom Carnack, whose operation stretched into the Californian desert. Her position had put her at odds with the objectives of the Cerberus personnel, and she had clashed with Kane, Brigid and Grant, along with another operative called Domi, whose skin was an eerie white the color of bone.

Carnack had been killed during the encounter with Cerberus, and his operation all but destroyed. Now a few splinter factions of Carnack's group remained, squabbling among themselves and with no clear leader emerging. And so Rosalia found herself once again out on her own, struggling to survive.

With no employer and no place to call home, Rosalia had found herself back in Hope, accompanied by the strange mongrel dog. What remained of the shanty dwellings had been reduced to a claustrophobic rabbit's warren, which suited Rosalia fine. She could hide here, another refugee among the population of strangers until she was ready to move on. There was the nunnery, of course, just over the border, where she had been trained.

Rosalia knew that she would always be welcome there if nowhere else.

Right now, however, she required rations and clean water, but she felt instinctively that revealing herself to Kane and his team would be foolhardy. Their business had not ended well. Better, then, that they thought her dead and dismissed her from their overly moralistic minds.

Rosalia hurried on, making her way from the church doors before ducking into a side street, the faithful mutt keeping pace with her. Rosalia had found the dog six weeks ago, while she had been wandering the Californian desert following the destruction of Carnack's base, and the two had become companions on the road. Not given to sentimentality, Rosalia had elected not to give the hound a name, merely calling it "Dog" or "Mutt" or "Belly-on-legs." The dog didn't seem to care, happy to have human company, sharing its warmth with Rosalia wherever she slept. The dog itself was a strange, nervous animal, inquisitive but slightly wary around strangers, often hiding behind Rosalia as they walked the streets. That nervousness served her well, for it meant the hound would wake at the slightest noise or movement and would bark at any shadow it didn't recognize. On more than one occasion, the dog's sudden barking had woken Rosalia and saved her from being robbed or attacked while she slept in one of the empty, ramshackle buildings that remained dotted around the fishing ville.

Dog whined, and Rosalia peered down at it. Like herself, Dog could feel the gnawing in its belly as hunger threatened to consume it. It wouldn't do to go hungry simply because of the Cerberus Magistrates and their interruption of her daily routine. If she didn't eat, she would become weak, and once that happened Rosalia would become a slave to circumstance, or she would never eat again and simply lie down in the street to die as she had seen others do.

There, she said in her mind as she looked back up the street, her predatory instincts rising. Exiting the church, a young couple made their way down the stone steps, going slowly so that their child could keep pace with them. The child was a toddler, and the mother held its hand as it slowly navigated the hard steps to the street. Rosalia's eyes were on the male's bag, small but full of rations and two bottles of purified water. The young woman cheered as the child clambered down the final step, and it looked up at her and laughed. They were simple folks, Rosalia recognized, naive and lacking street smarts. Ville folk turned refugee with the destruction of Beausoleil or Snakefishville, most probably. Educated to be idiots.

And if the child starved because of her actions?

Better the child than me, Rosalia reasoned.

Beneath the waxing moon, the couple turned into the side street where Rosalia waited by the wall, hidden in the shadows of the brickwork. She was about to step forward, planning merely to brush past them and take the bag before bolting in the manner of a common street thief, when she saw movement at the far end of the narrow street. Two tough-looking youths had followed the couple and their child, clearly harboring the same idea as Rosalia. She saw the glint of metal catch the moonlight as one of the young men unsheathed a switch-blade, and the whisper of a smile crossed her perfect lips. It was a bored smile, the kind that came when one could finally sense a break in the tedium. This would be Rosalia's break from tedium.

One of the young punks began laughing, a sinister, braying sound that echoed off the walls of the enclosed street. It was meant to terrify, and the young couple walked faster, glancing over their shoulders as they rushed down the street. Then the two punks began to sprint, rushing along the street and surrounding the young couple in an instant, like a pack of wild dogs, howling and laughing as they did so, the animalistic noises echoing off the walls. Two more young thugs had appeared from the far end of the alleyway, and another stepped out of a doorway on the far side from Rosalia's own hiding place, where he had been waiting just out of sight, a bend in the alley hiding her from him.

"Got something we want, Mr. Man," one of the punks announced, pointing to the modest bag of rations he had acquired from the church.

"Keep away," the man spit, reaching for his woman's elbow and urging her onward.

The five-strong gang paced around the young couple, hemming them in and laughing among themselves. Another knife appeared in one punk's hand, and Rosalia noted how weedy he looked, the arm that held the knife little more than skin pulled over bone.

"We went to eat, but they didn't feed us enough," the leering leader of the punks explained, his tone mocking. "We want more."

Ironically, Rosalia could well believe that. These punks looked emaciated, wasting away like the fishing town around them.

The man stopped, standing protectively before his partner and child even as the group continued to circle them. "Get away," he instructed. "We need to eat, too."

"No, Mr. Man," the lead punk said. "Not you."

Rosalia stepped forward then, while the eyes of the teenage gang members were fixed on the man and his wife, intimidating them with the threat of casual violence. With two long-legged strides, she was next to the nearest punk, and without warning her hand jabbed out and drove into the soft, fleshy part beneath his rib cage. He yelped and fell to the ground, his eyes wide and his tongue lolling in his open mouth. Though he didn't know it yet, his kidney had ruptured under the impact, and internal bleeding would fill and devour him in the next two hours.

As one, the group of would-be robbers turned to see the hooded woman in their presence.

"Who th—!"

Rosalia didn't give the little punk enough time to even finish his sentence. Already her right leg was swinging high off the ground to kick the gang member in the face, and his nose exploded in a hideous burst of scarlet.

As the punk fell backward, Rosalia dropped and lashed out behind her as another of the gang slashed at her with his knife. The blade whizzed over her head, and Rosalia continued backward, driving the sharp corner of her crooked elbow into the young hoodlum's groin. The punk screamed out as white-hot pain speared through his genitals, and Rosalia heard something soft squelch beneath the impact of her savage blow. The knife-wielder toppled forward, his cry of pain echoing in the enclosed space of the narrow street, and Rosalia snatched the blade from his hand as she flipped him over her back and into the next gang member, who was running toward her.

The running gang member collided with his flailing

comrade, and both of them crashed to the street with finality.

Still low on the ground, Rosalia turned to see the final would-be robber grab the woman's hair and drag the knife he held across her exposed throat, just short of cutting her but still close enough to make her cry out. Behind her, Rosalia's dog barked once, but she dismissed him from her mind, her hands a practiced blur of movement. An instant later, the stolen knife left her hand and sailed through the air, connecting in less than a second with the final gang member's right eye, plunging deep into the eye socket. The punk screamed as he staggered backward, the hostage he had been holding forgotten.

"You fucking bitch, you blinded me," the punk cried as he staggered back against the wall behind him. The knife was embedded in his eye, viscous liquid oozing down his cheek.

"No, I haven't," Rosalia told him calmly as she stood up and approached her struggling foe. "Not yet." With that, she pulled her own eight-inch blade from its hiding place in her voluminous sleeve, and thrust it into the worthless punk's remaining eye socket, ramming it so hard that she heard the bone crack.

As the frightened young couple ran down the street away from the scene of carnage, their child wailing in terror, Rosalia checked the pockets of her fallen foes. Riffling through their possessions, she snagged a half-dozen ration bars and two bottles of water. Not much, but enough for her and the mutt. The dog whined hopefully as it saw its mistress break the foil of a ration bar, snapping the end off. Rosalia handed the mongrel the broken end of the ration bar, telling it to make the food last, even though she knew it wouldn't understand or heed her advice.

As the gang lay there, groaning and struggling to recover from the woman's deadly attack, Rosalia and the dog exited the street and disappeared into the night.

Life in Hope could be hard. Only the strongest would survive.

Chapter 3

The Cerberus trio had spent the night in the spare rooms of the church warden, an aging man whose name was Vernor, but they awoke early and made their way out to the beach at Brigid's insistence.

"We spend half our lives cooped up inside a mountain," Brigid had insisted, referring to the hidden Cerberus redoubt in Montana where the team was based, "and the other half fighting for our lives. Let's go take a look at the ocean and remind ourselves what it is we're fighting for."

Grant agreed and, albeit with a reluctant grunt, Kane ultimately agreed, too. He'd much sooner spend another hour in bed, catching up on some much-needed rest, but he knew there was no reasoning with the red-haired archivist when she got like this.

When the three of them reached the beachfront, Brigid rushed off toward the rolling waves while Grant hung back to talk with Kane.

"Everything okay?" Grant asked, his voice a low rumble like distant thunder.

"What, with me?" Kane replied. "Sure. Why do you ask?"

"You just seem—" Grant shrugged "—I dunno, like you'd sooner be somewhere else."

Kane looked at Grant, fixing his trusty partner in his steely stare. "No, this is… Well, it's nice," Kane said, sweeping his hands before him to take in the vista of the sandy beach and the churning turquoise waves of the Pacific as a quintet of seagulls swooped across its surface, squawking to one another. "Just makes a weird change from the usual."

"Beating the crap out of Annunaki stone gods and their screwed-up minions, you mean?" Grant asked lightly, the humor clear from his tone.

Kane laughed. "Yeah, something like that." With that, he and Grant joined Brigid at the ocean's edge, where she had removed her boots to wade in the spume-dappled water.

Though meant in jest, Kane knew that Grant's statement had an air of truth to it. Just ten days before, Kane and Grant had found themselves battling with a stone-like being called Ullikummis, who had returned from the stars after almost five thousand years in exile from his Annunaki brethren. The Annunaki had been a constant thorn in the side of the Cerberus warriors since their earliest days as a team. Once mistaken for space gods, the Annunaki were lizardlike, alien visitors who assumed different aspects in their ultimate quest to subjugate and subvert humankind, denying it from reaching its full potential. Primary among those so-called gods was the ruthless Enlil, whose subtle planning and mastery of deception made him a formidable foe.

Ullikummis was, in fact, Enlil's son, his lizardlike body genetically altered to serve a specific purpose—to be his father's personal assassin. But approximately five thousand years ago, something had gone wrong in Ullikummis's assassination attempt on a god called Teshub, and Enlil had disowned his scion, exiling him to space, imprisoned within an asteroid.

Less than a month ago, Ullikummis reappeared when

his rock prison crash-landed in the Canadian heartland, and the stone-clad Annunaki prince had soon indoctrinated a small group of loyal followers from the local populace. Three Cerberus operatives had been among those would-be followers, including Brigid Baptiste herself, who had found the stone lord's Svengali-like instruction almost impossible to resist. Accompanied by their colleague Domi, Kane and Grant had led an assault on Ullikummis's stone base, freeing Brigid and the others and destroying the eerie headquarters that Ullikummis had created from the rocks and named Tenth City. Ullikummis himself had been pushed into a superhot oven by Kane, where his rock body had been blasted with jets of fire until it was reduced to ash.

"Come on, guys," Brigid called, her cheery voice intruding on Kane's somber thoughts.

Kane looked up and saw Brigid wading in the shallow waves of the ocean, her pant legs rolled up to just below her knees.

"It's lovely and cool," Brigid told them.

Grant had located a large, flat rock, which he used as a seat while he removed his own boots and carefully folded his trench coat. "My feet have been in boots so long I think they're getting engaged," Grant rumbled as he wiggled his dark-skinned toes.

Kane snorted at his partner's remark, wondering for a moment how long it had been since *he* had last been dressed for anything other than action. His gaze swept out across the rolling ocean, watching the early-morning sunlight play on its ever-changing surface as it rushed to meet with the shore. Even this early, Kane could see several small fishing boats making their way out into open ocean. Then he turned, taking in the beach and the little fishing ville that had been built along its edge, the clutch of little two- and three-story buildings that sat as a solid reminder of man's tenacity to survive. Down there, a little way along the beach, a few struts of rotting wood marked where the fishing pier had once stood, jutting into the ocean. Kane had been on that pier when it had collapsed, battling with a beautiful, sword-wielding dancing girl called Rosalia. As Kane smiled, recalling the antagonistic nature of the dancing girl, his eyes focused on two figures crouching in the shadows of the broken pier. Definitely human, neither figure was moving.

While Grant and Brigid kicked at the water with their bare feet, Kane padded silently across the sand, taking to a light jog as he made his way toward the pier and the figures underneath. Kane noticed the remnants of a little camp fire as he approached the pier, a clutch of broken shells—two dozen in all—littered all around it. He could see now that the figures at the pier were quite young, still teenagers, a boy and a girl.

"You okay?" Kane called as he slowed his pace to a trot.

Neither teen acknowledged him; neither even looked up at the sound of his voice. They were sitting on the sand, very still, the girl's legs stretched before her while the boy had pulled his knees up and had his arms wrapped around them as though to stave off the cold.

"Hey?" Kane tried again. "You guys need some help?"

An alarm was going off in the back of Kane's mind, an old instinct from his days as a Magistrate, recognizing danger before he had consciously acknowledged it. There was something wrong with the teenagers, something eerie and out of place. They were just sitting there unmoving, like statues.

When he reached the wrecked underside of the pier, Kane crouched beneath the low-hanging crossbeams and made his way to the two figures waiting there. They were too still, and Kane unconsciously checked for the weight of the Sin Eater handgun that was strapped to his right arm, its wrist holster hidden beneath the sleeve of his denim jacket.

"You kids all right?" Kane prompted again, slowing and looking around the shadow-thick area of the pier as he warily approached the young couple.

The girl had dirty-blond hair that almost matched the wet sand of the beach, and she was dressed in a T-shirt and cutoffs that showed off her girlish figure. The boy had dyed his short hair the color of plum, and wore a ring through one nostril that glinted in the early-morning sunlight over the fluffy beginnings of an adolescent's beard. Like the girl, he was dressed in cutoffs, though his shirt was long-sleeved where hers stopped just past her bony shoulders.

For a moment Kane took them to be dead, but then he saw the slight rise and fall of the girl's chest. She was still breathing at least, and Kane scrambled over to her, grasping her by her shoulders and shaking her.

"Wake up," Kane urged. "Come on, now." In his days as a Cobaltville Magistrate, Kane had seen people in various states of semiconsciousness and delirium, and he knew the first thing he had to do was try to rouse the suspect. He slapped lightly at the boy's face to try to pull him out of whatever trance he had fallen into. "Hey, hey—snap out of it."

Brigid and Grant had left the sea and traipsed over the beach to join Kane at the little shelter beneath the ruined pier.

"What's going on?" Grant asked as he ducked his huge frame to peer beneath the wooden crossbeams.

Kane glanced up at his colleagues, seeing that Grant wore his coat and boots once more, while Brigid Baptiste remained barefoot, carrying her own boots in one hand by their wide openings.

"I thought they were dead, but they're not," Kane explained briefly. "But I can't seem to wake them up."

Brigid made her way beneath the jagged crossbeams and knelt beside Kane, while Grant stood at the opening.

"I'll go back into town and see if I can get some medical help," Grant announced. "Stay in touch," he added, tapping the side of his face with his finger before turning to make his way up the beach. He meant by Commtact, and didn't need to spell that fact out to his colleagues.

"What's happened to them?" Brigid asked as she shook the girl gently, trying to rouse her while Kane focused his attention on the boy.

"No idea," Kane admitted. "Flesh is cold so I'd guess they've been out here all night, but this is more than simply the effects of exposure."

"I concur," Brigid agreed as the blond-haired girl finally started to groan as if waking from a deep slumber.

"Wh—" the girl groaned. "What is…it?"

"It's okay," Brigid told her in a sympathetic voice. "You're okay, you're safe."

The teen boy was waking up, too, and Kane reassured him in a sharp, professional tone as he held his head steady and stared into his eyes. The pupils were normal and reactive, and there was no trace of blood in the whites.

"What happened to you guys?" Kane asked, turning his attention from one to the other.

The girl was staring at Brigid, her eyes wide. Slowly, she reached up and grabbed a lock of Brigid's vibrant hair. "It's so colorful," she muttered. "Does it hurt?"

"My hair?" Brigid asked, perplexed. "No, it doesn't hurt. It's hair, just like yours."

The girl shook her head, smiling with disbelief. "There are things in your hair," she said, "hidden in the angles. They live in the shadows, making the tangles their home. The tangles of your hair turn back on themselves, creating non-space, like a tesseract. That's where the things live. That's where you hide your memories."

Brigid looked at the young woman, a disconcerting sense of fear gripping her. At first she had thought that the girl had seen lice there, but that wasn't what she was describing at all. A tesseract was a dimensional anomaly, a place that appeared bigger on the inside than it did from without. An advanced mathematical concept, a tesseract was something that a girl of that age wouldn't normally be speaking of, Brigid reasoned. And yet, the way she had used the term, it was as though she could see it as she looked into Brigid's glossy mane of sunset-colored hair. To see the impossible.

"My name's Brigid," the woman offered, trying to remain calm despite the strange turn in the conversation. "What's yours?"

The teenager looked at Brigid, her blue eyes fixed on the older woman's curls as she ran them through her fingers once more. "Pam," she said. "I'm Pam. Your hair hides lots of secrets, Brigid. I wish mine could do that."

Beside Pam, the other teen had started muttering,

too, and Kane helped him to his feet and led him out of the dark shelter of the pier with Brigid bringing the girl along shortly after. "Watch your head," Kane instructed as he ducked into the sunlight. "Let's walk it off together, okay?"

Kane walked the youth in a little circuit across the beach, instructing him to take deep breaths and get himself together. As they walked, Kane's Commtact came to life and Grant advised that he had found the local doctor and would be along shortly.

A couple of minutes later, having quizzed the teenagers some more and assured themselves that the two were all right—physically, at least—Kane took Brigid to one side and asked what she made of them.

"They're whacked out on something," Brigid concluded. "The girl's seeing visions wherever she looks. She told me the sea was being dragged to and fro by the moon."

Kane grimaced. "That's kind of true, I guess. You know, with tides and so on."

To Brigid, it sounded as if Kane was trying to convince himself. "Teenage girls don't say things like that, Kane," she told him. "She was talking about a tesseract being hidden within the angles of my hair. A place where I kept my memories."

"They've been smoking something, all right," Kane growled, looking around the campfire for evidence of cigarette butts or drug-taking equipment. There was nothing there; all he could see were the shells of smoke-damaged shellfish, cracked and empty.

"Or perhaps eating it," Brigid realized as she crouched by the empty mollusk shells to put her boots back on. "I think they had a little snack out here, Kane—look."

Kane cocked an eyebrow as he picked up and

examined one of the empty shells between thumb and forefinger. "Breakfast?" he suggested.

"More likely a midnight snack," Brigid told him, gathering up several shells and peering at them. They were different sizes, and each had been burned so that they were streaked with black, but they appeared to be of the same creature type.

"What are they?" Kane asked.

Brigid peered at them for a long moment, turning them on the palm of her hand, her brow furrowed.

"Baptiste?" Kane urged when she didn't respond.

"I don't know," Brigid admitted, mystified. In another person, this admission may have seemed innocent, but Kane knew that Brigid Baptiste had a phenomenal knowledge base, augmented by a rare natural quirk known as an eidetic memory, which meant she could visually reproduce in her mind's eye anything that she had ever seen. And as an ex-archivist and natural scholar, Brigid Baptiste had seen quite a lot. In many ways, she seemed more like a walking encyclopedia than a person when challenged to produce theories.

When Brigid looked up, she saw Kane's puzzled expression.

"No ideas?" he asked.

"It's from the same genetic strain as mollusks and crustaceans," Brigid assured him, "but I can't place the type. Not off the top of my head, anyway."

"And that's a lot of head," Kane mumbled.

As they spoke, Grant returned, accompanied by the church warden and a local medical practitioner called Mallory Price. Price was a tall, gangly woman with a gaunt face and thin blond hair, and she looked very much as if she had just been woken up.

"What do we have?" Mallory asked as she approached

the two teenagers, glancing over at Kane and Brigid. Her voice was husky, as if she had spent a lifetime shouting or smoking. Kane couldn't tell which.

"I found them in a trancelike state under the pier," Kane explained as he joined the medical woman. "They just didn't seem to want to wake up."

"The girl said some stuff," Brigid added as she walked over to join them, her boots back on her feet once more. "Unusual things, not what you'd expect from a teen."

Price checked the two teenagers briefly, but other than their general disorientation, she could find nothing ostensibly wrong with them. "They're both suffering a little bit from exposure," she told Kane and the others, "but they're young. They'll be fine."

"What about their altered state of mind when he found them?" Kane asked.

The woman shrugged. "Teenagers being teenagers," she said. "Who knows what they're getting hooped up on. You probably did the same when you were their age."

Overhearing this, Grant laughed. "Oh, you don't know Kane," he muttered.

Kane opened his fist and showed the mollusk shell to Mallory. "Have you seen one of these before, Doc?" he asked, letting her handle the little shell.

The medical woman turned it over in her hands. "What is that?" she queried. "Some kind of snail?"

The church warden, an older man called Vernor, with thinning hair that was turning gray at the temples, had made his way over by then, and he sucked at his teeth as he peered at the shell in Mallory's hands. "Could be a crab, maybe?" he suggested.

"Could be a lot of things, Vern," Kane agreed.

The old church warden looked up at Kane with an expression of concern. "Seen a few of these things wash up just lately. You think this has something to do with how these kids are acting, Kane?"

"Let's get these kids inside and see whether we can make any sense out of all of this," Kane suggested noncommittally.

"I KNOW."

The words came as a whisper from the thin gray lips of a creature called Balam. He was fifteen hundred years old and he had been born as the last of the Archons, a race that confirmed a pact between the Annunaki and the Tuatha de Danaan millennia before.

He was a small figure, humanoid in appearance but with long, thin arms and a wide, bulbous head that narrowed to a pointed chin. Entirely hairless, Balam's skin was a pink so washed out as to appear gray. Within his strangely expressive face, Balam had two wide, up-slanting eyes, as black as bottomless pools, their edges tapering to points. His tiny mouth resided below two small, flat nostrils that served as his nose.

He reached out before him, spreading the six fingers of each hand as if to stave off something that was attacking, and a gasp of breath came from his open mouth.

There was a child playing in the underground garden that spread before him. She was human in appearance and perhaps three years old, wearing a one-piece suit in a dark indigo blue that seemed to match the simple garment that Balam himself wore. The child turned at Balam's words, her pretty, snow-blond hair swishing behind her in simple ponytail, her large, blue eyes wide with curiosity.

"Wha' is it?" the child asked, peering up from the

daisy chain she had been making on the little expanse of lawn before Balam's dwelling.

Balam looked at the child with those strange, fathomless eyes and wondered if she might recognize the fear on his face, the fear that had threatened for just a moment to overwhelm him.

The child smiled at him, chuckling a little in that strange, deep way that human children will. "Uncle Balbal?" she asked. "Wha' is it?"

"The Ontic Library has been breached," Balam said, his words heavy with meaning, fully aware that the child could never comprehend the gravity of them. "Pack some toys, Quav. We're going to visit some old friends."

With that, Balam ushered the child—known as Little Quav after her late mother—back into their dwelling in the underground city of Agartha and prepared her for the interphase trip that would take them halfway around the world. It had been almost three years since Balam had last spoken with the Cerberus rebels, but the time had come to do so once again.

Chapter 4

The Cerberus warriors made their way back to the church hall, along with Vernor and the two teenagers, while Mallory returned to her surgery. The kid with the dyed hair—Tony—was getting edgy, and he started to ask some awkward questions. He'd been in trouble before, Kane realized, recognizing the signs, and he wondered if the youth might bolt before they could question him more fully about his altered state of mind.

Noticing the teen's discomfort, Grant took the lead. "Hey, Tony," he said, "you want to see something cool?"

Tony looked at the towering ex-Mag, visibly swallowing. "I didn't do anything wrong," he said.

"I know you didn't," Grant said reassuringly as they approached the stone steps that led into the church building. "Come on, we'll catch up with these guys in a minute." With that, Grant led the way off to the side of the two-story building with Tony tentatively following.

By contrast, the girl—Pam—seemed to have automatically slid into an air of unquestioning trust of the adults who were trying to help her. Kane reasoned that she had most likely grown up in a walled barony and was thereby indoctrinated to trust Magistrates and similar authority figures. Once again, Kane was struck by the difference between ville folk and outlanders.

Walking ahead, Grant didn't bother to look back to check on his charge, thereby demonstrating his trust in the teen boy. They walked around the side of the church building, along a wide service road that led to a side gate that opened on an open-air storage area. Grant pointed to the gate. "Take a look inside," he encouraged. "It won't bite."

Warily the plum-haired teenager worked the catch of the wooden gate, keeping one eye on Grant as the towering ex-Mag watched. "What's in there?" he asked.

"Take a look, son," Grant said, a smile on his lips.

Grant recognized the anticipation on Tony's face, both excited and fearful, wondering if a trick was being played on him. When the boy didn't open the gate, Grant reached over and pushed it gently until it swung open on a creaking hinge.

"Whoa!" Tony uttered, unable to contain his excitement. "Is that real? What are they?"

Two bronze-hued aircraft waited in the rough scrubland of the church hall garden. They were huge vehicles, with a wingspan of twenty yards, and a body length of almost fifteen feet. The beauty of their design was breathtaking, an effortless combination of every principle of aerodynamics wrapped up in a gleaming burned-gold finish. They had the shape and general configuration of seagoing manta rays, flattened wedges with graceful wings curving out from their bodies, and an elongated hump in the center of the craft providing the only evidence of a cockpit. Finished in a copper, metallic hue, the surfaces of each craft were decorated with curious geometric designs, elaborate cuneiform markings, swirling glyphs and cup-and-spiral symbols that covered the entire body of the aircraft. These were the Mantas, transatmospheric craft used by the Cerberus team for long-range missions. They were alien craft, discovered by Grant and Kane during one of their exploratory missions to the Manitius Moon base. While the adaptable vehicles were mostly used for long-haul and stealth missions, Kane, Grant and Brigid had employed them on this occasion as robust workhorses, able to convey the heavy crates of rations in collapsible storage units that had been attached to their undercarriages for transportation to Hope.

Grant chuckled as he answered Tony's question. "They're real, all right," he assured him. "Me and my buddies flew here in them."

Tony turned to Grant, his eyes wider than ever. "You flew them? Are you some kind of spaceman or something?"

Grant placed a friendly hand on the teenager's shoulder and guided him closer to the Mantas as the early-morning sun played off their metallic shells. "No, we're just like you, kid," he said.

Tony ran a hand along the wing of the nearest vehicle, touching the swirling patterns that had been engraved within its surface. "They're beautiful," he said.

He had come down from his high, Grant realized, just an excitable kid once more.

"Do you think you could ever fly one?" Grant asked.

Tony beamed. "I'd love to. How fast do they go?"

"Real fast," Grant assured him. "You could cover the whole of this ville in five seconds."

Tony was amazed. His was a world of poverty and survival; he had almost no inkling that such wondrous technology existed. While he looked at the engines at the back of the Manta craft, Grant brought up the subject of the mollusks and learned that the youth had found them on the beach while he was down there with his girlfriend. They were both hungry, it seemed, so they had decided to try eating them. They tasted lousy raw, so Tony had cooked them, starting a fire like his father had showed him. That kind of stood to reason, Grant thought, and he quietly admired the kid's adventurousness.

A few minutes later, Grant and the fourteen-year-old entered the church hall to join the others as they, too, discussed the mysterious mollusks.

Inside, Kane and Brigid had separately established that Pam had cooked and eaten the strange mollusks with Tony.

"We found them along the beach, near the old pier," she explained.

"Were they alive?" Brigid asked.

Pam shrugged. "I don't think so. They didn't try to get away or nothing."

"So they probably washed up on the tide," Kane concluded.

Vernor concurred. "I saw a few things like that lying on the beach when I walked Betsy the other day." Betsy was his dog, an old mutt who spent most of her day sleeping in her basket passing gas.

"Recently?" Kane asked.

"Must have been—" Vernor thought back "—the day before yesterday. Didn't really pay them much attention, and Betsy—well, she doesn't let stuff like that worry her no more." That was an understatement, Kane knew. Betsy didn't let anything bother her anymore; she seemed to be content just counting the days until she finally croaked.

Kane turned his attention back to the teenager, running through a logical series of questions as his analytical Magistrate training had taught. "Were there a lot of them?" he asked. "How many?"

Pam thought for a few seconds, her eyes looking up as she tried to remember. "We ate…maybe fifteen. Some were dead small, though."

"That's all right," Brigid assured her. "You haven't done anything wrong. Just tell us."

Pam nodded. "My mom will be getting worried. I should be at home."

Kane's eyes met with Grant where he had entered the hall with the other teen, and the huge ex-Mag nodded infinitesimally.

"You two head home, then," Kane instructed the kids, "but I want you to report to Doc Price here if you get any stomach problems, okay? We're not sure what's in those things you ate, and I wouldn't recommend that you eat them again."

"Are we going to die?" Pam asked, her voice taking on a whining quality.

"No," Brigid assured her, shaking her head firmly. "You just might have an upset tummy for a little while. You've both been rather silly eating these things. They could have been poisonous."

Apologetically, the two teenagers gathered themselves up and, hand-in-hand, made their way through the shadowy porch and off down the street.

Brigid laughed as she watched them go. "Young love."

Kane sighed, shaking his head in despair. "Let's get back to the problem at hand, Baptiste," he growled. "The flesh of these mollusks has some kind of psychotropic property when eaten."

"That's not that unusual," Brigid told him. "It may not even be particularly dangerous."

Kane offered a self-deprecating smile. "Trust me, Baptiste—it's always dangerous. Whatever it is."

Grant chuckled. "You're getting to be a real cynic in your old age, Kane."

"This area is overpopulated and hungry," Kane stated. "If these things start washing up on shore in greater numbers, we may very well see a spate of drug-related problems arise as more and more people start hallucinating after eating them. We have a rare opportunity to nip this problem in the bud. So, I want to know what they are where they're coming from."

Grant and Brigid nodded. "Agreed."

Church warden Vernor proposed to spread Kane's warning to the local fishermen, and he went off to make a start with Betsy in tow.

"Sea creatures often swap shells," Brigid pointed out, "but if we can catch a complete one we could take it back to Cerberus and show it to Clem."

Kane looked mystified for a moment. "Clem?" he asked. "The cook?"

Brigid smiled. "Chef. And Clem Bryant is a brilliant oceanographer, dear," she teased.

"He cooks a mean toasted sandwich," Grant added. "I know that much."

"Not helping," Brigid chastised him.

Kane shrugged. "Okay, I'll take your word for it. Let's go take a look along the beach and see if we can find us a little something to show to Clem."

"Heh. Maybe he'll cook it for us." Grant chuckled.

Brigid glared at him. "Still not helping."

The trio made its way out of the church and down the steps, heading toward the beach with jocularity despite their concerns.

"So," Kane asked, "how did Clem end up chefing for the tired, hungry masses of Cerberus?"

Brigid looked exasperated. "Why don't you ask him?"

Kane gave her his most innocent look. "Well, I just assumed you knew everything, Baptiste."

"You know what happens when you assume?" Brigid challenged.

"No, what?" Kane challenged back.

"I kick you in the nuts, smart guy."

"Yeah, that sounds familiar," Kane agreed.

AT THE CERBERUS REDOUBT located high in the Bitterroot Mountains in Montana, adventuring geologist Mariah Falk sat alone at her private desk in the laboratory, watching as the results of a spectrographic test appeared on her computer screen. Beside the desk, a single crutch rested, propped up against its side. Mariah had been testing the same batch of rocks ever since she had got back from the escapade in Canada that had seen her, along with Brigid Baptiste and another Cerberus man called Edwards, caught up in a deadly ordeal that sucked the very will from the Cerberus teammates. During that ordeal, Mariah had almost killed herself in supplication to the stone being known as Ullikummis.

Mariah was a slender woman in her forties, her dark hair cut short and showing traces of white throughout. Though not conventionally pretty, Mariah had an ingratiating smile and a fiercely inquisitive nature that made her a fascinating and engaging companion. She had recently been spending more of her time in the company of Cerberus oceanographer-turned-chef Clem Bryant, and their attraction to each other was clearly mutual. Both Mariah and Clem hailed from the last days of the twentieth century, where they had been part of a military program that saw them cryogenically frozen until the nuclear hostilities were concluded.

Mariah grimaced as she checked the spectrographic results for a second time. Despite every incredible thing she had seen in Canada just three days before, there was nothing on these charts to indicate that there was anything out of the ordinary about the rocks she had brought back. Frustrated, Mariah sighed and wondered at what else she could do.

As she sat there thinking, Lakesh stepped through the doorway and greeted her. The nominal head of the Cerberus organization, he was a tall man who appeared to be in his midfifties, with refined features and an aquiline nose. Known to his friends as Lakesh, Dr. Mohandas Lakesh Singh was in fact a 250-year-old man who had been involved with the Cerberus redoubt back before the nuclear conflict had all but destroyed civilization. Though ancient, Lakesh had had a degree of his youth restored by Enlil in his guise of Sam the Imperator. Over recent months, Lakesh had begun to suspect that that blessing had in fact been a curse, for he was worried that he would begin to age once more, and at a far more rapid pace than was normal.

The slim doctor made his way over to where Mariah sat and lowered himself so that he was at the same eye level as her. "How are things going here, Mariah?"

Mariah sighed once more and showed him the results of her analysis. "Not good," she admitted. "There's nothing untoward about the rocks I brought back with me."

Lakesh offered a friendly smile. "This must be a new definition of the term 'not good.' Would you care to explain?"

"The asteroid that we believe held Ullikummis

is nothing more than metamorphic rock. Its original source was probably igneous and originated right here on Earth," Mariah explained. "Both spectral and carbon analysis place the rock at over six thousand years old, but it's difficult to be more specific without an idea of where it came from. This rock type is so common it would be impossible to be that specific," Mariah added.

"An educated guess…" Lakesh encouraged.

Mariah shrugged. "A tropical climate, possibly Africa or the Middle East. I honestly don't know. There are also traces of radiation, but it's at a very low level and that's as likely from its travel through space."

"I see," Lakesh mused. "And the other material?"

Mariah picked up a slate-gray chunk of rock. "It's just schist," she explained. "You'll find it all over Canada. It's a good building material, but it has no special properties whatsoever."

"You sound disappointed," Lakesh observed as he lifted himself up and gave Mariah's results the once-over.

"I saw this stuff *move*," Mariah reminded him, "like it was alive. That monster—Ullikummis—built a wall with it, and not with his hands. A rock wall *grew* out of the soil, and it then proceeded to follow his commands, moving as he willed it. It was alive, I'd swear it."

"It was granted life," Lakesh corrected pensively. "Instructed to act as it did."

Mariah looked at him with wide blue eyes. "Is there a difference?"

Lakesh took the chunk of gray rock in one hand and meaneuvered it across the desk, using its sharp edges like feet. "Consider a puppeteer," he suggested, "bringing his creations to life. Are they alive or is their life merely illusory?"

Mariah smiled. "I take your point." She was about to say something else when the public-address system burst to life, and Donald Bry's voice came over the speakers, calling Lakesh back to the ops center. Lakesh initiated the comm unit on Mariah's desk and asked Donald what the situation was.

"We have a visitor," Bry explained, his voice sounding as urgent as ever. "One you'll want to meet. I think you should come right away."

Lakesh excused himself, and Mariah watched the elderly cyberneticist leave the laboratory and hurry off down the corridor. Alone once more, she looked around her, wondering whether she'd been wasting her time these past few days trying to find something that wasn't there. As Lakesh had said, maybe the rocks were just puppets, and Ullikummis their puppeteer.

Something dawned on her then, and she struggled to suppress the shudder that ran up her spine. She had seen the great stone form of Ullikummis pushed into a viciously hot furnace and suffer the fate that he had intended for her and others who had failed in his harsh training regime. His body had been reduced to ash in a half minute, superheated until it was incinerated to nothingness. But his body was stone. And if his body was stone, a thing that he controlled and shaped with such ease, might it not also be possible that he had replaced himself with a double as he stepped into those flames? Could it be that he had pulled a switch and cheated death?

"I've been sniffing test tubes too long," Mariah muttered, shaking her head. It was time to take a walk and get a cup of coffee. Maybe she could get one in the cafeteria and find out what Clem was up to.

Slowly, Mariah Falk reached across the desk for the crutch that rested against it. Then she eased herself up and, using the crutch to support her left leg, slowly hop-walked to the door and out toward the cafeteria. Mariah had taken a bullet to her left calf during the final assault on Ullikummis, and the pain still sang through her leg with every movement, despite the painkillers she had been prescribed.

"That bullet saved your life," she reminded herself as she struggled along the windowless corridor of the redoubt toward the elevator that would take her up to the facility's cafeteria. "Brave heart, girlfriend. They say you're not a real Cerberus operative until you've taken a bullet."

THE CERBERUS REDOUBT, originally a military facility, had remained forgotten or ignored in the two centuries since the nukecaust. In the years since that nuclear devastation, a strange mythology had grown up around the mountains, their dark, foreboding forests and seemingly bottomless ravines. The wilderness area surrounding the redoubt was virtually unpopulated. The nearest settlement was to be found in the flatlands some miles away, consisting of a small band of Indians, Sioux and Cheyenne, led by a shaman named Sky Dog.

Tucked beneath camouflage netting, hidden away within the rocky clefts of the mountains, concealed up-links chattered continuously with two orbiting satellites that provided much of the empirical data for Lakesh and his team. Gaining access to the satellites had taken many hours of intense trial-and-error work by the top scientists on hand at the base. Less than a month ago, both satellites had been damaged in a freak meteor shower, and the people of the Cerberus operation suddenly found themselves cut off from the outside world and feeling very vulnerable. Thankfully the satellites had been repaired so that Lakesh and his team could draw on live feeds from the orbiting Vela-class reconnaissance satellite and the Keyhole Comsat once again. But the fraught period of blackout had served to remind the Cerberus team how much they had come to rely on technology. Delays associated with satellite communication notwithstanding, their arrangement gave the people of Cerberus a near limitless stream of feed data surveying the surface of the planet, as well as the ability to communicate with field teams, such as Kane's team in Hope, in near real time.

Hidden away as it was, the redoubt required few active measures to discourage visitors. It was almost unheard-of for strangers to come to the main entry, a rollback door located on a plateau high on the mountain. Instead, most people accessed the redoubt either by Sandcat personnel carrier or the miraculous Manta craft that Kane and his field team currently employed, or via the teleportational mat-trans system housed within the redoubt itself.

The mat-trans had been developed toward the end of the twentieth century as a means to transport military personnel and equipment across the vast United States of America. Employing a quantum window, the mat-trans worked through the principle of a sender and a receiver unit, utilizing point-to-point transfer of matter through teleportation. Though eminently adaptable, the system was limited by the number and location of the mat-trans units.

More recently, the Cerberus personnel had discovered

an alien designed system that functioned along similar principles, but relied on a naturally occurring network of energy centers called parallax points. These parallax points existed across the globe and beyond, and could be exploited by use of a device called an interphaser, which was portable enough to be carried by one person in an attaché-style case. The interphaser was limited in other ways, not the least of which was the location of the parallax points, but proved a more flexible system to operate, bypassing the fixed location limitations of the mat-trans network, and no longer limiting the team to primarily U.S.-based locales.

The Cerberus base itself had served as the original center of the U.S. military mat-trans network, and its operations room was geared to monitoring its use. A vast Mercator relief map stretched across one wall above the double doors, covered in lights and lines that indicated the pathways and usage flow of the mat-trans system in the manner of a flight path map.

Two aisles of computers dominated the room, each one dedicated to the monitoring of the mat-trans and the feed data from the satellites.

In the far corner of the huge ops room was an antechamber that housed a smaller cubicle, its walls finished in a toughened, smoky brown armaglass. This was the mat-trans gateway itself, fully operational and able to fling an individual's atoms across the quantum ether in a fraction of a second.

As Lakesh entered the ops room, he could tell that the mat-trans had been functioning very recently, could smell the smoke it had emitted that was now dissipating in the air around him and could hear the air conditioners working overtime to clear it. Along with a handful of other operatives, Donald Bry crowded around the entrance to the mat-trans unit where two figures had emerged. Both figures were quite short, one no more than two feet tall. Like the other personnel in the redoubt, Donald was dressed in an all-in-one white jump suit with a blue, vertical zipper at its center. He had a mop of copper-colored curls, and his face showed its usual expression of consternation, switching to momentary relief when he saw Lakesh stride across the room toward him.

"Who do we have here, Donald?" Lakesh asked, his firm voice carrying loudly across the hushed room.

While two armed guards held the newcomer in their sights, Donald stepped aside and Lakesh saw the familiar face clearly for the first time. It was Balam of the First Folk, and he was accompanied by a human child with white-blond hair whom Lakesh assumed immediately to be Quavell's daughter. Ordering the guards to stand down, Lakesh approached the curious-looking pair.

"Welcome to our home, Balam," Lakesh said, stretching his hand out to greet the familiar alien.

Balam nodded his bulbous, pink-gray head once in acknowledgment. "Salutations, Dr. Singh. It's been a long time."

"Indeed it has," Lakesh agreed as he brushed his hand over Little Quav's hair, making her giggle with glee.

"I am afraid," Balam began with gravity, "that the nature of my visit is not a social one."

Chapter 5

Kane's field team returned to Cerberus in the early afternoon, using their Manta craft to travel cross-country and back to the hidden mountain base. They carried with them a small clutch of the strange mollusks that they had found washed up along the Hope beachfront. They had found a half dozen in all, each a different size but with the basic sluglike body inside a whirling, oily-rainbow-colored shell. Each one was dead when they found it, but neither Kane, Brigid nor Grant could locate any live examples in their brief jaunt along the coast. All three had tried digging into the sand in a few spots, both wet and dry, in case the unusual mollusks were burying themselves, but they failed to find any further examples. It seemed that the creatures really were just washing in on the tide, a whole host of dead animals from who knew where.

Travel by Manta was swift and almost silent as the slope-winged vehicles powered through the skies. The Mantas were propelled by two different types of engine—a ramjet and solid-fuel pulse detonation air spikes—allowing them to operate both in atmosphere and beyond it as subspace vehicles.

When Kane, Grant and Brigid arrived back at the Cerberus hangar bay, they were instructed to meet with Lakesh immediately in one of the secure interrogation rooms located in the subbasement.

"Do we have time to wash up?" Kane asked.

"And maybe get a consult on these?" Brigid added, brandishing a small clear plastic pouch full of the recovered shellfish.

The guard on duty shrugged, urging them to meet with Lakesh immediately. "Those were my orders, guys," he explained. "Lakesh seemed pretty serious about it."

Grant shot Kane a look as the trio exited the hangar area and headed to the internal stairwell. "'Serious' doesn't sound good," he muttered.

Kane offered a lopsided grin to his partner as he brushed dark hair from his face. "Maybe he's throwing us a surprise party," he proposed.

"You don't believe that, do you?" Grant questioned, chuckling a little despite himself.

In response, Kane held up his hands innocently as he started to make his way down the echoing staircase.

Taking the bag from Brigid, Grant told them he would go find their resident oceanographer while the pair of them placated Lakesh. "I'd sooner get these checked out as quickly as possible," he explained.

At the bottom of the stairs, the subbasement featured one long corridor painted a dull shade of off-white, with stairwells at both ends and a goods elevator located centrally along one wall. The corridor stretched almost the complete length of the Cerberus redoubt, a vast distance in all, and there were numerous rooms located to the left and right, among them a firing range, vast storage lockers and several interrogation and incarceration rooms. At the far end of the corridor, a set of double doors led into the recycling area, where food and other trash were deposited so that the facility could remain fully self-sufficient in case of an extended siege.

Kane pulled open the heavy fire door at the base of the stairs and led the way down the corridor, still light on his feet despite the extended period he had spent cooped up in the cockpit of the Manta. Brigid followed, gazing left and right in an effort to locate the room where Lakesh was working. Roughly one-third of the way down the long corridor, two armed guards stood to attention as they saw two members of the fabled Cerberus field crew enter.

"Dr. Singh has requested—" one of them began when he saw Kane and Brigid, but Kane brushed the remark away.

"We've heard this tune already, second verse same as the first," Kane assured him. "Just tell us which door."

The guard led the way to an interrogation room located close to the goods lift on the left-hand wall. "In there," he explained.

There was a wide pane of reinforced one-way glass along the wall, and Kane peered through it, looking at the occupants of the bland, simple room. There was a standard table, bolted to the floor as a security measure, along with a smattering of chairs, some of them stacked at the side of the room farthest from the table. A large cork notice board occupied one wall, with a similar, smaller board decorating the wall opposite the one-way glass.

Inside, Kane could see Lakesh and Donald Bry sitting on one side of the desk, addressing questions to their visitor. A little way across the room, much to Kane's surprise, Cerberus physician Reba DeFore was jiggling a little girl on her knee as she proceeded to give her a health checkup. The girl had feathery white-blond hair tied back in a ponytail, and wide, expressive blue eyes.

As Kane watched, DeFore, whose ash-blond hair had been tied up in an elaborate braid that left corkscrew-like strands dangling beside her ears, tickled the little girl's tummy to make her laugh before peering into her mouth with the tiny light of her handheld otoscope.

Kane turned his attention back to the weird humanoid figure that sat at the far side of the desk with Lakesh and Donald, recognizing it instantly. "Looks like Balam's come to pay us a visit," he growled as his beautiful colleague joined him.

"And is that Little Quav?" Brigid asked, tapping at the glass to indicate the blond-haired child who sat on Reba's lap. Brigid was clearly delighted to see the girl. "She's grown so."

Kane reached for the door, turning the handle. "Why don't we go say hello?"

With that, the tall ex-Mag pushed open the door and made his way inside, like a jungle cat stalking warily into a cage.

"Balam, pal o' mine," Kane spit through clenched teeth, his eyes focused on the weird, alien form at the desk, "it's been a long time."

"Not too long I hope, Kane," Balam chirped, his doleful eyes gazing at the new entrants as they filed into the room.

"It could never be too long," Kane growled sarcastically.

Lakesh and Donald turned from the desk, and Lakesh gave Kane a warning look. "Now, Kane, let's show some hospitality toward our honored visitors."

"Hospitality," Kane repeated, speaking the word as if it were something jagged that had just cut his tongue. "Right."

Feeling the tension in the room, Brigid stepped

forward and diffused it with her bright, sincere smile. "How have you been, Balam? How's Little Quav?"

"I have been keeping myself to myself," the gray-skinned alien replied simply in his softly spoken manner. "Quav seems to have settled into life in Agartha well. We have found some places where she may delight in play."

Brigid laughed when she heard that, turning her attention from the strange, alienlike humanoid at the far end of the room to the playful child on Reba's lap. "Listen to you, you old softie," Brigid said. "I never pictured you for the doting parent type." This was not entirely true, of course, for Brigid knew that Balam had at least two sons who had been raised in the underground city of Agartha. Still, it did genuinely amuse her to hear Balam speak with such a gentle tone of real emotion.

"Children change us," Balam admitted, his sinewy, six-fingered hands weaving through the air in a nervous tic. "They have the ability to show our true faces, no matter how we try to hide them."

Resting against the wall, Kane remained tense. His steely gaze had not left Balam since he had entered the room. "So, what?" he challenged. "This a social visit?"

Balam shook his huge, bulbous head ever so slightly, and his lips mouthed the word *no* so quietly that Kane wasn't sure that the visitor had actually spoken at all. "It saddens me to have to come to you at this time, but I have been made aware of a situation that requires urgent attention."

Brigid Baptiste pulled up a free chair to join Balam at the desk, while Kane took several steps closer until he loomed over them all, his shadow dark on the alien's domelike pate.

"What sort of a situation?" Brigid probed gently.

Balam raised his head slightly, and Brigid could not be sure if his fathomless eyes were staring at her or through her. "Many millennia ago, the Annunaki established a store that would house all of their knowledge," he explained. "This storehouse was called the Ontic Library, for it contained all of the caveats that defined the real from the imagined or the spiritually malleable."

Brigid nodded, aware of the philosophical resonance of the term *ontic*.

"Over the past few days I have felt things in my head," Balam continued, clearly referring to his telepathic nature, "that make me suspect that the library has been breached and may, in fact, be being broken apart."

Kane shrugged, clearly unimpressed. "So it's a library," he said. "Big deal."

Balam turned to face Kane, staring at him with those strangely expressive black eyes, but he took a long, calming breath before he actually spoke. "This is not a library as you understand the term," he explained. "This is a storehouse for the very rules governing this reality. Should it be broken apart, destroyed, there is a significant risk that 'the real'—that is, your world—will cease to hold integrity."

"So, the world is under threat?" Kane asked, incredulous.

"More," Balam stated, "the very rules that underpin the world are threatened. The Ontic Library is a store of knowledge so powerful that it holds the structure of 'the real' in place. Without it, your world, your universe may very well cease to hold together."

Kane looked uncomfortable at the thought, and his brow furrowed with irritation. "Why would they do that? Why create something that could destroy everything around you?"

"Is your knowledge of human history so poor?" Balam challenged in his soft-spoken manner. "Or have you conveniently forgotten the bloodshed caused by humankind barely two centuries ago at the push of a single button?"

"But a library," Kane said, still trying to comprehend the concept. "Why would they—?"

"The Annunaki are multidimensional beings, Kane," Balam stated. "Do you concern yourself that food may spoil in your larder, or that a pot might overboil while inside your oven? Everything has a risk, even the retention of knowledge."

Kane nodded, still feeling uncomfortable at the notion he had just been presented with.

Sitting at the desk, Brigid leaned forward to regain Balam's attention. "So, where is this Ontic Library located?"

"Beneath the ocean you call the Pacific," Balam stated emotionlessly, "off the coast of the barony of Snakefishville."

"Hope," Brigid breathed, a horrible realization knotting the pit of her stomach.

"Had to fucking be," Kane growled, clearly irritated that he hadn't realized it before now.

BACK IN THE FISHING VILLE of Hope, a separate Cerberus field team agents had been operating out of the shantytown area that surrounded the main ville. Like

Kane's group, this team was also a three-person operation, but they had journeyed to the overwhelmed ville using an interphaser unit and had traveled the remaining distance on foot, carrying much-needed medical supplies to the area. Right now, the three operatives were handing out antibiotics to a youthful family that was suffering a bout of skin rashes due to the poor sanitation of the area.

Domi looked at the eldest of the six children in the covered shack where her team had set up base. The child was a dark-haired boy of perhaps four years old, and Domi recognized the fear in the child's eyes. He was afraid of her because she looked different, Domi knew, but she wasn't here to make friends. Instead, she ignored him, turning her attention to the busy dirt street that ran between the slanting temporary dwellings while her colleagues, Edwards and Johnson, doled out the relevant medical supplies.

Domi was a small-framed woman, standing barely five feet tall, with the slender build of an adolescent girl. Her skin was a vivid white the color of chalk, and was complemented by similarly colored hair, cut short in a pixie style. She wore a simple outfit that left much of her unusual skin on display, cutoff denim shorts that sat low to her belly and finished high on the hip, and an abbreviated crop top in a dull tan color that clung tightly to her small, pert breasts. Contrary to her usual style, she had elected to wear shoes while round the refugee camp, a pair of muddy pumps with a gripping, cushioned sole; she would prefer to go barefoot given the choice.

Domi was a child of the Outlands, having grown up far from the protective walls of Cobaltville, where she had ended up prior to joining the Cerberus team. As such, her outlook was quite different—and often less diplomatic—than that held by her colleagues. A fearsome six-inch knife was strapped to her ankle, and she wore a Detonics Combat Master handgun in a leather holster slung low on her bare, chalk-white hip. Overall, Domi looked like a human figure that had been carved from bone. But it was her fiercely darting eyes that added to the feeling of otherness in the people who saw her. In stark contrast to her pure white flesh, Domi's eyes were a deep scarlet color, like two glistening pools of blood.

Right now, Domi's bloodred eyes were scanning the street, watching the many figures trotting along it with their meager belongings, their buckets and bowls of water, moth-eaten blankets and clothes. Mangy dogs and flea-bitten cats stepped out of the way to avoid the humans as they went about their business, and the street itself stank of human waste. Domi wrinkled her nose at the stench, all the more repulsed for her senses were unusually perceptive. Where Edwards and Johnson had become used to the unpleasant reek of Hope, Domi remained disgusted and a little nauseous despite being there for over a day.

A group of people was making its way down the street, six in all. Dressed in rags like the others around them, they seemed somehow different to Domi, giving her the impression that they were much more organized. She watched them for a moment, realizing that despite their ragged appearances, they were walking in perfect time, like soldiers at a parade. Not soldiers, she realized—birds. They moved like flocks of birds on the wing, turning as one.

Domi watched as the six people strode past, their

faces masked behind the hoods of their dirt-caked cloaks. Weird, she thought.

From behind her, back in the shack where her colleagues were distributing medicines, Domi heard Edwards growl. She turned just in time to see the tall, muscular man lunge up from where he sat, knocking a vial of medicine from the table in his haste. An ex-Magistrate, Edwards was a powerfully built man, dressed in his preferred garb of combat fatigues with shirt open to show the drab-olive undershirt that clung to his chiseled pectorals. Edwards's hair was shaved very close to his scalp, and the start of a beard was forming on his chin now in what seemed an almost comical imitation. His right ear was misshapen where it had been clipped by a bullet during an escapade on Thunder Isle.

Sitting beside Edwards, Henny Johnson gazed up at him with openmouthed surprise as he lunged up from the table. A little taller with a little more flesh on her bones than Domi, Henrietta Johnson wore her blond hair cut into a severe bob that ended just below the lobes of her ears. She was a freezie from the twentieth century, one of a number of U.S. military personnel who had been cryogenically frozen and placed in the Manitius Moon base before the nukecaust had hit. Awoken two hundred years later, Henny was one of over three dozen freezies who made up the bulk of the personnel at the Cerberus redoubt. Her field of expertise was artillery, but she had a solid working knowledge of medicine so she had taken point on this mission. If they came across anything serious, Henny was instructed to seek local help or to converse with physician Reba DeFore back at Cerberus headquarters.

"Everything okay, gunsmith cat?" Henny asked,

fixing Edwards with a stern look as the people who had come for their help scampered out of his way as if avoiding a rampaging bull.

Edwards looked puzzled for a moment, rubbing at his forehead as though in pain. "What?" he asked, his voice strangely distant as if he were just now waking up.

Henny calmed the other people in the open shack with a few hushed words and a gesture before rising to consult with Edwards. "You just freaked out a little there, cowpoke," she said in a low voice.

Edwards wiped his fingers against the ridge of his brow, playing them along the bridge of his nose so hard that Henny saw white streaks of pressure appear there before fading once more into his natural skin color. "My head's killing me," Edwards growled. "Came on all of a sudden, a real pounding bastard of a thing."

"Do you ever suffer from migraines?" Henny queried.

"Me? No." Edwards shook his head. "Probably just tired, being cooped up in here for a day treating the locals in their filth. Reminds me of the Tartarus Pits back…" Edwards stopped. He was about to say "home" but realized he hadn't been a Magistrate for a long time now, and the Tartarus Pits were a thing of a past best forgotten.

Domi watched from her position by the door, checking the street again to see if any more locals were waiting for their services. The strange group of six was gone, departed amid the labyrinthine alleyways that made up the shantytown. In fact, the streets seemed suddenly clear, a much-appreciated lull in the stream of locals needing help. "Why don't you go for a walk?" she suggested to Edwards. "Clear your head. Me and the Hen can man the fort for a while."

Edwards nodded lethargically, his head still sore, before brushing past Domi and off into the street of dust. "Thanks, doll, you're an angel."

Domi shook her head. "Don't ever call me that," she told him with semiseriousness, recalling a rather unpleasant incident in Russia where she really had been mistaken for an angel.

As Edwards ambled off down the street, Henny arched one blond eyebrow as Domi came over to join her. "'The Hen'?" she asked.

Domi shrugged. "Rule of the Outlands. Adapt and survive."

GRANT FOUND CLEM BRYANT in the Cerberus cafeteria. The chef was busily deep-frying some chicken in batter, while other personnel rushed back and forth, dressed in white with their hair held back in nets.

"Looks fattening," Grant observed as he approached Clem at the deep-fat fryer.

Clem glanced at him and smiled, a mischievous twinkle in his blue eyes. "But fattening is tasty," he said, "and we all deserve a treat once in a while." Clem was a tall man in his late thirties, with dark hair that swept back from his high forehead, and a trim goatee beard on his chin. An oceanographer by education, Clem was one of the Manitius Moon base freezies who had awoken to a world two hundred years after he had been placed in cryogenic stasis. With little need for his skills in a mountain redoubt, Clem had turned his attention to the culinary arts and found himself quite skillful at cooking, soon taking a permanent position with the facility's cafeteria staff. Besides being an oceanographer and a chef, Clem was a quiet but personable individual, who enjoyed his own company and revelled in the completion of a puzzle, be it filling in a Sudoku number grid or finding a challenging cryptic crossword among the vast archives of the Cerberus facility. In short, Clem was an obsessive thinker whose mind regularly deconstructed problems to view them from an alternate perspective. "So, how may I help you, Grant?" he asked in his treacle-rich voice.

Grant held up the clear plastic bag he carried. "I want you to take a look at these," he explained, unzipping the top of the bag.

Grant held open the mouth of the bag and Clem peered inside, seeing the mollusks resting there in their glistening shells. "Would you like me to cook them?" he queried.

"No." Grant laughed. "I want you to identify them. You're the ocean guy, right?"

Bryant nodded before reaching for the handle of his fryer and shaking the sizzling contents. "Oh, yes, I'm the ocean guy," he agreed. "Why don't you find yourself a table while I finish up here, and I'll join you outside in five minutes."

"I'll go snag a coffee," Grant said and he made his way from the kitchen area with the little bag clutched in his grip.

A few minutes later, sans hairnet, Clem walked over to the plastic-covered table where Grant was blowing on a steaming cup of java.

The cafeteria was a large room filled with long, fold-down tables that stretched to seat a dozen people on each side. The tables were covered in a wipe-dry plastic coating. The walls were painted in warm colors, and a line of horizontal, slit windows ran close to the ceiling along the length of the wall farthest from the double door entrance. Because of the size of the room and the amount of available seating, it occasionally doubled for a conference area when something important needed to be announced to all staff, since it lacked the austerity of a more formal venue, which was something Lakesh preferred to avoid. Right now, however, the cafeteria was almost entirely deserted, with just a few personnel sitting finishing a late lunch or enjoying a relaxing drink while they took a well-earned break from their shift. As ever, the room had that scent of all cafeterias the world over, the indefinable musk of warm foods served at strange hours for hungry personnel.

"Well, then," Clem began in his warm, friendly voice as he took the seat opposite Grant, "let's take a look at what you have there, shall we?"

Grant tipped the bag upside down and carefully laid the six dead crustaceans on the table between them.

Clem reached for the largest of them, then retracted his hand, clearly thinking better of it. "Are they dead?" he asked.

"Oh, yes," Grant assured him. "We couldn't find any live ones. Believe me, we looked."

Fascinated, Clem took the largest of the mollusks—roughly circular and about seven inches in diameter—and held it up to his eyes, turning it over and over in the light. "Where did they come from?" he asked, still gazing at the coruscating patterns on the strange creature's oil-like shell. The light seemed to waver across its surface, as if seen through a heat haze, and Clem was already speculating that it in fact had a double shell, the dark one below the clear surface shell that created the slightly disarming optical effect.

"We picked these up on the beachfront at Hope," Grant explained, "off the Snakefishville coastline."

"Snakefish," Clem muttered, as though doing a quick calculation in his mind. "You mean California."

"I mean Snakefishville," Grant growled, the ancient frame of reference largely lost of himself, a child of the twenty-third century.

Clem placed the first mollusk down and examined one of the smaller creatures, using a pen to poke at the inside of the shell until the dead creature inside plopped out. It looked like a slug, finished in a dull gray-pink color, and it was clear that it was now wizening up in death, wrinkles marring its fleshy skin. "It's definitely some kind of shellfish, but I must admit that I don't recognize the specific type. Where did you say you found this?"

"Hope," Grant repeated.

"No, I mean—" Clem looked up, smiling self-consciously "—in what circumstances?"

"They're washing up along the shoreline, just a few here and there, but enough so you can find them if you go looking," Grant explained. "We found a couple of teens out of it, like they were on something, and it turns out they'd cooked some of these things and been eating them. Figured maybe they had some hallucinogenic properties."

Bryant swept his hand over the little array of dead sea creatures that were spread out on the plastic-coated table between them. "You'd need a lot for a decent meal," he observed.

"The people in Hope are starving, Clem," Grant told him. "We were there on a mercy mission to distribute nutrition bars, stuff like that. Domi and Edwards are still there now, helping with basic medical needs with someone…can't remember her name. Penny something, I think."

Clem looked at the broad-shouldered ex-Mag as he tapped at one of the hard shells of the unknown creatures. "I'll check a few reference tomes and see what I can come up with if you'd like. Would you mind if I take one?"

"Be my guest," Grant encouraged. "We brought them back for you to study."

"Then study them I shall," Clem announced as he pushed himself up from the table, gathering the half-dozen shells and placing them back in the plastic bag.

Grant finished his coffee as he watched the slender figure of Clem speak to his coworkers before making his way from the cafeteria. At the door, Grant saw, Clem met with Mariah Falk, the geologist who had been reduced to walking with a crutch after what had happened out in Tenth City. Clem showed her the plastic bag and the pair of them exited together.

Grant took one final swig from his coffee cup. "And I guess I'd better go find out what's cooking downstairs," he grumbled to himself as he stood up, oblivious to the joke he had just made.

Chapter 6

His name was Dylan and he had once been a farmer—a month ago, a lifetime ago. He was forty-two years of age, his dark hair was cut short, and the beginnings of a beard marred his chin now as he trekked through the pouring rain on his way to who knew where. He walked with a slight limp as he made his way along the rain-slick dirt road where it turned to mud, and his right shoulder slouched a little where he had taken a bullet. His right ear, too, had taken a bullet and now his head was patched, a damp bandage held in place by tape where the Cerberus warriors had helped him before they had departed, leaving him and the others to fend for themselves as detonations racked the stone ville of Ten, the brief home of Dylan's god and master.

Three weeks ago he had been a farmer, selling his produce in a town called Market out in the Saskatchewan wilds in the northern area once known as Canada. That was before the world had changed, and a god had arrived on Earth to bless him.

Dylan was a simple man, firm in his narrow-minded belief that physical strength could somehow conquer all obstacles, glorying in his ignorance. He was what his wife called temperamental or, when he was out of earshot, angry. Dylan had lived his life in the mistaken belief that he would someday be important, that he, too, might make the decisions of gods, and so when the god had shown interest in him, he had mistaken this for a sign of his own importance.

The rain soaked Dylan's dark hair, pasting it to his head and leaving his clothes wringing wet. He didn't notice. Nor did he think about his wife anymore, not since meeting with his god.

There had been a moment, out in Tenth City, where he had seen his old life, embraced it again as though the god had never come. But once the Cerberus warriors had departed, the comforting tone in his skull had begun again, where the stone god called Ullikummis had buried a tiny piece of himself like a farmer sowing a seed.

Now Dylan walked across the uninhabited countryside, searching for the next town. Once there he would spread his message, spread the word of Lord Ullikummis, and so provide the world with its savior, as so many others were doing across the continent.

And if the people didn't listen…?

Dylan smiled, his hand playing across the pocket of his pants until he felt the clutch of tiny stones that waited there, buds from the body of Ullikummis that would guarantee enlightenment.

They would listen. One way or another, they would listen.

As he made his way past a small copse, Dylan saw the lights twinkling in the distance and heard the sounds of music and laughter. There was a settlement here, a handful of cottages where the people farmed together in their struggle for survival. So much of the world remained barely populated, even now, two hundred years after nuclear hostilities had brought them to the brink of extinction, but Dylan knew if you walked far enough in a straight line you would find people.

He strode onward, smiling as he felt the satisfying chink of the pebbles in his pocket, like that ancient story of Jack with his magic beans. He would take enlightenment to the people around him, and they in turn would spread the gospel of Ullikummis, as others had already begun spreading it into the south.

Enlightenment was coming, Dylan knew. Enlightenment was coming and the world would change because of it.

Enlightenment through obedience.

His name was Dylan and he had once been a farmer; now he was the first.

Reba DeFore had finished her examination of Balam's adopted daughter, and she took the time to find a few things for the little girl to play with while she remained locked in the interrogation room with her foster parent, Balam. The playthings were a sterilized medical bowl and some rubber gloves that Kane volunteered to inflate into balloons so that the girl had something to occupy herself besides the weird little doll she had brought with her. She seemed happy enough, bouncing the rubber-glove balloons against the wall and scooping them up with the bowl. Balam watched her with a beatific smile on his lips, and Kane was struck by the sense of pride he seemed to have in his human charge.

The Cerberus personnel then excused themselves from the room and left Balam alone with his foster child, so that they could privately discuss the ramifications of his revelation.

"Kid seems happy," Kane observed as he peered through the one-way mirror window.

"She's healthy," Reba assured him, patting Kane gently on the arm.

There was a strange bond between Kane and the girl known as Little Quav. Although apparently human, the child was the daughter of a hybrid woman called Quavell who had died shortly after childbirth. However, it was unclear who the father was, or if indeed she had a father at all and wasn't the result of advanced genetic manipulation. One popular rumor was that Kane had fathered the child, and perhaps not willingly, but Kane had dismissed this as fabrication.

Though called "Little Quav" after her mother, the child was actually a genetic template in infant form of the reborn Annunaki goddess named Ninlil. Upon Little Quav's birth, the Annunaki overlord Enlil had sought to bring the child into his custody, for he contended that Ninlil was destined to be his wife as she had been millennia before. When his attempts to take the child had resulted in a Mexican standoff with the Cerberus rebels, an uneasy pact had been formed that saw the acknowledged neutral party of Balam take the child for safekeeping. It had been three years since that decision had been reached, and the Cerberus team had not seen the child or Balam since then. Until today.

"As long as he's feeding her human food," Kane muttered before finally turning away from the observation glass.

Standing across from the window of the observation room, Lakesh stretched his hands before him in an open gesture. "The people in this room have had more experience with Balam and Quavell than anyone else in this facility," he began. "So, what does everyone think of his story?"

Kane turned his attention to the pane of glass for a

moment before speaking in an irritated snarl. "Balam can be a cagey son of a bitch at times, but he's not one to outright lie," he said. "I don't know what this Ontic thing is all about, but I guess he wouldn't come here willingly if it wasn't important."

Brigid spoke up then, addressing Kane's query but speaking to everyone in the room. "The word *ontic* is used to describe what is there, the real or factual existence of a thing, as opposed to theories held about it," she explained.

"Like *chair* versus, I don't know, *thought?*" Kane suggested, trying to clarify the concept in his mind.

"Kind of," Brigid said. "It's not simply about the physical existence of a thing, however. Francis Bacon famously proposed that different languages rely on the same ontically anchored linguistic structures—if they didn't, they would simply be jumbles of nouns with no ability to explain larger conceits."

Kane nodded. "So, this ontic thing is like the structure that everything conforms to."

Brigid winked at him. "We'll make a philosopher of you yet, Kane."

"Not unless he can arm-wrestle the other philosophers you won't," Reba suggested, shaking her head. Kane glared at her, but his hostility was tempered with an appreciation of her dry humor.

"So," Lakesh said, "this concept underpins reality at a very basic level. If what Balam has described is true, then his Ontic Library is a physical manifestation of the concept itself, and its destruction could lead to irrevocable cataclysm, my friends."

"It already has," Brigid said calmly.

Lakesh's blue eyes widened in astonishment. "My goodness, Brigid, why ever would you say that?"

"We found something out on the coast," Brigid explained, "in Hope."

"Which lies in the extended territory of Snakefishville on the shore of the Pacific," Kane grumbled, catching her point.

"Now, this may be a big load of coincidence," Brigid continued, "but there's some stuff washing up on the beach that I haven't seen before. Mollusks, by the look of them—and they are very, *very* dead. We brought a handful of them back and Grant's running them by Clem right now, but I wonder if Balam might have some insight."

Lakesh stroked at his chin absentmindedly as he thought. "What makes you believe that the two are connected, Brigid, my dear?" he asked, wording his question carefully.

"Instinct," Brigid admitted.

Lakesh gasped when he heard that, unable to contain his surprise.

Beside him, Donald Bry reminded the older man of something he had been known to say from time to time. "Aren't you the one who says coincidence can be a very tricky thing, Dr. Singh?"

Lakesh nodded in acknowledgment. "Let's show Balam what your team brought back with you," he instructed Brigid, "and we'll proceed from there."

FIVE MINUTES LATER, Grant appeared at the observation room that overlooked the interrogation chamber where Balam waited with Little Quav. He was surprised to find himself the center of attention for Lakesh and the other staff.

"Whoa," Grant requested, holding his hands up in surrender. "I don't have them."

Donald Bry pierced the towering ex-Mag with a concerned frown. "You've lost them?"

"Lost them nothing," Grant retorted. "I just caught up with Clem, who's looking them over now, trying to identify what they are. Why? What's the big rush already?"

From the rear of the observation room, Kane spoke up, his voice so droll it seemed to be stripped of all emotion. "The world's going to end because of those seashells."

Grant looked at his longtime Magistrate partner, wondering if he was kidding. The look on Kane's face immediately disabused Grant of any such notion. "World—end?" he said, as if suddenly unable to construct proper sentences.

"Possibly," Brigid said, trying to be reassuring. "There's an underwater facility somewhere off the coast of Hope that Balam tells us is disintegrating."

Grant shot a significant look at the scene playing out through the one-way glass. "Yeah, I saw that our little jackalope has come back," he grumbled.

"Those shells may be one sign of this facility's disintegration," Brigid continued. "If it is destroyed, the whole world *could* come to an end."

"Could?" Grant queried. "I thought Kane said…"

Brigid waved her hand in the air dismissively. "Kane's just being melodramatic."

But Lakesh spoke up, immediately correcting her. "No, he isn't," he said. "While we haven't established a definite link between these mollusks you brought back and Balam's alarm, it's probable that the two are related."

"So we'll revise the alert to probable end of the world," Kane muttered. "Big deal."

Brigid sighed theatrically, but she knew that Kane was right. This was a huge deal, and it was likely to get a lot worse if they didn't act fast. "I'm going to go get more info from Balam," Brigid decided, "while you guys find Clem and see what he's turned up on our find, okay?"

Kane and Grant nodded in unison before making their way from the observation room and down the corridor toward the nearest stairwell. Once they had gone and Brigid was off in the interrogation room, Lakesh let out a long, strained sigh.

"Is everything okay, Dr. Singh?" Donald Bry asked, and physician Reba DeFore also gave the aging cyberneticist a significant look.

"Just tired," Lakesh explained as he thanked them both for their concern. Then he excused himself and made his way to the nearest washroom just a little way down the bland, subbasement corridor.

GRANT ACCOMPANIED KANE up the stairwell and they made their way to Clem Bryant's quarters. "Sounds like some serious shit is going down," he growled.

"That about sums it up," Kane agreed. "You didn't miss anything."

Grant sighed wearily, shaking his head in despair as he followed Kane out of the gray-walled stairwell. "You ever miss the days when you could just shoot stuff until it keeled over?"

Kane looked back at his partner and offered a sly smile. "I don't remember."

Outside the stairwell, the redoubt corridor was painted an austere shade of charcoal with unsympathetically fierce lighting that did little to take off its edge. Clem Bryant's private quarters were located midway down the corridor, and the two ex-Mags could detect the soft strains of music coming from behind the closed door as they approached. Gently but firmly, Kane rapped on the door until Clem's clear voice replied, bidding them to enter.

Within, they found a small, boxlike room, where the tall figure of Clem Bryant was pacing up and down, a large hardback book resting open in his hand. A single military cot was pushed against one wall, and Mariah Falk was sitting on the cot examining the strange shells in the light of a desk lamp that rested on the cabinet by the bed, her crutch leaning against the wall there. Above the bed itself, a cramped-to-overflowing shelf of books threatened to spill over, and orchestral music emanated from twin speakers lodged among the books. The music was up-tempo, with a certain level of pomposity to its resonance.

Clem glanced up in acknowledgment when Kane and Grant entered before turning the page of the book he held. "Can I help you, gentlemen?" he asked.

"It seems we've got a lead on our pond life," Grant began, making his way into the room.

Clem peered over the top of his book, his eyebrows raised in surprise. "That was certainly quick. You only brought them to me an hour ago." He sounded amazed.

"We're thinking they may be related to something a little more esoteric than we first thought," Kane explained, "and it just so happens we have an expert in the esoteric on-site."

Grant gathered up the half-dozen samples in their plastic bag. "We're hoping he can identify these for us," he said.

Clem nodded. "Do you need me to come along to offer my input?"

"Wouldn't object," Grant told him, and he led the way back to the corridor with Clem at his heels, explaining enthusiastically what little he had discovered.

"Even no discovery is a discovery," Clem chirruped.

Grant scowled at the bookish oceanographer. "You were clearly never a Magistrate."

"Establishing what we don't know is a vital step in confirming what it is that we do," Clem admonished as he followed Grant down the stairwell.

Back in Clem's quarters, Kane waited a moment to talk with Mariah Falk. He had been part of the operation in Canada that had seen her get shot, and he felt a strange, dislocated sense of guilt at seeing her using a crutch to walk on her shattered ankle.

"How are you doing, Mariah?" Kane asked. The authority had gone from his voice, replaced instead by kindness.

"I've been better," Mariah said, clearly uncomfortable in Kane's presence.

"Domi had to do it, you know," Kane told the geologist. "She didn't want to. I've taken a few wounds in my time. I know what it feels like and it's not good."

Mariah blurted a single laugh at that as she reached across for the crutch she was now using to help her walk. "'Not good' is an understatement. It hurts like… heaven knows. Makes it all the worse when I think how Edwards came out of it without a scratch."

"Yeah, well, luck can be an insensitive bitch sometimes," Kane grumbled. With that, Kane made his way to the door, glancing back at Mariah as she rose slowly from the bed. "You work on a painkiller addiction for me, okay?"

Finally relaxed, Mariah giggled, her blue eyes twinkling bright. "I'll do that, Kane. But only because you asked so nicely."

BRIGID SAT WITH BALAM in the interrogation room, a smile forming on her full lips as she watched Little Quav bounce the inflated rubber glove against her doll's head and laugh in delight.

"She seems happy," Brigid stated, taking in Balam's own somber expression.

Balam nodded once, his pale, bulbous head moving down then up like some bizarre perpetual-motion executive toy. "She doesn't know the danger that she is in," he observed quietly. "I have shielded her from that all her life."

Brigid began to speak, but she stopped, allowing Balam's words to sink in. "Do you believe that she's in danger right now?"

Balam gazed at the innocent child with his dark, fathomless eyes. "She has been in danger since the day she was born," he stated, "and indeed, before then, when she was conceived. You know her position in the Annunaki pantheon, Brigid Baptiste. I hardly need remind you, of all people, of the dark path of destiny that stretches before her."

"No, of course not," Brigid agreed. She had been there when Little Quav had become a bargaining chip in the hostilities between Annunaki Overlord Enlil and the Cerberus team, was well aware of how Balam's intervention and graceful solution had saved countless lives. Still, there was something in Balam's voice, the way he had raised this point now, that nagged at Brigid's mind, even though she could not put her finger on it.

"Would this Ontic Library have any bearing on Qua—Ninlil," Brigid corrected herself, using the child's predestined Annunaki name. Little Quav glanced up for a moment at the start of her name, then turned back to her game.

In answer to Brigid's query, Balam nodded solemnly again, his lips sealed.

"How?" Brigid asked, the question barely a whisper.

"The knowledge held in the library would doubtless show of her renewed existence and would be sufficient to locate her," Balam stated, balling his fingers into a fist, "and hence take her. Potentially, an individual with that knowledge could fold space, reach for her out of the ether like some astral kidnapper."

Brigid felt suddenly cold, as though someone had stepped on her grave. A few feet before her, the light-haired three-year-old girl continued to play, singing to herself now and then as she drummed her palms against the medical bowl Reba had left her in lieu of other toys. As if sensing Brigid's eyes on her, the blond-haired girl turned and handed her the inflated rubber glove. Brigid bounced the five-finger balloon from one palm to the other before knocking it in the air and batting it back to the laughing little girl. "Here you go, munchkin," Brigid said quietly, the last word so subtle that it was almost indistinguishable from a breath.

Brigid had had a child, a little girl called Abigail who had been taken from her when she was five years old. Except Abigail had never existed; she had been a part of a false memory that had ensnared the Cerberus warriors within a hell cage called the Janus Trap. Abi had never existed, and yet she had awoken something within Brigid, triggered something that Brigid had only barely been aware of up until that moment.

Balam looked at the beautiful redhead for a moment, a quizzical furrow appearing on his immense brow.

Brigid shook her head, partly in response and partly to clear it of the morbid and pointless thoughts that teased her of Abigail, the girl who never was. "Would it be likely that the Ontic Library is simply breaking apart of its own accord?" she asked. "Perhaps through age?"

"Never," Balam told her. "The place has been accessed, most probably for the first time in many millennia, for it dates as far back as Anu himself."

Anu, Brigid knew, was the first of the Annunaki to visit Earth, a spiritual forefather to their invading race.

"Only an Annunaki would access this place, Brigid," Balam told her with gravity. "No one else."

"Not even by accident?" Brigid asked.

"No," Balam assured her. "The librarians would never allow that."

"Librarians," Brigid said with a knowing smile. She herself was a librarian by trade, which was to say an archivist in her days in Cobaltville.

"You'll see," Balam said, and the trace of a smile crossed his own pasty features. As Balam spoke those words, Brigid watched his expression alter slightly, wondering that she saw something in his oddly shaped face. She felt it was a glimmer of something not altogether kindly.

Chapter 7

Inside the washroom, Lakesh ran his hands under the faucet, dampening them with water before splashing it over his face in an effort to revive himself. He really did feel tired, but wasn't sure whether he was just imagining physical symptoms or was mentally exhausted.

He was getting old; he recognized it from the last time, when he had reached almost 150 thanks to organ transplants and other medical magic. When Enlil, in his guise as Sam the Imperator, had granted Lakesh a nanobot-rich nutrient bath that revived a measure of his youth, Lakesh had never expected it to have hidden strings attached.

"Curse me for a fool," Lakesh muttered as he watched the water drain down his lined face in the washroom mirror before the basin.

Everything that Enlil ever did had had strings attached. The man—creature?—was Machiavellian in his planning, every loss a win, every benefit a blight. And so it was proving this time, and Lakesh cursed himself once more for being surprised.

Lakesh looked once more at the man in the mirror, the familiar lines around his eyes and over his forehead and at the corners of his mouth.

"What now, old man?" he muttered, wiping the last

of the dripping water from his face with a paper towel from the dispenser beside the basin. "What now, you old, worn-out thing?"

WHEN HE RETURNED TO THE observation room, Lakesh found Donald Bry, Kane, Grant, Clem Bryant and Reba DeFore talking in muted tones among themselves as they waited for him. The tiny room felt cramped and warm with all those bodies in it, and Lakesh found himself backed up against the closing door. While the others spoke, Lakesh noted that oceanographer Clem was peering with some interest at the weird, alien figure of Balam through the one-way glass, a look of vexation on his usually calm features.

"Are these the creatures?" Lakesh asked, indicating the bag in Grant's hand as he held out his hands.

"This is them," Grant growled, passing the bag to the Cerberus operational leader.

Lakesh peered in the bag for a moment, before distracting Clem's attention away from the alien figure sitting a few feet away on the other side of the reinforced glass pane. "Do you have any idea what they are, Mr. Bryant?"

The ever-unruffled Clem Bryant looked faintly self-conscious for a moment, letting out a single bark of laughter before he spoke. "I have an idea, of course," he began.

The other people in the room had ceased their own conversations to listen to Clem's clear explanation now, and the man embraced taking the lead and playing to this small, intimate audience.

"I must say that I could not identify the specific

type, given the rather limited time I was given with the creatures, but certain things are immediately clear from examining them." Clem removed the largest of the mollusks from the bag, holding it up and pointing out certain aspects. "The shell is quite thick for such a small creature, and it employs a double layer between which is a vacuum—nature's equivalent of insulated glazing. This implies it is designed to withstand exceptional pressures, and that leads me to believe its natural habitat is deep in the ocean, where water pressure is that much greater—the equivalent of living in an environment with very heavy gravity."

Clem turned the shell over in his hand, allowing it to catch the light so that the oil-slick rainbow pattern played across its surface. "There is almost no color to the shells themselves," he explained. "The rainbow coruscation effect you see is created where the outer and inner shells meet. In the darkness of the ocean, these creatures would likely appear a dull, muddy brown, so they would seem to have no use for color—they're certainly not attracting mates or repelling predators through such vibrancy, and it's worth keeping in mind that many deep-sea creatures don't see color anyway.

"They do have a complex genetic structure, however. The double shell is one indicator of that, and I'm certain that fuller analysis would yield some fascinating information."

"So what are they?" Kane grumbled impatiently.

"That is an answer I don't have," Clem admitted, "but that shouldn't come as a surprise. The deepest levels of the ocean have remained a largely unexplored environment, but we do know that there are creatures there that would be unable to survive in shallower waters, much as we cannot survive indefinitely beneath the waves."

Nodding, Kane leaned across Clem and pressed his extended finger on the one-way glass. "So, spin it for us quick, Clem—are these things naturally Earth critters?"

Clem looked bemused for a second until he realized that Kane was pointing at the unearthly frame of Balam. "There's no evidence here to suggest that these creatures don't belong on our planet, Kane," he assured the ex-Mag.

Kane threw a significant look at Grant, the two of them now certain that this was the first inkling of what it was they were about to deal with.

"Earth stuff we've got a chance with," Grant rumbled in reply to Kane's unspoken question.

Lakesh opened the plastic bag and invited Clem to replace the shell before he led the way out of the room and through to the interrogation chamber itself, with Clem, Kane and Grant following. Reba and Donald remained behind, watching through the one-way glass of the observation cubicle in case they were needed.

Inside the interrogation chamber, Brigid continued to speak to Balam, her tone soft. "Does it have locks?" she asked him.

Balam shook his huge, egglike head. "It has no need of such," he explained. "The librarians take care of all intruders."

"Then if we go there," Brigid began, "you could show us…"

"No," Balam said, an infinite sadness in his voice. "I must not travel to the Ontic Library. I would be unwelcome there, and I have other responsibilities, as you can appreciate."

The munchkin, Brigid thought.

Brigid turned then as the door to the interrogation

room opened, her emerald eyes flashing as the quartet of personnel shuffled in. She was somewhat surprised to see Clem Bryant among them, knowing that Clem had largely been kept out of the hands-on side of their operations, sticking primarily to his role in the facility's cafeteria. Ever polite, Clem nodded once in acknowledgment of Brigid, but she could see his blue eyes yearning to openly stare at Balam.

"My friends," Balam said in his soft-spoken manner as Lakesh took a chair before him on the other side of the empty table.

Carefully, his eyes fixed on Balam for any trace of reaction, Lakesh placed the plastic bag on the desk between them and shook loose the contents. "Do you recognize these?" he asked.

Balam visibly reared back in his seat, dragging his long-fingered hands across the desktop and away from the dead creatures in their sparkling rainbow shells. As ethereal and graceful as he was, the movement seemed somehow out of place with Balam's normal manner. Finally, noticeably bringing himself back to his usual serenity, Balam spoke. "Have you or your people touched these, Lakesh?"

"Yes," Lakesh said with a definite nod. "What are they?"

"They are exactly what they appear to be," Balam said. "Genetic information taken form in flesh."

Kane, who had taken up a position before the doorway in subconscious imitation of a guardsman, growled a single word. "Meaning?"

"The library holds information within its reef," Balam explained, gesturing to the unusual mollusks. "This is the library. This is a part of the storehouse of all Annunaki knowledge."

Kane shook his head, anger and exhaustion vying for prominence in his mind. It was always like this with Balam, he recalled—like trying to figure out a riddle in a dream. "Couldn't they have just written it down in books?" he challenged.

"DNA sequencing is a far superior way of containing dense reams of information," Balam replied with no sense of malice. "Far more elaborate than the modified grunts of a race of semievolved monkeys."

The room fell to silence as the Cerberus personnel took in the gravity of that statement, but the silence lasted only for a moment. Little Quav began to sing again, running across the room on her stubby legs until she was standing beside Balam. She stood there, looking up at him, her small hands tugging at his indigo robe. "Pick up, Uncle Bal-bal," she said.

Balam leaned down and scooped the child from the floor, holding her close and rocking her in his arms, stroking at her white-blond hair with his inhumanly long fingers. "We shall be leaving soon, Quav," he told her in his soft, reassuring voice. "Not long to wait now." As he spoke, Balam's dark eyes flicked up, looking across to the Cerberus people he considered allies if not actual friends.

Brigid nodded, seeing the whole picture now in her mind. The Annunaki were masters of genetics. Little Quav was a genetic sequence, a code designed like a butterfly's chrysalis that would one day open into the goddess Ninlil. These mollusks were the same, sequences of DNA that held codes and protocols and a thousand other subtleties than humankind might never fully comprehend.

"I know you can't join us, but would you show us how to reach the Ontic Library?" Brigid asked.

Balam nodded his great, bulbous head once again, the human-hybrid girl still clutched in his arms. "I was beginning to wonder when you would ask me that," he said in his strange, lilting voice. "There is a problem, one that you should already suspect."

Lakesh drummed his fingers on the desk for a moment before inspiration struck. "The interphaser should be able to access an Annunaki stronghold," he realized, "but you would have already tried that."

"Essentially yes," Balam agreed. "In fact, no parallax point was ever established in the Ontic Library, for the knowledge it contained was considered too great to be left vulnerable like that."

"Aw, no," Grant espoused, and Kane and the others turned to him in surprise. "We're going to have to swim, aren't we?"

Balam smiled. "Make friends with the undertow. I'll proceed in drawing a map."

While Donald Bry produced a map of the West Coast and the ocean beyond on which Balam could add his notes, Brigid took Lakesh aside to discuss something preying on her mind.

"What concerns you, Brigid dear?" Lakesh asked.

Brigid glanced behind her, her eyes drawn for a moment by the curious way in which Balam clutched the pen he had been given with which to mark up the map. Around the pen, the six long fingers of his hand seemed less like a man working a tool than like a boa constrictor grasping and crushing the life from its prey. She dismissed the thought, turning back to gaze into Lakesh's crystal-clear blue eyes. "Not here," she said, her voice low and filled with meaning.

With a nod of acknowledgment, Lakesh led the way through the door and out of the room. As if sensing something was wrong, Kane took the opportunity to follow them, and the three made their way back to the observation room at the side of the interrogation chamber where Reba DeFore watched the scene playing out in the interview room.

"We need to find out what these mollusks do," Brigid began once Kane had closed the door behind him.

"From what chrome dome was saying in there," Kane said, gesturing to the one-way glass, "us hairless monkeys aren't capable of getting it."

Brigid's eyes flicked to Kane, like twin emeralds in the semidarkness. "Those kids 'got it,' Kane."

"They were tripping out, Baptiste," Kane reminded her brusquely.

Lakesh looked from one to the other, until Brigid quickly recounted the story of the teenagers they had found out in Hope beneath the pier. "So what do you propose, Brigid?" Lakesh asked.

"Somebody needs to ingest one of these things," Brigid said, "to see what it really does."

"Ingest?" Kane repeated incredulously. "You mean eat it? Are you crazy?"

Brigid turned to him, and Kane saw then that her expression was deadly serious. "We'll be going into this Ontic Library based on hearsay, Kane—all we have is what Balam's told us," she said. "We need to know what it is we're getting into."

Lakesh nodded. "Forewarned is forearmed," he agreed. When Kane glared at him, he added, somewhat self-consciously, "It's a cliché, Kane, but it's a cliché for a reason."

"So, what are you proposing?" Kane asked Brigid. "That we cook ourselves up a side of mollusk au gratin and trip our brains out?"

"Not we," Brigid said. "Me."

Kane muttered something under his breath, shaking his head with resignation. "Always the same," he finished.

Reaching forward, Brigid placed her hand on Kane's arm. "I'll be fine," she assured him. "Those kids we met were whacked out, but there were no aftereffects."

"That we know of," Kane corrected her.

Brigid fixed him in her gaze, peeking through the curling bangs of her sunset-colored hair. "I'll be fine," she repeated.

Kane took a deep, steadying breath, tamping down the angry words of concern he wanted to express. He and Brigid were *anam charas*—soul friends—whose emotional bond ran deeper than merely that of colleagues. There was a mystical aspect to their friendship, one that spoke of an eternal love that traversed time and space, a bond that had existed in them in times past, when they had worn different faces and been known by different names. The full nature of the *anam chara* link remained unclear, but it had proved the key to their survival in otherwise dire circumstances before now. They were not lovers; their bond was more like that of siblings. Whatever the nature of the *anam chara* link, Kane remained fiercely protective of Brigid Baptiste, a combination of his Magistrate instincts and that deeper, more personal bond.

As Kane let out a long, slow breath, concern buzzing around in his thoughts, Lakesh added his own spin on the situation.

"I'll join her," the Cerberus leader said.

Both Kane and Brigid were taken aback by the statement that had come from the elderly scientist's lips, but it was Kane who spoke first. "What did you say, Lakesh?"

"I'll join her," Lakesh affirmed. "I grew up during a period of immense change. I was in my twenties during the 1960s, when experimentation with mind-altering substances became briefly very fashionable among the intelligentsia."

Kane and Brigid both accepted Lakesh's words at face value—born two hundred years later, they had no frame of reference for what he was telling them.

"The phrase, if I recall it correctly," Reba DeFore suggested wistfully, "urged that one should turn on, tune in and drop out."

Kane's lips moved as he repeated the phrase silently. "Drop out of what?" he finally asked.

Lakesh laughed, never more conscious than at that moment of how different his life had become in the two-hundred-plus years since their birth.

"The point is, dear friends," Lakesh continued, "it is time for me to free my mind, as the hippies used to exhort."

Bemused, Kane and Brigid looked at each other for a moment, then they shrugged. Whatever it all meant, the old cyberneticist seemed keen to follow this ancient advice, and clinician Reba appeared to be in agreement.

So, PERHAPS I AM GETTING OLD, Lakesh told himself as he accompanied Brigid to the kitchen area of the vast redoubt complex along with their companions.

Here was something an old man could do—a field mission of the mind.

And perhaps that made Lakesh reckless, more so than he had been in times gone by. Would his precious

Domi have allowed him to do this were she here? Would he have let her? Perhaps it was desperation, a need to prove himself still capable, still active and useful, and not some withered old desk jockey who gave orders like one of those terrible generals from history who had sent young men to their deaths but never dared set foot on the battlefield themselves.

All of this, perhaps, was true. But then, an awareness of one's own mortality could do strange things to a man. And so it was that the normally levelheaded, sensible Mohandas Lakesh Singh led the way into an exploration of an unknown, mind-altering substance that had scared Balam, one of the most knowledgeable beings on the planet.

Danger be damned, Lakesh told himself. He would take the risks that he could, and let others judge him as they would.

But despite his rare intelligence, the one thing that Lakesh had overlooked was that, sometimes, when a man felt he had something to prove, he could become foolhardy in the pursuit of his goal.

Chapter 8

There were just two prison cells in all of Hope and each cell had a sign up by its great wooden door. One sign showed a man in silhouette while the other showed a woman, because that was the only reason anyone in Hope had ever thought that you might need two separate cells, simply to keep the men separate from the women.

Hope had been a fishing ville, a small community where everyone knew everyone else, and so there had been little need for cells and Magistrates and all the things that came with the towering, walled villes like Snakefish, Cobalt and Beausoleil. Although rarely used, the cells had housed a few people over their time, mostly drunks and occasional wife beaters and one time a guy who had been caught stealing fish out of old man Walsh's nets. Indeed, the local drunk, Ivan, knew where they kept the key, and it wasn't unheard-of that he would lock himself up just so he had somewhere to sleep till his wife came to find him. Hope had been that sort of a place.

When the refugees had flooded in, the cells had seen more use in one week than they had in the whole of the preceding year. The locals had held a committee meeting where they had spoken about getting more cells, maybe starting a local Magistrate division, policing the ville to keep these new strangers in line. And while the who's and the where's and the why for's had been discussed, the refugee population had grown and grown, and before anyone knew it crime was the second-biggest industry in Hope after fishing. Which was to say, the locals had somewhat underestimated their need for cells.

While arrests had been made on an ad hoc basis, it was true to say that the cells had seen more people drift through them in the past three months than the whole of the prior decade. The band of stick-up artists who had tried to jack the remaining rations from the church hall had been slung in the cells by the local fire chief, with the help of three of his brothers, and left there to cool off. Those who needed medical attention had been seen to by Mallory Price, including the young man who had received a face full of boiling hot soup, while they awaited their final punishment.

And so, junior stick-up man Richie now found himself sitting against the wall of the cell he shared with his crew and some dozing old bastard who stank of liquor and shouted in his sleep, tightening the screw that held his broken spectacles together. He hadn't worn them on the stick-up job, hating the way they made him look, like some genius whitecoat or something. Instead the glasses had been in his pocket during the whole operation, and when that angry bull of a man had upended the table as he leaped onto it, he had fallen hard and the glasses had been beneath him when he landed. Now, the left arm was bent out of shape and the hinge wouldn't sit right so that, when he placed the specs on the bridge of his nose, they rested at a comical angle that did nothing for his temperament.

As Richie worked, a shadow cut across his sight and he glared up to see what—or who—was blocking the light. The who in question was Hunch, another member of his little crew who had helped out at the failed robbery. Inevitably, Hunch's head was bent at an angle as he watched Richie work.

"Hunch," Richie growled, "you want to maybe get the fuck out of my light, already?"

"Sorry, Rich," Hunch murmured, taking a few steps to the right until he was over with the other members of the gang, his head still held at that odd angle that he seemed to favor. The others were passing around a joint as they stood or sat around the lone old table, its paint scabbed over like a wound.

Seth, Richie's older brother and the brains of their street gang, peered up at Richie's outburst. "And what's got you so pissy, little bro?"

"What do you think? That bastard fucked up my glasses, Seth," Richie explained. As if his brother couldn't see what he was doing!

"You should wear those when we're out," Seth said helpfully.

With a snarl, Richie put the glasses on his nose. They perched there for a moment before sliding down on the left side until they hung at a ludicrous angle. "Should I, Seth? Should I really? Fuck."

Seth got up from the paint-peeled table and padded slowly across to where Richie sat in the cell, his face held in that serious I-know-better way he adopted whenever he was about to lecture his kid brother. "Why don't you just calm down," Seth said when he reached Richie, keeping his voice low.

"Calm down?" Richie spit, thrusting his broken glasses up to Seth's face. "They're fucking ruined, man. I look like a fucking retard."

Seth crouched on his haunches, bringing his face

roughly to the same level as his little brother's. "We'll get you new glasses once we're out of here, Richie," he said calmly. "Now, just bring it down a notch, okay?"

Richie shook his head, bearing his teeth angrily. "I'm going to beat the crap out of—"

"No, you're not," Seth cut in. "We're all going to play nice and get ourselves out of this cell and back on the streets. These people here, they're weak, man—they're idiots. They'll talk rehabilitation and all that shit and then we'll be home free, and no one will care about you or your glasses and that's exactly what we want." He looked at Richie, locking eyes with his brother. "Isn't it?"

Reluctantly, Richie nodded, his head moving so slowly that it looked like a colossal burden on his neck.

From a darkened corner of the cell, the old sot began coughing, an ugly hacking thing that ended in the spitting of a glistening hunk of phlegm.

"Dirty bastard," one of Richie's crew snarled before turning back to his colleagues for another drag on the joint.

The old man ignored the comment and wiped spittle out of his beard before pushing himself up from where he lay on the wooden bench. Slowly, still wiping at his tangled beard, he shuffled across the gloomy cell, his feet barely rising from the floor.

As Richie went back to working at the hinge on his glasses, he became aware that the old man was standing nearby, watching him with glistening blue eyes beneath beetling brows. "Can I help you, old man?" Richie challenged. It was definitely a challenge, not a question.

"You boys know what a utopia is?" the old man said, his voice little more than a mutter.

"A you-what-i-pa?" Richie snapped, irritation clear in his voice. Richie had never been known for his patience.

"A utopia is likc heaven," the old man explained, clearly needing no encouragement. His breath and clothes stank of alcohol even now, Richie noticed, even from this distance. "Like the best of everything a man could possibly want. Sounds good, don't it?"

Richie just glared at the old man, wondering whether he'd be able to get away with knifing the bastard here in the cell. He figured probably not.

"This place," the old man continued in his murmuring, muttering way, "was kind of like that once, a utopia. The ville, I mean. They called it Hope because it was something special that came out of the awful times that had come before. Didn't need Magistrates—the people took care of themselves."

"Sounds like shit on toast, Granddad," Seth said from where he sat with the others of the gang. He had been watching the oldster warily, distrustful as he was of strangers.

"But that weren't really utopia at all," the old man explained, turning to Seth and his other cell mates, warming to his rambling story. "See, utopia is finding that paradise, that reward that gives you everything right here on Earth. I'm a traveler like you—came south from old Canada. I came here to find it."

Already irritable, Richie had had enough. He stood up, his wiry frame looming over the bent form of the elderly man, clutching his broken glasses in one hand. "What the hell are you jabbering about, you old fool?"

To Richie's surprise, the old man didn't seem intimidated by him. "If you accept it, utopia will come," the old man stated. "I'm going to tell you guys a word—a name, in fact—and I want you to repeat it. That is, if you want to take the first step in tasting heaven here on Earth."

"You're crazy," Richie growled, stepping closer to the old man, his empty fist raised threateningly. The other members of his crew had stood up now and were surrounding the old man like jackals around a lame antelope.

"That name is Ullikummis," the old man said, "and he shall be our savior."

Richie had had enough. He had been cooped up in this crap hole of a cell for eighteen hours, and he damn well wanted something to hit. And so he swung the first punch, his right fist powering through the air at the old man's nose, forcing Richie to miss him entirely.

What happened next, Richie would swear, was impossible. This old drunk, this shuffling pile of rags that stank of gin and piss, somehow stepped through the arc of Richie's punch.

Driven by his own momentum, Richie staggered forward, his feet scrabbling across the cell floor as he struggled to regain purchase there. He turned then, scowling as he tried to comprehend what it was that he had just witnessed. It had been a blur, a thing not fully seen. Noiseless and impossibly quick, the old man had taken a half step to his left, a fraction of movement but enough that he was entirely free from the path of Richie's thrown punch.

"What the hell?" Richie growled, turning once more to face the old drunk, shoving his glasses into the pocket of his grimy jacket. "What the hell kinda trick is that supposed to be?"

All around him, the other members of his gang

moved closer to the old man to ensure he couldn't get away from their colleague. They need not have bothered. The man just stood there, a beatific smile showing beneath his gray whiskers.

Richie's second punch was low, aiming for the old man's gut, and he followed through with an immediate left cross. Once again, the old man effortlessly avoided the blows, stepping through them with such speed that he was like a ghost or something made of smoke.

"What's the game?" Richie snarled, reaching into his jacket and pulling out a small switchblade he had secreted there. The local authorities had taken his blaster from him before tossing him in the cell, but Richie always had something hidden on him. The knife's blade was barely three inches, but it would be enough to teach this grinning buffoon a lesson in respect.

"No game," the old man replied calmly, and Richie smelled the reek of alcohol on his breath once more, alcohol and something else—disease.

"Hold him!" Richie ordered and his crew obeyed.

Hunch hooked an arm around the old man from behind, and the man just carried on smiling, as if he didn't have a care in the world. Two others snatched at the drunk's arms, holding them out from his rag-clad body, while another gang member stepped across to the cell bars, checking that no one was coming.

Seth stepped forward then, warning Richie that maybe this wasn't such a good idea. "He's just an old drunk, Richie," Seth elaborated. "They find out you stabbed him and—"

"They won't know," Richie insisted, anger reddening his face. And without another moment's hesitation, he leaped forward and drove the blade at the old man's gut.

In the ineffectual light of the cell, the blade seemed to disappear into the old man. But when he pulled it back there was no blood. The man was wearing several layers of clothing, Richie realized; the abbreviated blade couldn't have cut through.

With a curse, Richie slashed the blade at the man's smiling face, driving it into his cheek—fit to carve his initials there if he had to—as the old man stood and took it.

The thing that stuck with Richie and the gang members who witnessed it was the sound that the blade made as it snapped. It rang like the sound of a small bell, tinkling in the silence as the blade broke away from the hilt and clattered to the hard floor.

Sometimes we don't really see the things we do in anger and other times we see them all too clearly, the adrenaline giving us the ability to recall an event in far more vivid detail than we normally might. Richie's anger embedded every nanosecond of that moment on the lobes of his brain.

The point of the blade hit the old man in the left cheek, in line with where his top gum would be, two back from his upper canine tooth at the second premolar. It was fleshy there, and the blade should have pierced the man's face with ease. Long gray-white whiskers of the old man's shaggy beard clawed up to hide that part of his face, and Richie's blade cut cleanly through two of them as it swished toward the wrinkled skin of his cheek. And then, impossibly, the blade had snapped in two, the point splintering away as a separate part to the main blade, which itself broke from the knife's little plastic handle.

Richie's fist carried on through the arc, still clutching the useless handle of the knife as its shattered blade dropped toward the ground in two twinkling parts, and his fist connected with the old man's face with a glancing blow.

The moment passed, and sound and vision resumed normalcy as Richie leaped back, howling in agony as he clutched at his fist. Where he had hit the man's face it ached with such a raw fury that Richie wanted to hit a wall in some illogical, primordial urge to make it stop.

Seth saw his brother fall to the floor clutching at his broken hand and weeping, and he turned on the old man. "What the hell did you just do to my brother, you old fuck?" he yelled, bringing his face just inches from the drunk's.

The old man didn't raise his own voice when he responded, nor did he show any outward signs of fear. "All you need do is say the word," the old man explained.

On the floor, Richie looked up with pleading eyes at his brother. Seth could see that his knuckles had been skinned, and there was a trickle of blood running between the joints of his small and ring fingers. "It was like hitting stone, Seth," he muttered. "Like hitting a fucking wall."

Seth turned back to the old man where he stood held in place by the other members of the gang.

"What's this word you're babbling about?" Seth demanded, his fists bunched as he wrestled with his urge to try striking the man himself.

"Ullikummis," the old man breathed.

"Bullshit," Seth spit back.

A wide smile appeared on the old man's face then, his yellowing teeth showing amid his shaggy beard. "Your gateway to utopia."

From where he crouched on the floor, Richie looked

up at his brother, seeing the strange intensity in his older sibling's eyes. "Utopia?" he snapped. "Look at my hand, man. Look what this old freak did to my hand."

With that, Richie held forth his right hand, the one that had held the short knife and had merely tapped against the stranger's face. A lattice of blood trickled along the grooves of the skin in a thin veinlike pattern. The little finger had bent inward, just slightly, but it was clearly causing Richie pain.

"What is it, Rich?" Seth asked with a frown marring his dark, handsome features.

"This freakazoid did something, man," Richie snarled. "He did something to my hand. It's impossible."

Warily, Seth turned his attention back to the old man, suddenly unsure of what to do. "Is that true?" he asked. "Did you do something to my little brother?"

The old man smiled, yellow teeth visible through the whiskers of his unkempt beard. "You saw for yourself," he said, his voice oozing like treacle. "I didn't lay a finger on him. He struck me—all I did was took it."

"Richie," Seth ordered, "get up here, let me see that hand."

Reluctantly, Richie stood up in the ill-lit cell and held his hand out for his brother's inspection. Like all younger siblings, no matter how old Richie got, he would always feel like a child when ordered to do something by his brother, always feel that he had to justify how he felt. "Feels like he broke something in there, Seth," he whined.

Seth reached forward and touched Richie's crooked little finger with the tip of his own. Richie flinched, spitting out a curse as he drew his hand away.

"Hey, fuck, Seth," Richie howled. "What the hell—?"

"I just touched you," Seth barked. "Calm down, you fucking girl."

Richie glared at his brother but said nothing more, holding his hand still so that Seth could examine it. The way it hung at a strange angle, the little finger looked broken. There was blood, too, but just a little from the graze and it was drying already, turning from red to brown as it lost its vibrancy. And Seth saw something else—dust, a charcoal-gray dust lining a single thin streak along the side of Richie's hand.

Seth turned back to the old drunk where he stood held firmly in place by the other members of the gang. The old man looked back at him without betraying any emotion. Taking a pace forward, Seth looked at the man's left cheek, searching amid the man's whiskers to see where the charcoal might have rubbed off. He could see nothing.

"Bring him over to the light," Seth instructed Hunch and the others. "Let's get a good look at him."

The old man didn't struggle but simply walked with the gang as they held him in their grip until he was standing directly beneath the single light bulb of the cell. The story was the same—the man's cheek looked normal, no sign of any discoloration, nothing there that would leave the mysterious dusting on Richie's hand.

"What are you looking for, Seth?" Richie asked, baffled. "I hit him, right?"

Seth shrugged. "Yeah, you hit him, Rich. But what hit you?"

"Ullikummis," the old man replied, his eyes intensely fixed on Seth.

"What is that?" Seth asked. "This some kind of game to you, you drunken bastard?"

The old man shrugged in seeming imitation of Seth's

own movement just a moment before, and the three members of the gang who held him lurched away, losing their grips as though they had been trying to trap running water in their hands. Two of them stumbled into the wall, so unexpected was the movement.

"What th—!"

"Hey!"

Free, the old man reached forward, the movement as swift as a hummingbird's beating wing, and his hand slapped against Seth's forehead with a loud crack that reverberated through the tiny cell.

Seth toppled backward, his feet kicking out from under him with the impact of the old man's subtle blow. Immediately, one of the other gang members, a seventeen-year-old called Turtalia, who had an emaciated frame and a chip on his shoulder, leaped at the old man, reaching his hands around the oldster's shoulders to drag him violently toward him. In a second, Turtalia head butted the old man, a blow almost guaranteed to shatter the man's nose, only to recoil back with a scream. As he fell away from the old man, Turtalia's forehead erupted with blood in a circular wound, almost as though he had been shot through the frontal lobe.

Turtalia crashed to the floor of the cell, blood pouring from his head wound and running into his eyes and down his face. "He ain't human," Turtalia shrieked as his colleagues readied their own attacks.

The old man stood waiting, his clothes and his breath stinking of the local still. It was clear that the gang had underestimated him now, that somehow this innocuous old drunk possessed a hidden weapon with which he could harm those who came into contact with him. Even so, it took three more attempts to fell him until Seth finally gave the order to quit. Throughout, the old man's movements seemed effortless, just the slightest of steps to avoid contact, and never once did he actually strike back after that initial blow to Seth's head. And yet, three fully grown young men, street fighters in the prime of their life, fell before him. And when they were done, the old man turned to Seth, who had finally ordered an end to the combat, and he smiled once more.

"This is the power he brings," the outlander hobo stated. "All you need do is accept it."

Without thinking, Seth brushed the hair from his eyes and felt at the rough skin there where the old man had slapped him. "What is it?" he asked. "This thing? This Ullikummis?"

"What you crave is power," the old man said, his voice lowering to something akin to a whisper. "Power over those around you, power over the situation you find yourselves in. What Ullikummis will give you is strength. And with strength, power must surely follow."

As he spoke, the old man waggled the fingers of his hands ever so slightly and, like a prestidigitator revealing a coin that he had palmed earlier in his act, two tiny pebbles appeared in between his fingers, one held in each hand. The pebbles were small, each one little bigger than a person's thumbnail, but as Seth watched he saw them begin to expand, to move and to grow like living things in the old man's crooked fingers.

"What are those?" Seth gasped, unable to take his eyes from the living stones.

"Your future," the old man replied, and he tossed first one stone and then the other at Seth and Richie as they waited before him, expressions agog.

Like scurrying animals, the twin stones embedded in the flesh of the two brothers and began to burrow beneath, hiding themselves below each brother's skin. And then the tiny cell began to echo as Seth and Richie screamed in absolute terror.

Utopia was upon them.

Chapter 9

Reluctantly, Clem Bryant had agreed to cook four of the six mollusks, warming them briefly in a hot oven, the way one might warm pastries for breakfast, in much the same manner that the Hope teenagers had cooked them in the fire before eating.

"I'm just warming them through," Clem explained. "All this will do is take the edge off, possibly making them taste less salty but otherwise changing nothing fundamental of their natural constitution."

"That is what we expect," Lakesh agreed as he stood beside Clem in the staff-only area of the cafeteria along with Brigid, Kane and physician Reba DeFore.

"Can I just confirm, for the record, that I am thoroughly against this line of inquiry?" Clem stated.

"But you agree that it is a valid line of inquiry," Lakesh said with a knowing smile.

Clem looked at him, seeing that roguish twinkle in the older man's eye. "I didn't say it was valid, Lakesh."

"We learn through experience, Mr. Bryant," Lakesh reminded him. "No amount of reading can replace actually experiencing a thing."

"And we're about to experience something very few people on Earth have ever experienced before," Brigid added. "We're going to eat some knowledge."

"Like the golden apple of Eris," Clem said. Then he opened the oven door and, using a cloth to protect his hands, pulled the heated tray from the oven. Atop the black metal tray, four glistening mollusk shells waited, white smoke pouring from their innards through a split in the shells, the fizzy sounds of bubbling coming loudly from inside. As Clem turned them with a fork, one of the mollusks spit, a dollop of fatty liquid sizzling on the tray. Carefully, Clem began spooning them onto twin plates that rested on the countertop beside the oven.

Brigid, Lakesh, Kane and Reba looked at Clem blankly, and Brigid asked him to explain himself.

"In Greek myth, Eris brought the Apple of Discord to Mount Olympus and sparked the Trojan War," Clem explained as he took the plates to a quiet corner of the large kitchen area. "It's seen as a metaphor for cognitive dissonance, that feeling one gets of holding two contradictory ideas at the same time. The world is round, and yet the ground we walk on is flat," he elaborated after a moment.

"That sounds surprisingly accurate," Kane said uncomfortably. "Those kids were seeing more than we were. They babbled, but it wasn't a directionless kind of rambling. They made sense. Kind of."

As Kane spoke, Brigid and Lakesh took their places at the table. The bubbling sea creatures waited on the plate before them, and Clem had already placed glasses of iced water and paper napkins at each seat. It seemed almost comical in its way, the genteel manner in which they were about to imbibe a potential hallucinogen that may contain all the secrets of the universe.

"On three?" Brigid asked, picking up one of the oil-patterned shells with the napkin. Even through the medium of the napkin, it was still hot to her touch, a sliver of steam trailing from its seam.

Lakesh picked up his own mollusk and brought it close to his mouth. "On three," he agreed.

A moment later, the two of them had the steaming shell openings to their mouths, and they sucked at the innards, pulling the tiny, jellylike creatures out of the cavity and taking them between their teeth. They tasted salty, the taste of the ocean. Brigid closed her eyes, swishing the bitter taste around her mouth, chewing on the pulpy flesh until she felt she could swallow it. Opposite her, Lakesh did the same. Between chews, Lakesh explained that it tasted a little like oysters or caviar, delicately holding his napkin before his mouth as he spoke.

Standing sentinel over the table, Kane watched as his two friends ate the weird shellfish and prepared for whatever would happen next. Beside him, Reba DeFore checked her wrist chron and unconsciously patted at the medical supplies that she wore in a purselike bag over her shoulder.

GRANT REMAINED WITH BALAM in the basement inter-view room, gazing with disinterest at its bland walls and empty notice board. Donald Bry was assisting Balam with his notations on the sprawling map of the Pacific, providing a selection of pens that their visitor might mark the place up clearly in different colors.

Dressed in her blue robe, Little Quav appeared to be getting anxious, and Grant took a step over toward her, towering over the little girl as she looked up at him.

"Hey, how's it going?" Grant asked.

The girl looked wary of Grant, and he realized that his domineering frame had to seem like a giant to her, used as she was to Balam's much shorter figure. The ex-Mag leaned down, gently offering the hybrid human girl his hand.

"I know it's all a little bit boring," Grant said quietly, "and maybe a bit scary, too, but you'll be out of here soon enough. Uncle Balam will take you home, okay?"

The girl reached forward, coiling the tiny fingers of her hand around just two of Grant's own, smiling tentatively at him. "Quav," she said.

"Grant," Grant replied. "I was there when you were born, right here, just upstairs. I saw you enter the world."

The girl didn't really understand his words, Grant knew, but she liked to hear his deep, rumbling voice. She had been starved of human contact for three years, hidden away from her own people, or the closest thing that existed to them on this planet now.

"Come on, Quav," Grant said, standing up and letting her hold on to his fingers still. "Let's go see if Uncle Balam has nearly finished."

The pale girl walked across the room, hanging on to Grant's hand. The ex-Mag shortened his strides, walking slowly to accommodate her pace. When the Cerberus team had agreed to let Balam take care of the girl they had never considered the fact she would not be interacting with her own kind. In keeping her from the Annunaki they had hidden her from humans, too, the very people her disappearance was intended to protect. If she should turn, if she should grow and embrace her destiny as Ninlil, the Annunaki queen, then Cerberus had no excuse—they had brought it upon themselves if the girl grew up loathing and fearing humankind.

At the desk, Balam peeked up from his work at the map with those dark, sorrowful eyes. "It's done," he said, placing a red pen on the table beside the others, extricating his eerily long fingers from its grip.

Grant nodded as he and the little hybrid human girl joined the alien at the table.

"You do realize," Balam said, "that I could have planted the information in your mind using telepathic suggestion alone, of course."

"I think we'd all sooner avoid any telepathic trickery," Grant replied. "It makes everyone uncomfortable."

Balam nodded in acknowledgment. "I respect that," he said.

IT TOOK TWENTY MINUTES for the effects to become manifest. It was strange, a little like slipping into a dream when you were categorically certain that you are still awake. The world, the kitchen around them, seemed normal. People continued to bustle about, pans burbled and bubbled and their lids rocked as steam struggled to escape. Something behind Brigid dinged, a timer assuring the mess cooks that their dishes there was done. Kane stood over the table still, staunchly watching as nothing seemed to change. And yet, as Brigid looked at him, his sleek, muscular, wolfish form standing guard above her like some faithful hound, she saw colors emanating from the exposed skin of his arms and face, like the rays of the sun peeking over a towering mountain.

Brigid had never seen Kane look so beautiful; he was like something from one of the pre-Raphaelite paintings she had seen in her archivist days. The way the light rippled upon him, the way it played across his dark hair and in the grooves of his taut muscles was like some wondrous dance conjured from the very fabric of the universe itself. Strange as it seemed to think it, the light seemed to enjoy running across Kane's skin, and in its joy it shone brighter.

To Lakesh, an eminent scientist and man of logic, the whole experience was a little like trying to look at one's finger while holding it up close to one's nose. He could see things, and yet the world behind them had somehow doubled, taken on two contrary aspects while remaining fundamentally whole. The table before him was solid enough. It looked as it always had, a flat surface made of lightly colored beech wood, the varnish marred in a few places where things had been scraped against it over the years. And yet somehow it seemed liquid, like something he could see through, see past. Somehow, in some indefinable manner, the grooves, the mars, the little indentations all seemed to be more solid than the tabletop itself, more real somehow. These were ruined things that could no longer change their properties for his eyes, could no longer be more than they really were.

Lakesh looked up then, peering slowly about the bustling room, taking in the strange details he had never noticed before. Had it always been like this? Had it always been so vibrant and multifaceted? It was like looking into a kaleidoscope, the patterns and the colors and all those incomplete shapes that worked at some subliminal level to create the world.

"You guys okay?" Kane asked, his voice sounding far away.

Brigid nodded, but she felt her head swim uncomfortably with the movement. "It's started," she told him, closing her eyes tight for a moment to shake a growing feeling of nausea.

"Lakesh?" Kane prompted.

"Started," Lakesh mumbled his agreement, the word seeming to take flight from his mouth.

When Brigid opened her eyes again, she was looking at Lakesh, his dusky skin seeming to smolder before her like the last vestiges of smoke from a campfire. "Lakesh?"

"Yes." The word came from Lakesh's lips, although he wasn't quite sure he had willed it. "It's quite wrong, isn't it?" he said. "Quite delightfully wrong."

Brigid reached forward, touching her hand on the second mollusk where it cooled on the plate. "Shall we eat the others?" she proposed.

Lakesh agreed. "I believe that it is time to find out how deep our rabbit hole goes," he said.

With that, Brigid and Lakesh each downed their second mollusk, drinking the flesh like some protein shake, which in a sense it was.

Kane watched the proceedings with an increasing sense of unease, with Reba and Clem standing beside him. Kane had an inherent dislike of things he couldn't grab, things he couldn't physically examine and battle with if the need arose.

GRANT AND DONALD ESCORTED Balam and Little Quav back to the operations room where they could comfortably access the mat-trans and be on their way.

"It has been a pleasure seeing you again, Grant," Balam said graciously in his weird voice. "A dubious and unfortunate pleasure, perhaps, but a pleasure nonetheless."

Grant nodded, tousling Little Quav's hair as she waited outside the brown-tinted armaglass door of the mat-trans chamber. "You take care of this little girl, okay?"

"I shall do my very best," Balam assured the Cerberus warrior.

"Try to remember that she's human, Balam," Grant said, and there was a warning to his tone.

"I shall never forget that," Balam promised.

Grant held his hand out and grasped Balam's. "We'll see you again."

"It seems inevitable that you shall," Balam agreed.

Then Balam picked up his human charge and carried the little girl into the mat-trans chamber, encouraging her to wave to their Cerberus friends one final time before they departed. From twin aisles of computer desks, the active personnel on shift in the ops center all waved back, the sight of the little girl breaking more than a few hearts.

The door to the mat-trans chamber closed, then Balam's interphaser unit activated. A moment later, Balam's silhouette disappeared into a gateway in the quantum ether, the little girl in tow. They were gone.

Grant watched solemnly, the thoughts ticking over in his mind. Balam was protecting the girl in the hidden city of Agartha, but was that enough?

CONTRARY TO THE POPULAR SAYING, it was the second time that proved to be the charm. Brigid Baptiste felt its effects almost instantaneously, and with such immediacy that she nearly fell from her chair. Nothing had changed; the kitchen was exactly as it had always been. She knew that as she stared around the room with wide eyes. But it was different, utterly altered into something Brigid had never seen before.

We are living underwater, she thought, trying to take in the new sense of being she could now perceive. That made no sense, of course, and the logical part of her brain rejected it, rebelling against such patent foolishness. It wasn't water, she realized then; it was *air*.

Kane's voice came from beside her, the concern clear in his urgent tone. "Baptise? Are you okay?" He had seen her sway in her chair, and he had worried for a moment that she might topple.

"We are living underair," Brigid muttered in response.

Still sitting at the table, Brigid found herself fascinated by the vignettes progressing around her. A human she was, and as human she had come to rely upon her eyesight as her most crucial sense, her primary means of sensory input. Seeing the world now, the room with its sizzling grills and bubbling fryers, it all seemed different. Not *new*—no, that wasn't it at all—just different, like seeing it all again for the first time.

Is this how a baby sees? she wondered. *In those first moments when it exits the womb and sees our world for the very first time. Is this what it sees?*

There was a medium before Brigid, she realized, the medium of air with its many components, its nitrogen and oxygen and traces of a dozen more free floating chemicals. Despite herself, Brigid found she was surprised at the water vapor, gathering in clumps around the sizzling cookers, the way it looked like droplets dancing amid this medium they called air. Her eyes turned to Clem Bryant, who was taking a mouthful from his glass of water, and she wondered at how he could move so freely within this cloying weight of air that pressed upon them all like a stifling blanket. Then she noticed the movement, the way the water shifted in the glass as though playing a game, its factions clinging together to hurry joyously down the incline as the glass was tipped toward Clem's lips.

Curiously, everything shone in this new reality, everything glowed and sparkled as if it had been sprinkled with icing sugar. The colors were so unusual, colors that Brigid's mind couldn't seem to truly grasp, had no name for despite seeing them, like a dream half-remembered.

Could it be that we never saw the things we had no name for? Were we blind to the world because we couldn't name everything within it? she wondered.

Brigid became conscious of something else, too, of the way her heart was beating in her chest, flurrying rapidly to keep pace with the emotions that were running through her. She felt hot, clammy.

Tentatively, warily, Brigid stood, her eyes roving around the kitchen.

"Baptiste?" Kane asked again, his voice strangely so close to her now, almost as though it came from within her. Perhaps that was the *anam chara* bond they shared, perhaps that was how it should manifest, as voices from each other's body, each other's soul.

She swayed as she tried to take a step, discovering that her sense of balance had altered. "It is the weirdest feeling, Kane," she explained, her voice seeming somehow to come from both her and him at the same time.

"Tell me," Kane said, his voice low and encouraging.

"Like seeing the building blocks," Brigid said in wonder. "The building blocks of time."

Lakesh was still sitting at the little table by the wall, but his reaction to the effects of the mollusk was very different. Where the hallucinogen had seemed to expand Brigid's sense of vision, Lakesh felt his own eyes burning. They were alien things, eyes not his own. This was true, for Lakesh had had new eyes implanted in his skull when his own had dimmed with age.

Unlike Brigid, he ceased to concern himself with external input and instead his mind turned within, a scientist looking for answers he knew he had to have. He felt his heart beating, drumming against the walls of his chest in its quest to keep moving, to keep pumping. The blood rushed through arteries and veins, with the fiery intensity of neat whisky.

Lakesh looked down, gazing at his hands as if they were things he held and not things he was. Ridges and bumps, a mountain range of age displayed in every trough and valley. Then, disconcertingly, he became aware of the layers of his hands, the skin that wrapped the parcel of flesh and blood and bone. He tried for a moment to flex his fingers, found that he couldn't, as if he had forgotten how to move. He closed his eyes, and beneath the lids he could see the veins there pulsing, rippling before his vision as red blood cells hurtled oxygen through his body. Somewhere deep inside, Mohandas Lakesh Singh felt his heart skip, his breathing cease and restart, as though his autonomic functions were failing; it was his brain he knew, the burning of the brain raging through him like a forest fire. He was witness here to something no person could prepare for, something no person should witness. A level of knowledge that went beyond simple fact, into a pureness that underpinned everything.

"Hold it together, you old fool," Lakesh chastised himself, though he could not tell if he had said the words out loud or merely thought them.

The aftertaste of the mollusk flesh swilled around his tongue, an acrid vinegar that he could not seem to shake even after swallowing the second dead creature.

Something moved before him, swirling in his vision, and he realized with a start that his eyes were still closed, that whatever he saw was only within him. Black on white, the stripes of a zebra, a pattern that promised to make sense but would not resolve, no matter how hard he studied it. Something else moved then, whirring in front of him, and he opened his eyes, seeing the figures moving all about him. It had been their shadows that had played on his eyelids, their movements that he had interpreted as zebra stripes amid the redness of his own skin. Brigid was standing, but she looked pained, her body bending in on itself like the crooked man who lived in the little crooked house.

As Lakesh watched, Brigid staggered, seemingly in slow motion yet still right, falling forward, stumbling into the wall before him and lurching onward, as if lost. The powerful figure of Kane was following just a few steps behind the redheaded woman, and Lakesh could hear his voice calling to her, but it wasn't in the room where he was. Instead the voice seemed to come from the far end of a torpedo tube, a muffled, eerie echo like the voice of a spirit, of Biblical God.

Brigid's hair seemed so bright in the lights now that it shimmered like flame, the reds glowing and burning, glowing and burning. In fascination, Lakesh watched it, wondering why it didn't hurt, what all those flames might hide.

Baptiste herself was muttering something over and over. Two paces away, Kane could hear them for what they were—nonsense words: *"Namu amida butsu."*

Brigid's lips continued to move and her eyes darted back and forth as she tried to make sense of sensory input that seemed to change too rapidly for her. The swirl of air hung before her, its currents moving around and around in circles and curlicues. It was hypnotic, drawing her full attention so that she had to make a conscious effort to not look at it, to not be trapped by it like some awful, mesmeric thing.

Beyond that swirl of air, Brigid saw the people and the shadows that they cast and, as she forced her eyes to focus past those beautiful currents of the air, she saw something hiding in those shadows as they played over the walls. The black of the shadows held red, a trace of rich scarlet amid the darkness. The word came back to her, horrifying and familiar, and suddenly her lips stopped their incessant *"namu amida butsu"* movement and she opened her mouth wide and unleashed an ear-piercing scream.

As Brigid began to scream, Kane reached and grabbed her, pulling her away from where she had lurched against the wall as if drunk, clutching her to his chest. "Baptiste," he urged. "Baptiste, snap out of it. Deep breaths. Snap out of it now."

Beside Kane, Reba DeFore was readying a hypo of sedative, wondering if she should act. She looked at Kane for approval and he shook his head.

"Wait," he instructed. "Give her a moment. She'll come around—won't you, Baptiste?"

Brigid seemed to ignore him. It was almost as if she was no longer aware of his presence. She pushed against him, leaning on his chest with all her weight, as though she was trying to shove him off his feet.

Kane stood firm, his legs well spaced to provide support as the screaming woman pushed at him. "Snap out of it, Baptiste," he urged again, drawing all the authority of his Magistrate vocal coaching into his command.

For a moment, nothing happened. And then, as abruptly as she had started, Brigid stopped shrieking, stopped pushing at Kane with all her might. Now, like a lifeless doll, she sagged against him as he drew her close, and Kane found himself propping her up as her whole body began to slump like a rag doll.

When he looked at her, Kane saw that Brigid had buried her face in his chest, hiding her eyes from the bright lights of the kitchen like a frightened animal. Her shoulders were moving up and down as if she was struggling to breathe, as if she were crying in great racking sobs. But she seemed normal now, no longer tripping out.

"It's okay, Baptiste," Kane said, emphasizing her name each time he spoke. "It's okay now."

Across the room, Lakesh still sat at the table with Clem Bryant standing close by. Lakesh had been silent throughout Brigid's strange episode, and he had barely moved since imbibing the flesh of the second shellfish. As Kane watched, the Cerberus leader drew his shaking hand close to his mouth and reached inside with the tips of his index and middle fingers.

"What the hell...?" Kane began, and he took a step toward Lakesh, still clutching on to the limp form of Brigid Baptiste.

Reba DeFore held up her hand to stop Kane from interfering. "I believe, even in his addled state, he knows just what he's doing," she explained.

As Kane watched, Lakesh gagged and then pulled his hand away from his mouth, a rush of vomit bursting forth and splattering over the empty plate and table before him. Kane cursed, and a few of the cooks in the immediate area called out, well aware of the hygiene implications of Lakesh's act. Clem hushed them with a word.

Lakesh continued vomiting, bringing up a watery

drizzle of oily yellow gunk until the gunk turned to nothing more than foamy spittle. After thirty seconds or so, Lakesh's vomiting subsided to dry heaving, and he drew a deep, pained breath. Clem knelt beside him, pulling a handful of fresh napkins from a loaded dispenser and handing them to Lakesh.

"Here, Lakesh," he urged. "Deep breaths and I'll get you some more water."

"Th-thank you, Clem," Lakesh said, his eyelids flickering as he struggled to take in the scene around him. After a moment, his eyes fixed on Kane, who still stood clutching Brigid's shaking form close to him. Kane helped her drink her own glass of water.

"How is Brigid?" Lakesh asked, his voice sounding a little hoarse from the strain he had just placed on his throat by forcing himself to disgorge the weird mollusks.

"She completely freaked out," Kane admitted. "What the hell were you two seeing?"

"Perhaps the wonders of the universe, my friend. I'm not sure," Lakesh said vaguely. "I started to become caught up within myself, trapped in the ego, I think—inner space—and I knew that if I didn't eject this stuff from my system it would overwhelm me. I'd be trapped looking inward forever."

"You're overreacting," Kane said, though he didn't feel as sure of his words as he tried to sound. "Those kids we saw in Hope came out of it and seemed normal pretty quick."

"How long between imbibing the flesh and their return to normalcy?" Lakesh queried.

Kane thought for a moment, then gave up. "Fair point," he said. "We weren't there when they ate the stuff."

After taking a long draw from the fresh glass of water that Clem had provided him, diluting whatever vestiges of the mollusks remained in his system, Lakesh began to speak once more. "This is a powerful—and I use this term with reticence—hallucinogen. Its effects began almost instantaneously..."

"You ate two," Kane reminded him.

"But neither was very big, Kane," Lakesh continued. "I can understand why Balam was so concerned about humans even touching them. They are quite exceptionally powerful and effective in altering one's perception field."

"Reckless is what I call it," Clem muttered, shaking his head.

"I agree," Lakesh said, "but, as I said before, sometimes one has to learn through doing."

Still propped up in Kane's arms, Brigid began to move, pushing herself away from him.

"You okay?" Kane asked, and Lakesh echoed his query a second after.

"My head is swimming," Brigid said, "but I wouldn't want to eat a plateful of those!"

Lakesh looked woozy as he sat at the table, where Clem had removed the vomit-drenched plate and was cleaning the countertop with a cloth dampened with sterilizing solution. "I would suggest water," Lakesh proposed, "and lots of it. It should dilute the effects Brigid is still feeling."

Reba agreed.

As Kane paced across the room to the water cooler, Brigid continued to speak, not really addressing anyone but simply following her natural instinct to archive information. "This is so weird," she said. "I should feel scared, but I don't. I feel tense, but not scared. Just a sense of discomfort. It's almost like I had too much sensory input at once and my mind couldn't process it. Whatever is in those sea creatures, it has a crazy effect on the human brain."

"I quite agree," Lakesh said, feeling the beginnings of a headache itching at his skull.

"Like Eris's Apple of Discord," Clem reminded them both. "You've seen simultaneous, conflicting views of the world and been unable to process which is the truth, for perhaps they both are."

Kane returned with a new glass of water, which he handed to Brigid. "I think it's time we all found out what this library is all about, then, don't you?"

Chapter 10

Less than an hour later, twin Manta craft soared through the air, glistening in the rays of the midday sun. They were like two streaks of lightning as they surged through the cloudless skies above the ruins of Snakefishville in their swift pursuit toward the coast. In the passenger seat within the tight cockpit of the lead aircraft, Clem Bryant peered through the thin window down at the shattered ruins below.

"Well, there's no getting away from it—I suppose I'm in the big leagues now," he muttered as the ruins rushed beneath him while the craft continued on its urgent errand.

Sitting in the pilot's seat before Bryant, his head entirely encased in a domelike helmet of the same color bronze as the graceful craft's sloping wings, Grant turned as if cocking an ear at his passenger. "What was that, buddy?" he asked.

"Nothing important," Clem admitted, idly stroking at the whiskers of his goatee beard. "I was just thinking about how this is a step up for me. Going on a field mission in one of these amazing spaceships. I rather feel like I've hired a limousine to take my sweetheart to the prom."

Grant shrugged, not entirely comprehending Clem's twentieth-century nostalgia. "Well, I'm no substitute for Mariah," he admitted.

Unseen by Grant, Clem sat up a little straighter in his seat, his eyes widening with surprise. "And why would you say that?" he asked.

Grant laughed. "'Sweetheart'? I just thought that you and Mariah were—" He checked himself. "Well, it's none of my business."

Clem turned his attention back to the view through the window once again, while Grant continued to pilot the almost-silent aircraft over the California coastline.

"It's funny," Clem said after a minute or so, "but this will be the first time I've been under the ocean's surface in, well, whatever it is—two hundred years."

"You're a freezie," Grant pointed out, aware that Clem had spent two hundred years in suspended animation on the Manitius Moon base. "Time's screwy for you. Why's that so funny?"

"Because it was only a couple of weeks ago that I was promising that I'd teach Mariah to scuba dive," Clem admitted. "Just before her...well, accident, I suppose you'd call it. It's the first I'd really thought about it in a long time."

Hidden beneath the faceplate of the pilot's helmet, a broad smile appeared on Grant's face. He knew from experience that love could make a fool of any man, but it was also the one thing that made everything that the Cerberus team endured worthwhile. Grant's own sweetheart—the beautiful Shizuka, leader of the Tigers of Heaven—had more than once saved his life, and not always in the traditional sense of removing him from harm's way. Having someone to live for could make all the difference in a harsh world.

As he considered that, Grant's thoughts turned unbidden to his colleagues Kane and Brigid. Neither one of them seemed to be able to commit to a real relationship, and the whole thing seemed all the more messed up because they shared their *anam chara* link, that special bond of soul friends. Some had proposed that this meant the couple would eventually be lovers; they had even been shown prospective futures where that appeared to be the case, although the validity of those visions was ever in question given the duplicitous nature of their many enemies. No, their bond to each other seemed to have settled into an almost siblinglike arrangement, not romantic love so much as a deep concern for the welfare of the other. Grant smiled. They sure as hell bickered like siblings; he had seen that with his own eyes.

Both Kane and Brigid had taken lovers, that was true. Most recently, Brigid had begun a tentative relationship with Daryl Morganstern, a handsome, advanced mathematician from the Cerberus personnel roster. Yet it seemed, to Grant at least, that the *anam chara* bond that his two friends shared somehow scuppered any chance of long-term fulfillment in a relationship, as if the pair's very closeness was their downfall. It was the old trap—they were damned if they did and damned if they didn't.

Grant turned his full attention back to piloting the Manta as a warning icon appeared on his all-encompassing heads-up display to inform him that they were coming within range of their destination. Whatever it was that Kane and Brigid did, he assured himself, they were fighting for something. Who knew? Maybe he was the only one of their tight trinity who needed to put a definite face on that nebulous goal.

FLYING IN FORMATION BEHIND Grant's vehicle, Kane piloted his own shimmering bronze Manta along the

Snakefish coastline and out over the sparkling, clear blue waves of the Pacific. Below, several fishing scows could be seen working near the shoreline, and Kane wondered if, even now, the fishermen might be netting more of the strange shellfish they had discovered on Hope's beach. He hoped not, given how Brigid and Lakesh had reacted—anyone foolish enough to eat them would be in for a tremendous surprise.

In the passenger seat situated directly behind the pilot, Brigid Baptiste sat with her eyes closed, going over everything Balam had told them in the preceding few hours. She was still feeling woozy from her experience with eating the mollusks. The effects had passed, but she had been left with an unspecified sense of discomfort, as if something had shifted deep inside her. In another time, in another situation, she might have called this feeling a hangover.

Kane flipped something on the dash console and the craft began to bank. He spoke briefly to Grant via their Commtact link, confirming their location.

"I'd guess we're about three minutes out, Baptiste," Kane announced in a louder voice once he had broken the radio contact. "You feeling any better?"

Brigid assured him she was. "Just a touch of nausea. Can you fly less bumpy maybe?" she joked.

"Sure," Kane agreed. For a moment, he concentrated on angling the graceful aircraft around, following the path Grant was charting through the cerulean skies. Then, partially by way of conversation, partially to air something that was preying at the back of his mind, he spoke up again, directing a question at his ferociously intelligent colleague. "Can you believe all this?"

"All what?" Brigid asked, concentrating on keeping her lunch down as turbulence rocked the aircraft.

"This whole undersea-library shtick," Kane elaborated. "Living creatures that work as books. Does that not strike you as a bit nutso?"

For just a moment, Brigid was taken aback. Kane was usually cool, not one to get himself too personally involved in a given situation. Perhaps, she thought, the sight of Little Quav had disturbed him.

"You hear me back there, Baptiste?" Kane prompted, raising his voice just a little over the sounds of air rushing all about their remarkable vehicle.

"I guess we're all 'books' of DNA," Brigid began, "if you think about it. There's so much we don't really know about the double-helix code that makes up living things. There are whole reams of data therein, right there within our own bodies, that appear to serve no purpose. They call it junk DNA, legacy data that has remained with us through the evolutionary cycle even though it's no longer required. Retrotransposons and pseudogenes—there's a lot of crap in our systems, Kane, much more than most people realize."

As Brigid spoke, Grant's voice sounded over Kane's Commtact once more, informing him that they were one minute away from their final staging point, after which there would be no turning back. Kane acknowledged that with a word, banking his Manta to stay in line with Grant's own Manta.

"So, all this junk DNA," Kane said, picking up on his discussion with Brigid, "could hold—what?—book-smart information?"

Brigid let out a sharp bark of laughter at Kane's obstinacy. "I rather suspect that the terms *book* and *library* are words of convenience that Balam employed to help us comprehend the rather unusual situation that we're entering."

"Which is to say," Kane said, "don't take them so literally."

"Exactly."

"It just makes my head reel when I think about this stuff," Kane admitted. "I mean, we've dealt with a lot of strange crap, but this—the stakes involved, the outright alienness of the whole concept—well, it's huge."

"The ocean is huge," Brigid reminded Kane, "and it makes up two-thirds of the planet's surface. There are life-forms that we've never seen. The Great Barrier Reef off the coast of Australia is home to untold thousands of different creatures, so many that no one has ever been able to adequately catalog them all."

"But are they all walking libraries?" Kane asked lightly.

"Who knows?" Brigid said with a degree more seriousness than even she expected.

Just then, Grant's voice came over the receiver of Kane's Commtact once again. "Staging point," he stated. "Say when."

Kane looked below, peering through the glowing data feed that the Manta's scanning equipment was providing on his helmet's heads-up display. They were eighteen miles out from the coastline, and it looked— rather disappointingly in Kane's opinion—like any other part of the ocean. Blue waters swirled below, the gentle waves making the afternoon sunlight twinkle across its surface, the white foam bursting into existence as opposing waves clapped together. Unlike at the coastline where the sea was an enticing, light cyan, here that blue seemed darker and more ominous.

"By your mark," Kane stated over the Commtact.

He and Grant had discussed their plan of approach before leaving the Cerberus redoubt, and it had been agreed that Clem Bryant should be in the lead vessel as, with his oceanographer background, he had the greatest experience of situations of this sort. Thus, Grant would lead the way through the watery depths on a curving vector while Kane would follow in his own Manta at a close clip, keeping pace with his colleague while in a suitable position to provide backup support if needed. What that backup might be, no one was quite sure. Neither Manta had any armament; their offensive capabilities were nil. But keeping within line of sight while under the ocean seemed the most practical approach; if one vehicle met with trouble, the other could hopefully assist while retaining a safe distance from suffering the same indignity. They had no real idea of what it was they were to face here, and Kane wanted to be prepared for any eventuality.

"Submerging in five," Grant confirmed.

"Acknowledged," Kane stated. "Stay sharp."

Seated behind Grant, Clem took a deep breath, listening as the pilot counted down aloud. Then, Grant powered the Manta high in the air, looping it as he gained momentum before entering the water like a sleek dart, the aerodynamic form kicking up the barest minimum of splash in its wake as it disappeared beneath the rolling blue waves. Behind Grant's Manta, Kane followed in his own craft, swooping so close to the ocean's surface that spume was kicked into the air by his vehicle's passage, before lunging into the air and banking back down to follow Grant into the ocean depths on a parallel course.

The two sleek, identical aircraft hit the water at a five-second interval, their aerodynamic wings cutting through the surface with such grace that they barely created a mark by their passing. The Mantas were transatmospheric and subspace vehicles, but they could also adapt to underwater environments, being utterly airtight and powered using air spikes.

And so they went. Down, down into the blue.

The ocean had its own currents, its own eddies. The surface turned and churned, glistening with a blueness that could seem inviting. But down, away from the sunlight, the ocean became a place of gloom, its creatures living lives spent in shadow. This was the environment that the Cerberus exiles now found themselves in.

In the lead Manta, Grant studied the sensory input from his craft's scanning device as an increasing amount of information made itself known on his heads-up display. The Manta crafts were surprisingly maneuverable under the ocean, and something within their makeup automatically adapted to the new environment, ensuring that they could travel seamlessly through the water. Perhaps not that surprising, Grant reminded himself— the alien craft's design seemed based on the undersea manta ray, which itself glided through the waters of the Pacific.

Still, the ocean buffeted the crafts like strong crosswinds, threatening to knock them from their intended path, and both Grant and Kane found themselves fighting with their control yolks as they hurried through the blue-green water.

Around them, fish and other creatures swam, darting out of their way as the metal hulks plummeted through the ocean depths. Things floated by, too, bubbling up to the surface in little pockets of air, and Kane felt sure he recognized several of the odd little shellfish that had washed ashore at Hope. Like so much else under the water's surface, the things were swirling with the current, tossed this way and that as they slowly drifted to the white sunlight above.

Gradually, the water became darker as they moved farther and farther away from the sunbeams, and Grant found himself increasingly reliant on the scanning equipment aboard the Manta. He took the opportunity to ask Clem if things were okay.

"It's peculiar," Clem admitted, "being back in the ocean like this. Especially traveling at such speed. I was seconded to some navy operations during my time back home," he said, recalling his work in the twentieth century, "which involved some use of small, two-man submarines. Nothing this fast, however. Do you know how fast we're moving?"

Grant checked his displays, but they were designed for airspeed. He gave Clem that figure, and Clem translated it as about thirty knots—fast for undersea movement.

The weird, muffling effects of the liquid made it seem that much more alien, and Grant watched the counter increase as they got deeper and deeper into the vast body of water.

"It's curious," Clem pointed out, "but I'm feeling no effects from the pressure. I wonder if we'll need to go through decompression when all this is over."

Grant checked his heads-up display, mentally calling forth the relevant information. "This ship is self-pressurizing," he told Clem. "It'll keep adapting no matter how deep we go. In theory, it should reverse the process when we're ready to surface."

"That's quite a relief," Clem said. "I had the bends once, early in my diving days. Not something I'd want to experience again, let me tell you."

The two mantas continued onward, two tiny specks

dropping through the vastness of the Pacific. Lower and lower they rushed, past shoals of brightly colored fish and poisonous jellyfish, past clumpy, floating plants and tiny crustaceans no bigger than a person's little toenail. Down and down, into the inky blue, lower and lower until Grant felt almost certain they had to be reaching not simply the bottom of the ocean, but the Earth's core itself.

Finally, after fully six minutes of rushing through the water at an almost perfectly vertical angle, the bottom of the ocean became visible, stretching to right and left, with hard rocks littering its smooth, silt carpet, and creatures large and small hurrying across its surface. Amid the silty banks, a vast hole waited in darkness absolute, the huge, gaping mouth to some gigantic cave or crater that sat beneath the lowest reaches of the ocean proper.

Grant engaged his Commtact, radioing through to Kane. "I have visual on our entrance," he explained. "Heading in on three."

Kane acknowledged the communiqué, assuring Grant that he was still just behind him.

Then Kane watched as Grant's vehicle swooped into the huge, gaping maw, disappearing from sight. For a moment, even the exceptional scanning equipment of the Manta seemed unable to follow Grant's passage, almost as if it was being deliberately blocked, and then a light winked back up on Kane's heads-up display and tagged itself as his partner's Manta. Thumbing the throttle, Kane followed, banking lower before racing through the opening and down into what lay beneath.

It was almost black down here; the whole area was shrouded in thick shadow. Refocusing his eyes, Kane flipped his attention from the heads-up display to standard visual, eyeballing the utter darkness of the vast cavern that they had entered. According to the sensors, the deep crater was at least six miles across, adopting an oval shape at the floor of the ocean and burrowing far deeper than the sea bottom that surrounded it.

"We are now entering an alien environment," Kane stated, the words shocking his passenger out of her own reverie.

"I can't see a freaking thing," Brigid complained as she peered through the slit windows to her left and right. "It's like a mine shaft outside."

The Mantas surged onward, gliding through the water with all the grace of their namesakes.

It took another two minutes, and even Clem began to wonder if they had somehow entered some other realm, given the seemingly impossible depth of the cavern, but finally the bottom came into view on the scanning equipment's far distance range.

"Instruments report that we are now nine miles below sea level," Grant announced.

Clem took a sharp intake of breath at that. The deepest known ocean trench—Marianas in the Pacific— was seven miles below sea level. They truly were in uncharted and slightly unreal territory.

And, as if to make it just that little bit more unreal, Grant's next announcement took Clem by complete surprise.

"Shit! We have incoming!"

Peering through the tiny slit of window in the back of the Manta, Clem suddenly saw something lunge at them out of the near-absolute darkness—and it was something huge.

Chapter 11

Rosalia awoke to the sound of barking. The noise was urgent and close to her ear, and it sounded strained. Automatically she reached for the stiletto blade that was hidden in its sheath beneath her sleeve, pulling the dirk free in a swift, practiced movement even as her eyes began to dart left and right as she took in her surroundings.

It was midday, and she had been napping for several hours. Like so much else in Rosalia's life, sleeping in the daytime was a habit that had been adopted as a precaution. A lone woman sleeping rough at night invited all sorts of trouble in the rotten ville of Hope, where a constantly shifting population absorbed and hid those who would prey on the weak. There was irony to that, of course—Rosalia herself was what psychologists would term an alpha predator, deadly, with her eyes open to any opportunity. Yet even she had to sleep, and that was when she was at her most vulnerable. While she had no love for the pale-eyed mongrel that seemed to have adopted her as its master, Rosalia knew there were benefits to keeping Belly-on-legs at her side.

She peered around, recalling the rotten husk of concrete and wood that she had taken to sleeping in over the past few days. It had been a storage garage for cars once, a long time ago, before the nukecaust had rewritten the lives of people and buildings and things. Now it was just a square with a roof, its floor moldy, its Swiss-cheese walls inefficient at keeping the wind at bay. Still, it was safe, secluded and offered a respectable view of the surroundings simply by merit of being high on a sloping road overgrown with weeds. Rosalia had jury-rigged a sheet of corrugated aluminium for the door. The sheet itself had been the roof of another dwelling before the tidal wave had leveled so much of the town.

Belly-on-legs was barking repeatedly, a strained sound as though he was shouting himself hoarse. The mutt rushed back and forth, tail swishing angrily as he circled around and around before returning to a position by the propped-up, corrugated-aluminium door. Something was out there, in the street, and the dog either wanted it or feared it; Rosalia couldn't tell which.

Confident that no one else had crept into the shelter with her, Rosalia silently made her way to the door, the soles of her shoes touching the concrete floor with the softness of a lover's gentle kisses, her eyes fixed on a gap in the top right side of the makeshift doorway. As she got closer, the olive-skinned woman leaned down and placed her hand—the one without the knife—on the mutt's head to calm him, stroking firmly between his ears. The dog yipped once before going quiet, its incessant barking giving way to a low growl from somewhere deep in its throat. The dog sensed something out there, perhaps a storm coming from the distance.

Warily, Rosalia peered through the gap in the door, dazzled for a moment by the brightness of the clear sky. Outside, a dirt track road ambled up the slope, bushes and stunted trees growing along its edges, weeds painting the road's surface a putrid shade of green. Three children were playing at the edge of the road, rolling pebbles across a flat area they had marked out with a stick in some derivation of jacks or marbles. Beyond them, about fifty yards to Rosalia's left, two women were talking, the volume of their conversation slipping as they dropped in snippets of gossip among the facts. Rosalia ignored them, turning her attention back to the children and then looking beyond, over the slope of the road. The dog at her side let out a plaintive whine.

There was a drop out there, where the edge of the roadway met the scrubland, and it fell in a sharp incline until it met another road parallel to this track, that one lined with run-down buildings from the original town along with the hideous in-fill of shanty dwellings. A half-dozen men were striding along that road, swiftly dismissing anyone who stepped into their path with a single gesture of their hands. It looked to Rosalia as if the hooded strangers were passing the locals money, but the transactions were so quick that she was certain that that could not be the case. Food, perhaps?

Rosalia's eyes narrowed as she examined the group. There were six of them, dressed in similar clothes with ragged hooded cloaks that left their faces in shadow, much like her own. People with something to hide.

The dog at her side growled again, and Rosalia mumbled soothing words as she stroked his head, not bothering to take her attention away from the gap in the door. As one, the walkers turned like flocking birds, their pace unchanging, and they began to stride up the sharp incline toward the dirt track.

Could it be? Were they coming for her? Impossible. No one knew that she was here. No one knew who she was.

Face pressed close to the gap in the door, Rosalia noticed something else then, something subtle and yet peculiar—a handful of other people followed from the roads below. Unlike the initial group, these followers didn't walk in step, but seemed more shambolic, almost as if they weren't sure that they should follow or not. There were just four of them, Rosalia saw, poking their heads out from here and there, turning to follow the group like children playing follow-the-leader. It was uncanny.

Rosalia felt the dog stiffen beneath her grip, his muscles becoming as taut as the half-dozen walkers continued to climb the slope. Unconsciously, her own muscles clenched, too, and she felt her grip on the handle of the knife tighten until her knuckles were icy-white lines in the tanned olive skin of her hand.

As the striders came over the lip of the slope, Rosalia saw how low their hoods sat, covering their faces almost entirely so that only their mouths were visible. Each mouth was a grim slit, turned down in determination. They carried themselves in a certain manner, not like Magistrates but with an authority, a presence, that Rosalia found herself contemplating. The heavy weight to their stride suggested they had rocks for boots, as though they were made of stone, statues come to life. Behind them, more casually, the others followed, clambering up the slope as if heeding the call to Mecca.

The lead group strode onward, its steps in unison, passing through the children's game, a casual kick of the leader's foot scattering the pebbles that they had been playing with. The kick was not deliberate, it seemed, just another stride, as though these people were ignorant of their surroundings, only truly conscious of their destination. But the leader dropped something from his hand as he passed, and Rosalia watched as one of the children picked it up and placed it in his mouth.

And then the group walked straight toward where

she hid in the wrecked garage, and Rosalia's breath tripped, a near-silent noise that seemed somehow loud in the darkness. She stepped back, ducking from the gap in the makeshift door, turning her attention to her dog and holding his head still with both hands as she looked in its freakishly pale eyes. The mongrel tilted his long head slightly and let out the beginning of a whimper, but Rosalia shushed it.

"Not now, Mutt," Rosalia whispered. "Keep quiet now or you'll get us both killed."

Curiously, the dog seemed to understand, for he went silent, looking at her with wide, anxious eyes the color of milk.

From outside, Rosalia could hear the group of six marching past, their footsteps in time like old-fashioned soldiers. She watched their long shadows cross the partition in the aluminium door, six heads moving across the bright gap in the darkness. And then they were gone.

Rosalia turned back to the door, one hand still patting at her dog's head lest he begin his yapping again. He had never been a noisy dog, but when he got scared he got scared. Pressing her head to the gap in the doorway, the dark-haired woman peered outside. Out there, out in the dirt track street, the six walkers were continuing on their way, heading toward a break between buildings through which they strode, finally disappearing from Rosalia's view.

It was an instinctive decision then, what they used to call female intuition or plain old gut instinct. Rosalia grabbed the small pouch of her belongings that lay on the floor—a tiny sewing kit that she had been using to repair a hole in her ragged cloak, two ration bars that she had remaining after her tussle in the street on the preceding night—and scampered back to the aluminium door on lightest tread, quietly encouraging the dog to follow.

"Come on, Belly-on-legs," Rosalia cooed. "This is something."

What that something was, she didn't know. But as she drew back the temporary doorway a little farther and let the dog run ahead of her down the dirt track road, Rosalita was certain that it was the sort of something she would want to know all about.

DOMI'S NOSE TWITCHED AS she peered around her, her scarlet eyes narrowing. She was still in the makeshift drop-in surgery that her Cerberus field team had established, and Henny Johnson stood beside her, cleaning the oozing arm wound of a middle-aged woman who had been bitten by one of the rats that roamed the shanty ville. Domi glanced once at the woman's weeping wound, assuring herself that Henny had the situation in hand, before stepping through the doorway and scanning the street.

Alongside Henny, Domi had spent much of the past hour or so patching wounds, administering tetanus shots and handing out vitamin supplements to malnourished locals. By her own admission, the albino woman had somewhat lost track of time, but it had been at least an hour since she had suggested Edwards get himself some fresh air and clear his head.

So where was he?

Engaging her subdermal Commtact, Domi patched a message through to Edwards. "Edwards? You out there, big man?" she asked.

After thirty seconds of silence from the Commtact, Domi felt certain there would be no response.

Something was up; it wasn't just her Outlands-refined instincts playing tricks on her.

"Don't take hour to clear head," Domi muttered, slipping into abbreviated outlander argot despite herself.

The street was busy, an endless stream of people wandering along its length as they sought food or work or whatever it was refugees sought in places like Hope when there was clearly no food and no work. It stank, that cloying stench of human movement, the smell of sweat and bodily functions. A young woman hovered outside one of the shacklike dwellings, wearing a short, tight skirt and a sweat-stained top that strained at her breasts, a dark cloud of hair bursting from a grimy headband that struggled to keep it free from her eyes. She was watching people wandering down the street, speaking now and then to some of the men who passed.

The dark-haired woman was what they used to call a gaudy slut—a prostitute—likely operating out of her own dwelling here in the butt end of a shanty ville. And, like all street people, the prostitute was probably more aware of the comings and goings around here than most.

Domi approached the street girl, gazing at the taller woman for a moment in open admiration. The prostitute turned, and Domi smiled as the woman literally jumped.

"Whoa, shit!" the woman spit. "Don't sneak up on me like that, freak."

"I need some help," Domi explained, ignoring the casual insult.

The taller woman appraised her for a long moment, looking the slender albino up and down as though eyeing the competition. "What's with the white skin?" the woman asked.

Domi ignored the question, moving the conversation along. "I'm looking for a friend of mine," she explained. "About six-two, thirties, Caucasian—"

The street girl interrupted, a confused moue shaping her lips. "What's Caucasian?"

"Means he's white-skinned," Domi clarified.

"Like you?" the prostitute asked.

"No," Domi said. "Normal white, like you."

"Pink," the girl said. "Why didn't you just say that?"

Tamping down her irritation, Domi ignored the comment and continued with her description of Edwards. "My friend was wearing an olive undershirt and pants, has a shaved head and his ear's all mangled like this." Domi folded her right ear over so that the top was crumpled. "Have you seen him?"

The street walker nodded, a smile appearing on her face. Domi saw then that one of the woman's upper canines was missing when she smiled, and her other teeth had been set crookedly, either a birth defect or after some especially poor dental work. "Tall guy, real big," the woman said. "Quite a honey, I'm guessing. Yeah, I seen him. Remember his ear, piece of shittin' work that was. What happened?"

"He took a bullet," Domi explained swiftly. "Now, he went off about an hour ago, maybe a little longer. Did you see where he went?"

"Sure, he passed here and went off down that way," the street girl said, pointing down the winding street in the rough direction of the sea. "Broad shoulders on that honey. I watched him go down there until he turned by the cart there—you see it?"

Domi saw an old wooden cart slumped to one side

where one wheel was missing. "Thanks," Domi said, and she left the woman to ply her trade.

The cart was about thirty yards along the street, and when she reached it Domi saw there was a rusting cage atop it where chickens were kept, clucking and blurting at random as they wandered about their cramped prison, in the way that chickens will. Her nose wrinkled as she stood by the cart, smelling the acrid stench of birds' fecal matter that spattered the floor of the chicken cage.

As Domi looked around, a man appeared, a dirty red fez propped on his head at a jaunty angle, puffing at a cigarette in a long plastic holder. "You like chicken?" he asked.

"No, thank you," Domi replied, dismissing the man as she looked all around.

Another lopsided alleyway crawled up a slope that led toward the beachfront ville of Hope itself, and Domi stood there, looking at it for ten seconds, wondering just what to do.

"You like egg?" the man in the fez asked, stepping before the shorter Domi's field of vision, an ingratiating smile on his tobacco-stained teeth.

"No, thank you," Domi said with rising irritation as she struggled to peer around the street trader.

The alleyway leading up was where the prostitute had indicated. Perhaps Edwards was up there. Domi could ask around, but the trail was an hour old and already going cold.

"You don't like chicken, you don't like egg?" the man in the fez asked, blowing out a plume of smoke from his lips. "What you eat?"

Domi looked at him, a feral smile appearing on her

ghostlike face. "People," she told him, her red eyes glaring.

The man in the fez hat suddenly found something more pressing that required his attention, and he couldn't apologize fast enough as he disappeared back inside his falling-down shack.

Domi shook her head, muttering something nonsensical under her breath. She was being paranoid. Edwards had gone off to clear his head, bullet-bitten ear and all. Surely an ex-Magistrate like Edwards could take care of himself.

Chapter 12

"Huge" was an understatement, Clem realized a second later, as he saw an incredible form rush toward them through the tiny slit of window in the rear of Grant's Manta craft. It looked like a swinging column of darkness, a vast line cleaving the water amid the dimness of the undersea crater.

Piloting the vehicle, Grant banked to port, turning the sleek craft over on itself as he avoided the thing he could see on the scopes. "Hang on back there, Clem," he instructed as he maneuvered away from the colossal creature that was hurtling at them through the ocean.

Kane's voice came to Grant over their linked Commtacts. "What's going on down there?" Kane demanded. "Just saw you take a sudden dive."

"We've got company," Grant summarized. "Big company."

As Clem was jostled about in the backseat of the Manta craft, he struggled to get a better look at the thing that had surged toward them out of the shadows. Even in the near-total darkness of the crater, he could see that it was colossal, comparable in size to buildings, not living creatures.

"Any idea what that thing is, Clem?" Grant shouted to his shipmate, raising his voice now over the straining sounds of the air pulse engine as it struggled to power them through the swift evasion maneuvers that he was running through. Up became down as they banked once more as the vast shadow swung toward them through the darkness, the waters churning in its wake.

"I can barely see it," Clem admitted, peering fretfully as the huge shadow rushed at them through the ocean gloom. "I'm not sure, but the size of it…could be a whale or…" He stopped then, watching the huge thing get bigger still as it came at them once more.

"Or?" Grant prompted, flipping the Manta over to avoid the huge creature that plowed toward them on the scope.

In that moment, Clem and Grant both realized that the thing that came at them had been merely a limb. Behind it a hulking shadow maneuvered through the darkness of the crater, powering itself through the ocean currents. The limb itself was the size of a building, it was like trying to navigate around a swinging skyscraper tossed at them from the ocean bed. And as for the creature behind that limb—neither of them wanted to guess at its size.

"Or it could be prehistoric," Clem finished finally, the words sounding uncertain even to his own ears.

The sensor readouts in Grant's heads-up display were going insane. Lights flashed and information scrolled so fast that he could barely take it in before a new blip of information vied for his attention.

"Kane," Grant barked, once again engaging the Commtact within his skull, "are you seeing this?"

STRAPPED IN THE PILOT seat of his Manta, Kane gripped the control stick, fighting for control as the backwash of the huge creature's movements threatened to send his own craft into a deadly spin.

"I'm trying to get to higher ground," Kane spit in reply to Grant's question, "but we're getting tangled up in the backwash."

Even as he said it, the engines whined and Kane found his Manta circling in a spin, almost entirely beyond his control.

"Dammit," Kane growled, "pull up, damn you."

Despite the safety harness he wore, Kane was slammed against the side of the craft as it hurtled through the ocean, entirely out of his control for a dangerously prolonged instant as it was swept up in the vicious current generated by the movement of the monstrous creature ahead of him. From behind, Kane could hear Brigid shouting something, her words unintelligible over the sounds of the straining engines. The heads-up display was flashing contradictory information, too, a blur of shapes and identifier tags popping up in strobe-light flashes before fizzing out again to be replaced by something new.

Kane wrestled with the control yoke, yanking it against the pull of the ocean current, urging the Manta out of its fearsome spin and back to a straight course. Ahead, he saw the outline of the sea creature, its shape drawn in glowing lines by the Manta's powerful sensor equipment. With no reference point, it was hard for Kane to accurately assess the creature's size, but he could guess it was well over two hundred yards from tip to tail, roughly the length of a Cobaltville block.

The Manta rotated again, its speed diminishing as Kane finally brought the vehicle under control once more, lifting it high over the vast shape of the monster that rushed just a few feet beneath him. The monster itself seemed to ignore Kane, instead busily pursuing his partner's craft as Grant's Manta sped through the ocean just a few dozen yards ahead of it.

"You okay back there, Baptiste?" Kane asked, aware that Brigid had been tossed about in the seat behind him.

Brigid groaned an affirmative, rubbing at her head where she had been slammed into the side of the vehicle during their fierce, uncontrolled spin.

As the Manta swooped through the ocean, Kane finally saw the full shape of the creature highlighted on his sensor display. It was roughly cylindrical in shape, bulging in the middle like a swollen torpedo. Eight vast, curling forelimbs dragged it through the ocean, each one of them curling and uncurling with each whirring movement as it raced after Grant's Manta, like the long tentacles of a squid. The thing moved with such speed through the ocean that it seemed almost effortless, despite its breathtaking size.

"I'm picking up an analysis now," Kane stated over the Commtact link he shared with Grant. "Looks like some kind of giant squid, and it's definitely alive. Scope here shows it's about 170 yards from nose to tail, plus those arms almost double its size."

GRANT GROWLED TO HIMSELF as he navigated out of the path of those mighty, swinging tentacles sweeping through the ocean toward him. He was working in darkness down here, but his sensor displays were alive with information, bright lights rushing across the field of his heads-up display inside the dome-shaped helmet. The Manta slipped between two swinging tentacle arms as the sea behemoth reached for the fleeing craft. Then, just as they appeared to be in the clear, another tentacle cut through the gloom, slamming into the bottom of

Get FREE BOOKS and a FREE GIFT when you play the...

LAS VEGAS
GAME

Just scratch off the gold box with a coin. Then check below to see the gifts you get!

YES! I have scratched off the gold box. Please send me my **2 FREE BOOKS** and **gift for which I qualify**. I understand that I am under no obligation to purchase any books as explained on the back of this card.

366 ADL E4CE   166 ADL E4CE

FIRST NAME

LAST NAME

ADDRESS

APT.#

CITY

STATE/PROV.

ZIP/POSTAL CODE

© 2009 WORLDWIDE LIBRARY. Printed in Canada.
® and ™ are trademarks owned and used by the trademark owner and/or its licensee.

7 7 7 Worth TWO FREE BOOKS plus a BONUS Mystery Gift!

Worth TWO FREE BOOKS!

TRY AGAIN!

Offer limited to one per household and not valid to current subscribers of Gold Eagle® books. All orders subject to approval. Please allow 4 to 6 weeks for delivery.

Your Privacy—Worldwide Library is committed to protecting your privacy. Our privacy policy is available online at www.ReaderService.com or upon request from the Reader Service. From time to time we make our lists of customers available to reputable third parties who may have a product or service of interest to you. If you would prefer for us not to share your name and address, please check here ☐. **Help us get it right**—We strive for accurate, respectful and relevant communications. To clarify or modify your communication preferences, visit us at www.ReaderService.com/consumerschoice.

the Manta with an almighty thud that made the whole vehicle shake.

Grant shouted unintelligibly as he struggled with the control yoke, trying desperately to regain control as the Manta flipped over and over in a dizzying spin. Behind him, somewhere to the rear of the Manta, the engines shrieked as they strained to right the vehicle once more, sounding for all the world like an animal caught in a trap.

The lights of Grant's heads-up display were flashing with increasing urgency, and a bright orange blip appeared to the upper right of his vision, assuring him that they were now in an emergency.

"I know, I know," Grant growled as the orange light winked on. He grasped the control stick with both hands, urging more thrust to the engines to try to level their course as they plummeted toward the great, squid-like beast that loomed beneath them.

Then, as Grant brought the Manta back under control, he realized that there wasn't just one beast out there; there were two.

"Kane?" Grant yelled over the Commtact as he yanked the control yoke hard to the right, neatly slipping past another of those swinging tentacles. "It's twins, buddy! We've got two of these things out here."

AT A HIGHER LEVEL, now just skimming the edge of the crater, Kane discussed Grant's message with Brigid, for she, too, was tuned into the communications via her own subdermal Commtact receiver.

"Well, any ideas, Baptiste?"

"They're the librarians that Balam spoke of," Brigid realized, the information coming to her as if from nowhere.

"What's that?" Kane shouted angrily, swinging the Manta through the waters to join his flailing partner, even though he had no idea what they were going to do to get out of this mess.

"While you were off finding Clem, Balam told me about the librarians," Brigid said. "He explained how only Annunaki are allowed access to the Ontic Library, that the librarians would never allow anyone else entry. That's why he wouldn't come down here himself." Of course, Balam was telepathic, Brigid realized, and it was entirely possible that that knowing smile he had offered her in the interrogation room had been as he placed a telepathic suggestion deep in her subconscious.

Kane checked the information scrolling across his scopes, confirming that there were two of the city-block-size creatures moving in the darkness. "Librarians, huh?" he snarled. "And they couldn't just shush us?"

"They're more like sentries or guardians," Brigid postulated. "I don't think they'll let us pass."

As Brigid pondered the crazy situation, Grant's voice came over the Commtact that linked them together. "Got two on my tail now, and they are closing real fast."

Kane urged more power from the Manta's thrusters, diving into the crater once more as he located Grant's vehicle on his readout display. "I'm on my way," he assured his partner.

"Kane?" Brigid snapped. "What the hell are you going to do? The Mantas are unarmed. We couldn't fight back even if we wanted to."

"Then we'll run interference until Grant can get himself clear," Kane snarled, "or I'll play the shortest game of chicken you've ever seen."

"No," Brigid muttered. "There has to be some other way. We just need to figure out what it is."

Kane piled on the speed, rushing faster and faster into the darkness. "Then you had better figure a whole lot faster!"

WITHIN THE COCKPIT OF the other Manta, Grant and Clem were reaching the same conclusion as their vehicle weaved dangerously close to the writhing tentacle arms of one of the squidlike behemoths.

"I'm not normally one to advocate the overt use of force," Clem said, "but I wonder if you might consider—?"

"Can't do it," Grant growled. "The Mantas don't have any weapons. We're unarmed."

"Has this never been an issue before?"

"Clem," Grant snarled. "Three words for you—not, the, time."

Clem put his hands together and closed his eyes as the bronze-hued craft was buffeted by the colossal movements of the creatures just beyond its frame. "Oh, I don't want to be Jonah," he muttered as the Manta lurched on the fiercely churning current.

Via the viewing displays, Grant could see the two creatures moving toward him through the darkened undersea crater. Despite their size, they moved through the water with exceptional grace and speed, their huge limbs uncoiling and rushing at him like rockets, dragging themselves forward. Despite himself, Grant physically ducked as one of those snakelike appendages cut through the water just a few feet above the bulge of the cockpit. He flipped the Manta, turning its belly toward the nearest creature and darting lower into the ocean depths. According to the sensor scan, they were at ten miles below sea level and there seemed to be no end to the depth of the massive crater.

"If you're going to pull something out of the bag, Kane," Grant growled, "you had better do it now."

GRASPING THE CONTROL STICK of his Manta, his hands slick with sweat, Kane powered the vehicle down toward where the monsters awaited. As he closed in, one of them turned and he saw it darting toward him, those colossal, swaying limbs preceding the bulk of its tubular body.

"Nothing's supposed to come down here," Brigid said, thinking aloud. "So these librarians investigate anything that does appear."

"I would call this a little more than investigation," Kane growled as the Manta craft was buffeted in the wake of another swinging limb a city block long.

"To us, maybe," Brigid agreed, "but from their point of view we're just interlopers, little more than flies buzzing around the room."

With a resounding crash, the tip of a tentacle skimmed against the wing of the Manta, and Kane clung tightly to the control stick as the vehicle spun once more, knocked from its path. In his sensor scope, he could see that Grant's own Manta was faring little better, just barely avoiding the slew of tentacles of his primary foe as it grasped for his vehicle through the shadowy depths.

In the backseat, Brigid wedged herself against the tight sides of the craft as she was tossed about in her chair, slamming against the starboard side as Kane struggled to right the ship. "There must be stuff down here for these things to eat," she reasoned, trying to focus on the problem of the immense squids. "Things would drift here all the time."

"Yeah, like us!" Kane growled as he zipped between two more of the colossal, writhing tentacles as they grasped for the Manta. "Come on, Baptiste, I thought you'd have an affinity with this shit." As he spoke, Kane urged the Manta ahead, rocketing just ten feet beyond the side of the nearest gigantic tentacle.

"Cut the power," Brigid said suddenly.

"Are you out of your mind?" Kane asked, struggling to be heard over the complaining engines as a tentacle swung at them through the water.

"Just do it," Brigid said, a firmness in her voice that Kane recognized from other escapades with the ex-archivist.

Despite harboring his own reservations, Kane cut the drive and felt the vibration of the engines cease as the Manta's system rapidly powered down. Behind him, Brigid Baptiste was relaying the same instruction to Grant via Commtact, assuring him that she knew what she was doing.

IN HIS OWN MANTA, whirling amid the grasping arms of the massive sea monster, Grant accepted Brigid's order without question, his fingers racing across the dashboard and cutting all power in a second. Where, just moments before, the Manta's complaining engine had been a whining shriek that grated on the passengers' ears, now it went deadly silent, the whole interior taking on the aspect of a mausoleum. The small bank of interior lights generated by the cockpit's dashboard winked out, too, leaving the whole craft in an eerily sudden darkness.

By contrast, the heads-up display playing across Grant's retina was in flux, as a dozen different warning signals vied for the pilot's attention. Grant ignored the flashing signals, wondering if any of the ancient Annunaki pilots who had once used these crafts had ever suffered epilepsy. "I fucking hope not," he muttered into the faceplate of the heads-up display helmet.

In the seat behind Grant, unaware of the order Brigid had given, Clem Bryant voiced his concern. "Are we hit? Are we sunk?"

"Oh, we're sunk," Grant said, "but it's all part of Brigid's plan."

"I have to say that sounds a lot less reassuring than it should," Clem voiced as the Manta began drifting in silence, its engines negated.

Just outside the smoothly curved shell, the two squid-like behemoths moved like planets orbiting the sun.

ABOVE GRANT'S VEHICLE, Kane's Manta continued along its course for thirty seconds or so, gradually arcing downward as its momentum was lost. "We're starting to sink," he informed his companion as a warning light blinked on in his heads-up display.

"Exactly," Brigid said, "and that's just what we want."

Behind them, remarkably, the huge squidlike monster seemed to have stopped grasping at them, and Kane saw that the same thing had happened below them, where Grant had cut the power to his own engines. Now the Mantas were gradually sinking.

"The librarian creatures are leaving us alone," Kane growled, equal parts astonishment and fury in his voice. "What the hell happened?"

"They're attracted to the heat of the engines or maybe just the unnatural movement of the crafts in their presence," Brigid postulated. "With no power in our engines, they're seeing us as no more threat than a sinking stone."

Kane shook his head in disbelief, the bronze helmet

swaying back and forth atop his neck. "Phew. When you pull it out of the fire, Baptiste..." he began.

As he spoke, Grant's jubilant voice came over the Commtact, broadcasting directly to the Cerberus warriors' subdermal implants. "We're all clear," he said. "Those big bads seem to be leaving us alone. I don't know how you did it, but it seems to have worked, Brigid."

As the currents of the ocean depths swirled slowly in their invisible dance, the two Mantas drifted gracefully toward the bottom of the crater, like two sycamore seeds caught on the autumn breeze.

THE CREATURES THAT BRIGID had identified as librarians did not bother the Cerberus warriors again, satisfied perhaps that the seemingly dead Mantas were no threat to their habitat. As they slowly sank toward the bottom, Kane wiped his sweating palms on the legs of his pants, and he stretched the kinks out of his muscles. It had been a trying few minutes.

"What I don't get," Kane said, "is how the Annunaki ever accessed this place. With those squids guarding the gateway, I mean."

"Presumably they had some way to soothe the savage beasts," Brigid suggested. "Maybe a sonic signal or something along those lines. Sound carries quite well in the ocean, albeit at a different rate to what we're used to. Whales communicate through song."

"Huh." Kane shrugged. "Kind of like a dog whistle, I guess."

Brigid smiled at the comment. Though his eloquence sometimes left a little to be desired, Kane's ability to hit the nail on the head was very often second to none.

Languidly, the two Mantas sank lower, gradually

dropping to the bottom of the undersea crater, whose proportions dwarfed even the vast creatures that the Cerberus team had tangled with. As they got closer to the bottom, the water became muddied, and Kane observed a number of tiny objects being picked up by his Manta's built-in sensors.

"There's a lot of debris around here," he stated as he took in the information on his helmet display.

Brigid peered through the slitlike windows in the back of the cockpit, but she was unable to see anything other than darkness now, even the bubbles of the Mantas' passing lost amid the intense gloom.

"Maybe it's the library itself," she suggested.

Her statement resonated within the confines of the cockpit, reminding Kane of how alien the whole concept of the Ontic Library truly was. Balam had intimated it was something like a coral reef, a living environment that sustained more life-forms on its surface, each of them contributing to the archive of information in some unfathomable, collective manner. These things in the water may very well be the same mollusk-type creatures that Kane's team had initially found along the seafront at Hope, the ones that had been eaten by the teenagers beneath the wreckage of the pier.

DRIFTING A LITTLE LOWER than Kane's Manta, Grant and Clem tensely waited in the near-total darkness, the only faint light coming from the display board that interacted with Grant's heads-up display.

"Are we nearing the bottom?" Clem asked, feeling strangely dissociated with real life in that ghostly environment.

"About a half mile," Grant said, translating the readings that whirred before his eyes. "But something's coming up," he added. "Kane? Can you see this?"

For a moment, the Commtact link was silent, then Kane's voice came, speaking slowly. "Just reading it now. What appears to be a huge undersea structure in a roughly cruciform design."

"Think this is it?" Grant asked, seeing the same outline on his own heads-up display.

"Stand by to reengage engines," Kane advised. "But let's not be too hasty. I don't want to get into another squabble with the guard fish."

"Roger that," Grant replied, watching in wonder as the heads-up display began to draw in details of the structure far below.

The construction was shaped something like a giant cross, with one arm stretching out to almost twice the length of the others. At its longest point, the structure stretched to three-quarters of a mile, large enough to house a village or small town. A cloud of debris came from a section close to one of the joints, a rent seemed to have appeared there and spewed a thick, inky liquid amid the stultifying gloom. From this distance, drifting in darkness, it was impossible for Kane or Grant to guess what the structure itself was made from; they could only marvel at its vastness.

Whatever it was made from, one thing was certain— they had found the Ontic Library.

Kane widened the range beam of his scopes to their maximum, bringing input from far above them. The huge, squidlike guardians of the depths remained dormant over a mile above them, uncaring of what was going on down here in the lower depths of the crater.

"Let's motor," Kane instructed over the Commtact, engaging his own engines once more as he did so.

Grant copied the request, and Kane watched on the heads-up display as his partner's Manta stopped sinking and began a more gentle arc forward, heading in a graceful curve toward the cruciform structure below them.

Still conscious of the leviathans above, Kane tapped a little power to the thrusters and followed his partner across the ocean bed toward the undersea palace.

"We're about one minute out," Grant advised as he angled his craft over the ridged surface of the Ontic Library. "I've located an entry gate off to the port side."

Kane checked his readouts and saw a signal flashing on his display, indicating the very entryway that Grant had just referred to. The Mantas were rediscovered Annunaki craft, and it seemed that certain information was preprogrammed into their amazing circuits for eventualities such as this.

Kane eased his hands across the control board, letting go of the control stick for a moment and allowing the Manta to glide toward the entrance under its own power. Thirty seconds later, he and Brigid were following Grant's craft into the belly of the undersea structure, taking another step into the unknown.

Chapter 13

Outside the dirt-caked garage, Rosalia followed the group of marching humans as they continued down the street toward the beach. Besides the six in hoods, four others followed, their movements less regular and more shambolic, almost as if they were sleepwalking.

Trotting along at her side, Belly-on-legs let out an excited yip, peering back over his shoulder.

"Hush, stupid mutt," Rosalia ordered, stepping into the shadows between the two nearest buildings, both of them ramshackle huts showing the heavy trauma of weathering.

Peering back to where the excited dog was looking, Rosalia saw another man pacing along the street, this one more upright with an almost military gait. Magistrate, she said to herself automatically. He had a shaved head, the start of a beard on his chin, and, as he came closer, Rosalia saw that his right ear was mangled where it had suffered some kind of wound. As she watched him pass, Rosalia saw the man lift his hand to his ear as if in pain.

"I can hear you, Domi," the tall man said as though to thin air. "Stop blabbering in my fucking ear."

Domi? Rosalia knew that name; it was another of the Cerberus people, the ones she had met with here just a few months before. Domi had been the curious-looking girl with the pure white skin. She had been a hellion,

Rosalia recalled, savage in her manners and brutal in her fighting techniques—an outlander, uncivilized despite her outward affectations.

Which didn't explain who the man with the bullet-bitten ear was, although it did heavily imply that he was part of the Cerberus team. They all communicated using some kind of internal electronic device, she knew, had seen it with her own eyes. Keeping her distance, Rosalia padded after the shaved-headed man, the pale-eyed mongrel at her side.

AT A LOWER LEVEL OF the favela, Domi had decided to follow the alleyway she had found by the jaunty chicken keeper. She engaged her Commtact communicator once again, trying to raise Edwards, but the response was the same as before—which was to say, there was no response.

"Come on, Edwards," Domi growled as she trotted past a crate of rotten fruit that three young children were busily picking through. The children wore no clothes, and they glared at Domi with feral eyes as she passed them. Ignoring them, Domi continued up the winding passageway between tumbledown dwellings.

"Cerberus?" Domi said, engaging the hidden pickup in her skull. "This is Domi. I need a favor."

A moment later, the cool voice of Brewster Philboyd, one of the mainstay operatives at the Cerberus redoubt, came back over the subdermal relay, pumping straight through Domi's mastoid bone. "I read you, Domi. What's going on?"

"I've lost Edwards," Domi explained as she danced beneath a low rail stretched across the narrow alley, a handful of clothes upon it having been left to dry in the sun. "Do you think you could use his transponder to give me a fix on his location?"

Over the Commtact link, Brewster Philboyd confirmed that he was doing so now. Transponders were implanted beneath the skin of each member of the Cerberus team, broadcasting a telemetric signal that provided the Cerberus nerve center with a constant stream of information about an individual's health, including heart rate, blood pressure and brain-wave activity. At a keystroke, these blips could be expanded to give full diagnostics for each member of a field team. With satellite triangulation, the transponders could also be used to track down an individual to within almost a hairbreadth of their actual physical location.

"So, how did you lose him anyway?" Philboyd asked as he brought forward Edwards's data feed.

"He went out for some fresh air and, um, gave us the slip," Domi explained a little self-consciously.

"Gave you the…?" Brewster sounded faintly amused. "I didn't realize Edwards was a prisoner."

"He's not," Domi agreed. "Which is why his disappearing like this is all the more worrying."

"Okay, okay," Philboyd mused, speaking as if to himself "Right, I've got Edwards tagged now. He's westbound, heading in roughly the direction of the ocean. By my reckoning, you're about three-quarters of a mile from his current location."

"Which way?" Domi asked, picking up speed as she hurried down the seemingly endless, foul-smelling alleyway.

"You're heading north just now," Philboyd told her. "You want to turn left as soon as you can and keep roughly to that course."

"Okay," Domi agreed as she saw a gap between two

of the broken-down huts. She rushed through the gap, ducking beneath a jutting strut of metal and weaving past a group of young mothers discussing something or other while they rocked their babies in their arms. The babies bawled incessantly, and the mothers ignored them, peering instead at the ghostly, chalk-white figure of Domi as she darted past them.

Brewster's rich voice came over the Commtact again as Domi headed on through the shanty ville. "I've just brought up the live satellite feed now, Domi," he explained. "That place is nothing shy of a maze and you're heading for a dead end."

"Dammit," Domi cussed. "See if you can raise Edwards from your side, while I find myself another route."

As she spoke, Domi reached the end of the current pathway, just as Philboyd had warned. A high wall loomed before her, its brickwork covered in damp lichen of a putrescent green shade with tiny mauve buds. To her left stood a ramshackle collection of aluminum cladding and wooden crates, somehow balanced together to create a rainproof structure—give or take a leak—within which dwelled a family of seven. Above the dwelling, a tin-can chimney contentedly chuffed billowing black smoke from the family's tiny cooking stove. To Domi's right, a similar building stood, its makeshift walls leaning at uncomfortable angles, apparently propping itself up in spite of the desires of gravity.

It was instinct, nothing more than that, but Domi felt certain that Edwards was in trouble. Assessing the two dwellings to either side of her, the albino woman reached up to the roof sill of the one to her left and sprang, her legs kicking out as she ran up the wall, pulling herself to the roof.

A holler of complaint came from the people below, but Domi ignored it. From up there, just one story above the ground, she could see across the immediate area. There were numerous run-down shacks, with smoking chimneys made from old piping or cans. The street plan, such as it was, was a labyrinthine mess of lefts and rights, abrupt stops in the roads where a new family of refugees from the destroyed villes had moved in and set up their home. But up here, on the rippled rooftop of corrugated iron, Domi could see a far easier way to travel through the run-down favela.

"Domi?" Brewster's voice came to her ear. "I've tried Edwards, but I'm having no success. A remote test shows his Commtact seems to be working. He just doesn't appear to be responding."

Ignoring the complaints coming from the grubby street below, Domi strode across the rooftop, speeding up to a run as she reached its end. "What does the transponder show?" she asked Brewster over the Commtact link. "Is he conscious?" As she spoke, Domi leaped from the rooftop to that of the next building. From there she kept running, moving with long strides of her bone-white legs, her pace quickening.

"He's moving," Brewster mused, "but that's not a definite sign he's awake. Stand by, I'm bringing up a full bio scan now."

Domi ran, her feet pounding lightly against the hollow roofs as she rushed over the heads of Hope's shanty ville populace. A moment later she had found a lower section of the moss-smeared wall, leaping over it in a single bound, her legs scissoring like a high jumper as she flung herself over the obstacle and headed west. On the other side, the petite albino woman found another rooftop, this one made of rain-damp wood. She ran onward, listening to Brewster's voice as she made her way toward the coast.

EDWARDS WAS STILL TREKKING after the silent, hooded figures he had found himself drawn to while he was administering medicines to the locals. There was something about them, he knew, something eerily familiar; he just couldn't place it. The irritating pain in his head didn't help matters, either.

Just then, Brewster Philboyd's voice reverberated in his skull via the Commtact, requesting that he respond and state his position.

"Hey, Brewmeister," Edwards said, keeping his voice low so as not to attract too much attention. "I'm...um—" he peered up at the position of the sun "—heading west, I think, following a group of suspects."

Edwards waited for Philboyd to acknowledge, but nothing happened.

"Suspects," Edwards repeated. "Perps. Whatever you non-Mags call them. People, weirdos. You getting this?"

Again there was no reply.

Irritably, Edwards continued along the shingle road between run-down tenements, wondering why his home base wouldn't respond. After all, they had called on him, not vice versa.

"Come on, Cerberus," he muttered, "answer the damn call."

Behind Edwards, stalking through the shadows, Rosalia followed the broad ex-Mag, her pale-eyed dog loping along at her heels. Rosalia wasn't being particularly subtle, she knew, and yet the wide-shouldered man seemed oblivious to his tail, as though his mind was too caught up on other things. She hurried along the street, her booted feet splashing the puddles that littered the pockmarked road.

"Okay, Magistrate man," she muttered, "let's see what you've got."

DOMI LEAPED THROUGH the air, bouncing from rooftop to rooftop like some out-of-control jack-in-the-box as she rushed through the shanty dwellings that lay at the outskirts of the fishing ville.

"Brew?" she asked between breaths as she leaped the gap between two more buildings. "You have that heads-up on Edwards's status yet?"

"Sorry about that, Domi. He's conscious," Philboyd responded after a moment. "His transponder is showing live brain activity and his heart is beating as normal. I just got a consult to double-check I was reading it right."

Bounding down from a two-story shack, Domi hit the ground running, weaving through a crowd of customers at a makeshift market stall as they bartered for the local produce. By the smell of it, the produce was already on the turn, but Domi had no time to consider that any further. "So he's alive," Domi said, "conscious and his Commtact appears to be operational. Any ideas what's going down?"

"I'm bringing in satellite surveillance now," Brewster responded over the radio link. "There's a crowd gathering out there, close to the coast. Keep on track and I'll guide you."

"How far?" Domi asked.

"You'll be there shortly," Brewster judged. "Take the next right and head up toward the hills."

Domi took the next right as instructed. Whatever

Edwards was involved in, he had better have a damn fine excuse for breaking contact.

THE HOODED FIGURES IN the distance had stopped, amassing in a block of scrubland that overlooked the ocean. Edwards halted to watch them, and Rosalia also halted so that she could watch both him and the figures in the hoods.

Other people seemed to be appearing from all around now, drawn to the hooded group as they waited. Some of them carried the pebbles that the people had dropped like calling cards all over the ville. Within a few minutes, the watching crowd had to have become forty or fifty strong, waiting in near silence for whatever it was to proceed.

Edwards made his way along the rearmost edge of the crowd, sticking to the shadows of an uneven wall, one eye on the hooded figures while he took in the faces here. They seemed to have been drawn here, called by something unseen, just as he had been. He reached for his face, rubbing at his forehead where that dull ache resided.

Suddenly, one of the six figures began to speak, a powerful orator, his voice carrying clearly over the crowd that had amassed.

"Come one, come all," he said. "Everyone is welcome here. This is where all salvation starts. Shall we begin?"

The crowd cried its assent, anticipation rising.

"We come among you today," the hooded leader explained, "to bring you utopia. A paradise that you cannot begin to imagine. But before we start, I must ask a question."

Edwards stopped walking as he reached the edge of

the wall that hid him, turning to face the speaker. The man reached his hands up and pulled back the low-hanging hood that had obscured his face. Around him, his five colleagues did likewise. Edwards narrowed his eyes, seeing something on each man's forehead, a circle no larger than a fingerprint.

"Who here already bears the mark?" the leader asked.

Several members of the crowd stepped forward, both men and women. They were the same people who had been following the group from down in the favela.

"Come now," the leader called, "there are more of you, I'm sure. There's no need to be shy."

Almost against his will, Edwards found himself stepping forward, edging away from a dead tree he had found himself standing beside, stepping away from the shattered wall. He could feel himself being drawn to the speaker, feel the man's hypnotic call inside his head. A part of him wanted to join the group, and—worse—that part of him seemed to be making the decision for the rest of him.

Edwards wasn't the only one. Others were emerging from the crowd, pushing their way to the front.

Suddenly a woman's voice spoke close by to Edwards's ear, just as he was about to make his way out from the wall and into the crowd.

"Sorry, Cerberus, but you're cramping my style."

Edwards felt a heavy blow to his head then, and he collapsed to his knees, before sprawling forward, a trickle of blood pouring down the side of his face from where the woman had struck him with a fallen branch from the tree. As Edwards's consciousness flickered and dimmed, the last thing he saw was the lithe, olive-skinned woman striding away, hiding herself among the crowd, her mongrel dog trotting along faithfully at her side.

As Domi HURRIED UP the mud steps toward the road that Philboyd was indicating over the Commtact link, the man's voice came to her again.

"Domi, we may have a problem," Philboyd stated from his position at the Cerberus redoubt in Montana.

"Go ahead, Cerberus," Domi instructed, her hand automatically reaching to check that her Detonics Combat Master handgun was still in its holster at her hip.

"Edwards's transponder just flatlined," Brewster explained. "He's either lost consciousness or—"

"Don't say it, Brewster," Domi ordered. "I'll be there soon enough." As she hurried up the steep steps, Domi just hoped that wasn't as ambitious a statement as it sounded to her own ears right now.

Chapter 14

Roughly twelve miles beneath the surface of the Pacific, two Cerberus Manta craft glided gracefully through the water toward the cruciform structure that waited at the bottom of the sea. After their tangle with the giant squidlike creatures, both pilots remained alert and cautious of what was going on all around them, and the tension in the cockpits of both vehicles was acute.

The whole approach was done using the heads-up sensor display and guided by an automated system that seemed to already know the position and entry route for the docking gateway that resided on one side of the immense coral-like cross.

Sitting behind Grant in the tiny passenger seat of the compact cockpit, Clem let out a long sigh of relief as he peered through the slit windows at the near total darkness.

Hearing this, Grant offered a note of reassurance. "Almost there now, Clem," he said.

"I feel like we just went ten rounds with the kraken of legend," the oceanographer said, sounding genuinely exhausted.

Grant loosed a single, sharp bark of laughter as he guided the Manta along the final approach. He could see from the sensor display that Kane was following in his own craft and there were no more sea monsters out there—at least for now. "Brigid called them librarians," Grant explained.

It was Clem's turn to laugh then, and it was the fulsome sound of relief. "The kraken was a fearsome beast, a sea monster," he explained, "that was said to roam the oceans around Norway and Iceland. Modern interpretations suggest that the kraken really was some kind of giant squid that generally made its home in the ocean depths."

"Sounds like our librarian, all right," Grant agreed.

Clem shook his head in astonishment, though Grant was too busy concentrating on the controls to see. "You're completely unfazed," Clem said in amazement. "You—the three of you—do this kind of thing a lot, don't you?"

"Define 'a lot,'" Grant replied as the Manta floated through a wide, coral archway within the cruciform structure.

A moment later they found themselves dipping even lower as Grant followed the tunnel beyond the archway, keeping to a slow, steady pace as his sensor array began bringing up reams of new information.

"Have entered some kind of tunnel construction," Grant informed Kane over the Commtact.

Kane's voice came back a moment later: "I've got your back, buddy. Entering the structure now."

The tunnel continued to sink, dropping at a thirty-degree angle as it burrowed beneath the ocean bed. Peering through the back windowpanes, Clem was delighted to see that the walls were visible, lit sporadically by some kind of phosphorescent moss that grew upon the walls in shades of pinks and orange-reds, the color of a peach's skin.

"It looks like a magical grotto," Clem said in wonder.

Up ahead of him, Grant peered past the heads-up display information, looking through the windshield at the otherworldly sight of the cavern that they were slowly traveling through. Clem was right; it really did look like something magical, like an illustration from a child's storybook. The tunnel's uneven walls seemed to twinkle with the strange lighting as the Manta followed its mysterious path.

"Do you realize," Clem said, the reverence clear in his tone, "that we are probably deeper beneath the ocean than any human has ever been?"

Grant eased up a little on the thrust to the engines, letting the Manta glide as the tunnel began to rise steeply once again. A moment later they found themselves emerging from the water in what appeared to be a vast cavern, filled with air and once again lit by the strange glowing lichen that clung to the walls in its obscure patterns. The cavern featured a huge circular pool in its center from which the Manta had emerged, with a border of flattened rock at its edges that led to an opening on the far side of the cave, its entryway approximately six feet across. To Grant's surprise, there were three Manta craft already waiting at the edges of the pool, their blisterlike cockpits drawn back and showing them to be unoccupied.

Grant examined the opening at the far end of the cavern, allowing the sensors to judge its width. "Too small for us to fit through," he muttered. "Looks like this is where we get out and walk."

"Excellent," Clem announced buoyantly. "I could do with stretching my legs."

Grant brought the Manta around, edging it on vertical

jets toward a spot against one rocky wall, away from the other docked Mantas, before bringing it to rest in the water. The water here was shallower, and Grant felt the bottom of the Manta's hull clunk lightly against a shelf that was hidden just a few feet beneath the water's surface. The shelf was at the perfect height to allow the Manta's wings to rest level with the rock circle that bordered the room, as if it had been designed as a kind of docking bay for these ancient craft of Annunaki design.

As Grant eased the Manta to a resting position, Kane's vehicle emerged from the circular pool, water streaming off its sleek lines as the red-orange light glistened off its mirror-bronzed surface.

"Docking bay," Grant explained over the Commtact link as Kane brought his Manta out of the water, hovering in place for a few seconds.

"So I see," Kane replied over the medium of the Commtact.

Inside his own Manta craft, hovering just a few feet above the surface of the water, Kane allowed the sensitive scanning equipment to analyze the cavern and what it could "see" beyond its walls.

"I'm picking up a nebulous reading of a lot of life-forms," Kane stated, "but the details seem unclear."

"It looks like a coral reef, a living habitat," Brigid stated from behind Kane's head, peering through the slit windows to either side of her seat. "We're likely to find a lot of things making their homes here."

Then, following Grant's lead, Kane brought his Manta down on the hidden shelf that surrounded the rim of the pool, taking one last look at the area through the complex scanning equipment aboard his craft.

Once he had landed, Kane removed his helmet and

opened the cockpit seal. Then he and Brigid made their way down one sloped wing of the craft and out onto the rocky border that circled the room. Already disembarked, Grant and Clem waited by the wing of their own craft while their colleagues made their way over to join them. Grant was checking the damage his vehicle had taken in the meeting with the colossal librarians, relieved to see just a few dents and scrapes. They'd been lucky.

Grant wore his favored Kevlar trenchcoat over his shadow suit, while Clem had added a padded jacket over his Cerberus jumpsuit, and he pulled the wings of the collar tight to his neck, staving off the cold of the cavern. In fact, despite being roughly twelve miles beneath the surface of the sea, the temperature in the grotto was surprisingly mild, just a little cooler than normal room temperature. Additionally, there was no breeze in the area at all, which seemed slightly peculiar for some unidentifiable reason.

The Mantas had been designed as space-faring craft, and their sensors had automatically informed their pilots that they were reentering a breathable atmosphere before opening the cockpit seals.

"At least we can breathe," Kane said as he deeply inhaled the atmosphere through his nostrils.

"Guess the lizards didn't like getting wet," Grant observed sullenly as he stared around the cavern. He had never been comfortable discussing the intricacies of Annunaki society or technology.

As Brigid joined them, Grant acknowledged her with a grim nod. "Hell of a slick move back there," Grant told her by way of thanks.

The Titian-haired woman acknowledged his thanks with a self-conscious smile before indicating the three abandoned craft within the cavern. "Someone else on the guest list?" she asked.

Clem narrowed his eyes as he looked at the docked Mantas in the pale light of the cavern. "If there is, they arrived a long time before we did," he said. "There are barnacles on the bottoms of the hulls, see?"

The other Cerberus warriors followed Clem's eye line, seeing the lumpy growths along the waterline of the sleek craft. The bronze metal had turned to green in ugly patches, too, and on closer examination, each craft appeared to be in a state of disrepair.

"Guess they've been here a while," Kane agreed.

"Their pilots are probably long since dead, then," Clem proposed jauntily.

"Could have been dead ten thousand years or more," Grant said, bringing his Copperhead assault subgun out of a hidden recess in his coat, and scanning the cavern and its sole above-water entry point warily. "Still, I'd rather we keep our eyes open just in case they're not."

Kane powered his own weapon, the Sin Eater pistol, into his hand from its hidden wrist holster. "Annunaki live for a long time," he reminded Clem. "Keep behind me."

With that, Kane led the way into the entryway tunnel that led from the docking pool.

Warily, the Cerberus field team made its way from the area that they had deemed the docking bay and into a corridor that stretched off into the main area of the undersea complex. The corridor was quite narrow, too tight for all four to walk abreast, and so Kane took the lead, his Sin Eater handgun clutched ready in his right hand. Though tight, the sides of the corridor stretched quite high, towering to almost fourteen feet above them, and narrowing to an archlike point that ran along its center. It was low lit, small pods glowing an eerie blue amid the structure of the walls themselves, and the light was too erratically spaced and too dim to cast firm shadows, instead rendering everything into a vague, foggy sort of blandness. Close up, the walls and floor seemed to be made of dried coral, and Kane was struck by its uncomfortable similarity to bone.

"Feels a little like an ossuary," Grant grumbled as he entered the corridor archway, bringing up the rear of the group. "Smells like one, too."

Grant clutched his Copperhead assault rifle, a fiercely powerful weapon and one of his favorites when in the field, purely because of its ease of use and the sheer level of rapid destruction it could bring. The grip and trigger of the gun were placed in front of the breech in the bullpup design, allowing the weapon to be used single-handed, and an optical, image-intensified scope coupled with a laser autotargeter were mounted on top of the frame. The Copperhead possessed a 700-round-per-minute rate of fire and was equipped with an extended magazine holding thirty-five 4.85 mm steel-jacketed rounds. Besides the Copperhead subgun, Grant also wore his own Sin Eater pistol in a responsive wrist holster like Kane's, where it could be called to his hand with the speed of thought.

Striding between the two ex-Mags, Brigid and Clem kept their wits about them, but showed more interest in the nature of the corridor itself. Clem especially was fascinated by the suggestion of sea life that he saw here. "An ossuary might not be so far from the truth," he proposed, running a gloved hand along the wall to his left. "I rather suspect that the foundation for this structure could in fact be a skeleton."

Kane glanced behind him for a moment, a look of

irritation furrowing his brow. "It'd be one hell of a big skeleton, Clem," he said, keeping his voice low.

"Those things we saw outside—the librarians—were creatures of exceptional magnitude," Clem reminded Kane.

Brigid pondered the walls for a moment, keeping her pace up as she followed Kane along the eerie, softly lit corridor. "If it is a skeleton," she said, "then it died a long, long time ago. The coral that's grown up here looks to be several feet thick."

Clem shrugged. "Things die all the time, Brigid," he said.

As they continued to make their way down the corridor, their footsteps echoing softly amid the dulling sound of water, Grant spotted something from the corner of his eye. He turned, automatically bringing the Copperhead subgun around to track whatever it was that had drawn his attention.

"Everything okay, partner?" Kane called back to him, halting in his own progress. His own senses were on high alert, and something nagged at the edge of Kane's consciousness; it felt as if he was being watched.

Grant stood stock-still for a moment, his eyes narrowed as he examined the wall before him in the dim light. Its bumps and ridges were like valleys, a miniature landscape full of peaks and caves. Three feet away from where he had stopped, one of the blue lights flickered a little and then, utterly soundless, it winked out.

"Grant?" Kane asked from along the corridor.

"Fine," Grant growled, lowering his blaster and turning away from the uneven wall.

The others began making their way along the narrow corridor, but even as Grant turned, there came a sound like needles dropping onto glass from very close to his left ear.

Grant turned, but he was almost too late to see the thing in the semidarkness. Something skittered across the surface of the coral, something no bigger than Grant's fist and with an abundance of long, whirring legs that propelled it along at incredible speed. "Whoa!" Grant cried as, in flinch reaction, he leaped back from the wall.

His companions turned at their friend's outburst and saw him jump sideways until he met with the wall on the other side of the narrow corridor. Grant spun then, looking left and right at the wall he had automatically propelled himself against. "There's something alive here," he shouted to Kane and the others.

Chapter 15

Kane raised his Sin Eater before him as he trotted back down the tight corridor to meet with Grant.

Brigid Baptiste gave Clem a reassuring look as she pulled a TP-9 from the holster she wore slung low to her hip. "Stay behind us, Clem," she said. "You'll be safe."

Clem nodded agreement, keeping his distance as he followed Brigid's slender form retreating down the corridor.

"What did you see?" Kane demanded as he pulled up beside Grant. As he spoke, another of the dull blue lights winked out behind them, casting the corridor into ever-deepening gloom.

"Only saw it for a second but it looked like some kind of spider," Grant explained. "Lot of legs and it moved real fast."

"How big?" Kane asked.

"About—" Grant began, then he saw another movement as something leaped from the craggy surface of the wall. "Shit!"

Whatever it was, it had jumped the gap between the wall and Kane, and the ex-Mag spun as he felt it land upon his back. "What the—?"

Without stopping to think, Grant swung the Copperhead around, jabbing with its butt at the skittering creature that was scrambling over Kane's shoulder. The creature dropped to the floor. Grant and Kane watched, disgusted, as the hand-size creature disappeared into a nook in the uneven coral surface of the floor, its long, spindly legs disappearing from sight.

"What was it?" Brigid asked as she caught up to her partners.

"I don't know," Kane admitted. "We're thinking spider maybe."

Brigid looked from Kane to Grant, conscious of the weight of the TP-9 in her own hand and how ridiculous the three of them had to look at that moment. The TP-9 was a compact semiautomatic, a bulky handgun with the grip set just off center beneath the barrel and a covered targeting scope across the top, all finished in molded matte black. To point it at a spider was very much like using the proverbial sledgehammer to crack a nut. Feeling foolish, Brigid eased her grip on the bulky pistol, relaxing from her ready stance.

Clem joined the three Cerberus warriors an instant later. "Where did it go?" he asked.

"Little bugaboo found a hole or crevice or something," Kane told him, toeing the ground with his boot, "just about there."

Clem crouched down on his haunches, his dark eyes furiously scanning the lumpy ground.

"You want to be careful there, Clem," Grant warned.

Clem looked up, and there was such a look of open fascination on his face that he seemed like a child on Christmas morning. "This could be a new form of life," he said enthusiastically. "It's our duty to catalog and—"

Grant shook his head. "You must be mistaking us with someone else, Bryant. We go in, we get the job done and then we get the fuck out of here. Right now I'm really looking forward to getting to point C in that list—you read me?"

Clem sighed, resigning himself to the facts at hand. "The mission comes first," he agreed, pushing himself back to a standing position. "But it does rather go against my ethos."

"Well," Kane growled, "it wasn't your ethos that got crawled on now, was it?"

Clem was about to respond when the spiderlike creature reappeared from a gap in the floor, and Grant shoved him to one side as he swung the Copperhead assault weapon to bear.

"Grant, no!" Clem shouted, but his instruction—or perhaps it had been a warning—came too late.

Grant unleashed a blast from the Copperhead, and a smattering of lethal 4.85 mm bullets peppered the ground about their feet, their explosion bright in the semidarkness of the corridor. The weird creature was instantaneously reduced to a messy pulp as one of Grant's bullets drilled through its hard carapace. It lay there in a pool of its own fluids, a milky-colored ooze leaking from the remains of its body as its legs twitched. Although it had been mashed up by Grant's bullet, enough of it remained that the Cerberus warriors could define its basic anatomy. It was roughly seven inches across, both length and width, in an almost perfectly circular form. The body itself was a dangling two-inch oval amid the spray of long, needle-thin legs, and milky ooze seeped from a ruined area at its back left edge as the legs finally stilled. There were eight legs in all, a neutral color like the body, the color of frosted glass. It made no noise, just continued to bubble in place as its white lifeblood seeped away into the uneven floor of the corridor, washing away in thin runnels as the liquid sought the path of least resistance.

"You were right," Brigid said to no one in particular. "It does look like a spider. Could be a crab of some sort. What do you think, Clem?" she asked, turning to the oceanographer.

Clem's eyes were fixed on a point just behind Brigid, a little way over her head. "Whatever it is, I think we're about to get better acquainted, Miss Baptiste," he said in a quiet, awestruck voice.

Brigid turned, as did Kane and Grant, automatically bringing their blasters to bear on the place Clem indicated. Up there, skittering along the walls and high arch of the roof, more of the glass-colored creatures were moving, their numbers lost to the darkness of the corridor. In the halfhearted blue light from the walls, it looked like a hundred needle-thin fingers reaching out from the walls at Grant, pointing at him in accusation.

"Clem," Kane asked, not bothering to look behind him, "best guess here—are these things likely to be deadly?"

Although Clem had never seen the creatures until today, his expertise was sufficient to extrapolate a reasonable risk assessment in a couple of seconds. "The ocean is full of numerous things that can be poisonous—and often fatal—to human beings. I'd suggest we don't touch their blood until we know what's in it."

As a hundred spiderlike creatures skittered across the walls, moving in a radial pattern toward the Cerberus heroes, Kane became aware of more movements at his sides, behind and all around him. He glanced briefly to the side and saw more of the spiny creatures emerging from crevices in the coral wall, their spindly legs reaching out as they clambered into view, even as another of the dull blue wall lights winked out. As Kane turned back to the mass of creatures at his rear, yet another of the ocean blue lights blinked out, plunging another chunk of the corridor into darkness in the direction of the docking bay.

"Let's keep going," Kane decided, his gun twitching this way and that as he spotted more of the ugly arachnids moving about the walls and skittering along the floor. "Baptiste, you're on point."

Brigid grabbed Clem by the elbow and hurried him down the corridor in the direction they had been going before Grant had stopped.

Three steps later and another of the ineffective blue lights fizzled out, leaving an increasing length of the corridor ahead of them in darkness, as was the whole of the tunnel length behind them. Clem slowed his pace, but Brigid urged him on.

"Come on, Clem, let's keep moving," Brigid insisted.

Clem looked at her, and Brigid saw his eyes flash in the eerie nonlight of the narrow corridor. "I don't relish walking into a situation blind," he said, though it was a practical concern rather than through any suggestion of fear on his part.

Even as Clem said it, bright beams of light appeared from behind him—first one, then two, as Grant and Kane flipped on their xenon-beam flashlights. Suddenly the whole of the narrow corridor was bathed in brilliance, the xenon beams the equivalent of five thousand candles of power.

It wasn't an improvement.

The bumpy, misshapen walls appeared to be alive with movement, the glistening, spiderlike creatures skittering across their surfaces as they reared away from the bright lights. On the floor, too, dozens of multi-legged creatures scurried for cover, clambering over the uneven floor as they vied for space. As Brigid watched, more of the creatures emerged, their pencil-thin legs wrapping around the ridges in the floor as they reared up, peering at the intruders.

"Kane…" Brigid began uncertainly.

"I see them, Baptiste," Kane said from behind her. "Let's hope that if we just ignore them—"

Kane didn't get the chance to finish his sentence. One of the spiderlike monstrosities disengaged from the wall before him and flew at his face, propelled through the air by a powerful leap, its spindly legs waving before it like a snapping claw.

Kane ducked, but as he did so things took a further turn for the worse. The leaping creature seemed to throw something at Kane, either spit or secreted through some other orifice, and a thin spurt of yellow-white liquid dashed through the air, whizzing just over his head.

To one side, Grant followed the little creature with the nose of his blaster as it dropped to the floor just behind Kane, its leap propelling it past its target. Without hesitation, he blasted off another round from the Copperhead close-assault weapon, reducing the fast-moving creature to a messy pool of goo and quivering legs.

Having avoided the thing's attack, Kane's eyes widened as he watched the pool of spit it had tossed at him. The venom, or whatever it was, was fizzing, bubbles appearing across its surface as it spewed a misty white trail of smoke, like caustic soda where it had pooled on the uneven floor. "We may be in trouble," he muttered as he raised his Sin Eater and scanned the walls ahead under the unforgiving light of his xenon beam.

The Cerberus warriors were absolutely surrounded by the monstrous creatures whose needlelike legs clicked as they raced across the hard surface of the coral structure.

At the front of the group, Clem took a step back, even as three more of the multilimbed creatures spewed streams of venom at him and Brigid. The venom streams rushed past him, creating smoldering trails on the ridged floor.

Brigid took aim with the TP-9, blasting off three shots in swift succession, destroying the attacking creatures where they clung to the walls. It was hopeless, she knew—the odds were simply too great. Like some mythological beast, kill one and a dozen more rushed to take its place. "Kane, we need a better solution," she announced, "and we need it quick."

Then Brigid shoved Clem to one side as one of the wall-crawlers leaped, its sharp legs poised ahead like blades. The creature sailed past where Clem had stood a second before, landing on the ground with a clack-clack of its legs and scurrying down the corridor toward where Grant waited with Kane.

"Stay awake, Clem," Brigid admonished, "we're in a danger zone here."

More of the creatures were dropping from the ceiling and walls, a whole cloud of them leaping through the air toward Grant and Kane.

Grant's Copperhead assault gun boomed in the narrow corridor, its loud blast muffled by the ridges of the tight walls. Several of the tiny monsters were caught in the blast, fizzling into fiery nothingness as Grant's bullets drilled through their fragile forms. Then they were upon him, six tiny bodies clambering over his chest and up his right arm, their needle-sharp legs pressing against his Kevlar coat and shadow suit.

Moving swiftly, Grant swept the creatures off his arm, and two of them went flying through the air while a third dug its spiny legs into his brushing hand. Grant yelped in pain as the needlelike legs prodded at his skin, before swatting the thing against the nearest wall. It moved fast, trying to get away from its promised fate, but Grant's lightning-quick reactions trapped enough of the creature against the wall to flatten its bulk.

Two more of the strange arachnids were racing across his chest, and one loomed over his breastbone, raising its carapace on those awful, sticklike legs before spitting a gob of milky venom at the exposed skin of his face. Grant closed his eyes, turning his head as the acidic spew sprayed past him, smelling something like gasoline. He heard the fizzing of the liquid spray as it whooshed past his ear. And then something slapped against Grant's chest. He opened his eyes to see Kane flinging the remaining creatures from him, using the muzzle of his Sin Eater. Kane flipped them into the air with a swift movement, blasting a flaring shot into one of them as it whizzed through the air while the other bumped against and clung onto the wall, scuttling up the ridges before disappearing into one of the shadowy crevices there.

More of the spindly-legged creatures were scampering across the floor and walls, their sharp talons skittering against the hard coral with a sound like raindrops on a tin plate. At the head of the group, Brigid was rapidly selecting her targets and drilling them with 9 mm bullets from her TP-9, missing about one in three thanks to the creatures' rapid movements. Suddenly, one of the monstrous things was on her foot, clambering to gain purchase on her leg, and Brigid kicked out, flipping the thing away in a graceless whirl of clacking limbs.

More of the creatures were dropping from above, and Clem danced on the spot as sprays of acid venom rained down all around him. Kane watched as one of the ugly, spindly creatures turned and spit a gob of venom at Clem's back. The gob fell just short, and Kane rattled off another blast from his Sin Eater, turning the little monster into a pool of dangling goo.

Another of the creatures pounced off the floor at Brigid, using its multiple limbs like a spring to charge forward, embedding itself in her leg. She roared with surprise as much as pain before turning her pistol on it and blasting a bullet through its colorless body. Even as its body exploded, another of the spiderlike creatures dropped from the ceiling, landing in Brigid's long hair and entangling itself there in a moment.

Brigid was struck by a weird sense of déjà vu, as she felt the thing scampering across her scalp. She sensed that she had been here before, done this very thing before. It was strange, and all the more so since Brigid Baptiste had an eidetic memory and the vague sense of déjà vu was, to say the least, very unusual in her because her powers of recollection were so potent.

She pushed the thought aside, blindly reaching into her hair and placing her fingers around one of the creature's limbs. In a second, she had tossed the thing to the floor, and she stamped on it as it struggled to right itself, crushing its body beneath the ball of her foot. Goop oozed out around her boot as the creature was turned to sludgy pulp. Brigid ignored it, turning back down the corridor and shouting for Kane.

"We need a plan here, and quick," she called.

"I know," Kane growled. He looked around, playing the bright xenon beam across the corridor that they were in until it hit Brigid in the face, and she blinked so hard it was almost like waking up.

A moment later, the beam lit on the scuttling creatures as his mind raced. The more prominent of the hard-shelled creatures reared back as the light struck them, diving into nooks and ridges as he tried to examine them while their smaller brethren skittered away, keeping their distance. "Light," he muttered. "They don't like the light."

"Stands to reason," Clem agreed as he sidestepped another creature plummeting from the ceiling, its claws outstretched. "Living down here in the darkness for so long."

Grant brought the beam of his own xenon flashlight around, adding its intensity to Kane's. "Put them together and keep going forward?" he proposed.

Kane peered back over his shoulder, saw the skittering bodies there as the spiderlike creatures rushed across floor and walls toward them. "They're going to keep following us," he concluded after a moment's thought, "and we can't light up the whole area."

"You want to bring that light around here?" Brigid asked, a rising sense of panic in her voice.

"Heads up," Kane called as he tossed Brigid the flashlight.

Grant blasted another shot from his Copperhead as yet another of the spindly creatures dropped from the ceiling, plummeting down toward where Kane stood. "I'll cover you," he said, "but let's keep moving, huh?"

"No," Kane ordered, reaching into a utility pouch at the side of his belt with his free hand. In a moment, he had removed three ball-bearing-like spheres—flash-bangs, part of the standard arsenal carried by all Cerberus field teams. The flash-bangs were tiny devices that could be hidden in the palm of the hand and used on unsuspecting enemies. Each compact sphere contained a volatile chemical mixture along with a small amount of ignition fluid. When activated, the flash-bang would do exactly what its name implied—flash and bang. Different mixtures were available to create other effects, such as masking smoke clouds and tear gas, but the basic premise remained the same for each—a relatively harmless defensive weapon that could be used to surprise an enemy so that one could disorient and overpower them. Right now, however, Kane would have to admit he hadn't expected that enemy to be some weird alien spider-crab hybrid when he had stocked up his arsenal for the day. "Everybody look away," he instructed in a firm voice, as the others continued toward the far end of the corridor.

As his colleagues ran, sweeping the rugged sides of the corridor with the fierce beams of their flashlights, Kane tossed three flash-bangs behind him, counting down in his head as they bounced off the hardpacked coral and rattled along the floor. Kane turned away before he reached the count of zero, waiting for the short flash-bang timers to take effect. Then, with cataclysmic fury, the trio of flash-bangs ignited, their cacophonous noise achingly loud in the confines of the narrow corridor, their bright lights illuminating the whole area like a savage lightning strike.

Eyes closed against the brightness that shone all around, Kane sprinted down the corridor, trusting his instincts and spatial awareness as he chased after his rapidly retreating colleagues. Behind him, he knew the hideous arachnids had to be scuttling for cover, their world turned upside down by the dazzling blast of light. If they cried out—if they were capable of such—Kane could not hear them over the ringing in his ears from the explosion.

Bullets whizzed all about Kane, blasting overhead and spraying the walls as Grant and Brigid picked off more of the creatures that were scuttling after their prey. As he ran, Kane felt something small land on his shoulder, clawlike appendages jabbing at the protective weave of his shadow suit. Opening his eyes to a narrow squint, Kane punched at the thing, knocking it from his body as it spit a thick stream of the yellow-white venom at his face. The spray splashed over his shoulder before looping over and over in the air as the spider-thing was knocked away. The venom fizzed there against Kane's arm for a moment, and the ex-Mag was remarkably grateful at that moment for the protective power of the shadow suit that he wore.

His feet crashed against the rock-hard floor, and Kane felt things burst as he stepped on the bodies of more of the weird arachnids.

An instant later he was at the end of the corridor, dark shapes visible before him in his narrowed eyes, and a strong arm reached around him, pulling him to a halt; it was Grant.

"You're okay, man," Grant assured him, his voice a deep rumble heard above the ringing in Kane's ears.

Kane opened his eyes wider, seeing the splurge of yellow-white that dripped from his shoulder. When he peered up, he saw that they stood in a vast chamber, the high ceiling a series of opaque panes that showed the inky darkness of the open ocean beyond. Augmented by the more diffused effects of the xenon beams in the vast room, there was enough light that Kane could see the huge scale of the chamber they now found themselves in. It was at least ten times the size of the grotto that they had docked within, its farthest reaches lost in a blue-green gloom.

"Well, where are we?" Kane asked breathlessly, though he didn't expect an answer from his colleagues.

"I think we're here," Brigid said, and she pointed to something in the center of the huge chamber.

A vast structure towered up into the rafters, dominating the center of the room. Kane saw it in sections as Brigid played the beam of the flashlight over its surface, so huge was the construct. It looked like an enormous upturned funnel, with eight great roots tangling outward from its lowest section, reaching across the coral floor like the arms of an octopus. As Brigid ran the beam across the center of the strange construction, Kane saw a majestic figure sitting there, and for a moment he thought that the still figure was simply a statue carved from stone. And then, as realisation dawned, Kane's heart thudded against his rib cage in alarm.

"Ullikummis," he murmured.

Chapter 16

In the scrubland overlooking the beach in the township of Hope, the speaker in the hooded robe began to explain the nature of the forthcoming utopia. As he spoke, Rosalia watched the members of the crowd out of the corners of her eyes, observing their reactions. The crowd seemed excited, hanging on the speaker's every word as he spoke of salvation and saviors and all the other reams of nonsense spoken by every preacher Rosalia had ever seen. It was uncanny, the way they listened with such intensity.

The crowd itself was made up of men and women, old and young. There were even a few children who, despite their youthful years, paid increasing attention to the speaker as he fed them his line of bull.

As she peered warily around, Rosalia began to spot a few faces she recognized. She noticed the group of street thugs from the altercation in the church hall the previous evening, when Kane and the others had employed their usual strong-arm Magistrate tactics to overpower them. Their leader, or at least the one who had led the attack that she had witnessed, wore glasses now, perched on the end of his nose at a slightly askew angle. He seemed entranced by the speech, as did his colleagues. That was strange—it wasn't normal that young predators like these gang members would fall for this kind of spiel, unless they were here to steal from the congregation.

Rosalia made to brush her dark hair from her face, taking a more careful look at the street thugs. They seemed to be utterly entranced, their expressions blank and...*soulless,* that was the word that came to her. She had seen people without souls before, and it was not a thing she wished to revisit.

An elderly man stood with them, an outlander type with a dirty, drink-stained coat and a grizzly beard. Rosalia did not recognize him, but he seemed to be leading them now. Perhaps one of the thug's fathers?

Rosalia turned her attention back to the speaker for a moment, as he continued espousing his mumbo-jumbo about heaven on Earth, a savior from the stars and some great god called Ullikummis. The name was new, admittedly, but the rest was depressingly familiar to Rosalia, who had grown up in a nunnery.

At her feet, Belly-on-legs began to bark, looking at someone in the crowd. Rosalia hushed the dog, turning her attention to her right to try to see what it was that had disturbed the idiot mutt. There were three children there, three familiar children. They were the same ones who had been outside her garage home when she had been awoken, tossing stones in a dirt circle in some derivation of jacks. They were normal neighborhood kids, maybe five or six years of age; she knew them from around, sometimes gave them scraps of food if she managed to scrabble up any extra that she could tell was only going to rot.

Three normal five- or six-year-olds, and yet they sat erect on the ground, saying nothing, listening to the speechmaker with rapt attention. It was uncanny.

Then the person next to Rosalia jostled her, and she

almost struck her in automatic reaction. She stopped short, looking at the elderly woman there. The gray-haired woman was passing her something. For a moment, Rosalia took it to be a communion wafer, for it was small and circular and a light tan color. But as she took it, she saw it was not a wafer—it was a tiny rock, nothing more than a pebble.

The woman passed a handful of these to Rosalia, instructing her to take one and pass the others on.

"If you have one already," the speaker was explaining in his proud orator's voice, "don't be greedy. Let others share in the future."

Someone off to Rosalia's right shrieked, something just a little more than a gasp really, and the ears of Rosalia's mongrel dog suddenly pricked up. The dark-haired woman crouched, soothing the mutt as he became visibly agitated, wondering what was happening.

"Shh," she told him. "It's nothing. It's okay. These people just want to be friends."

As she spoke, Rosalia felt something digging into her right hand, and she opened her palm to see the stone she had held there was now burying itself, working through her skin like some burrowing insect. She gasped despite herself, reaching for the rock with her other hand and plucking at it with her nails, pulling it swiftly free. The hard stone rolled out of her fingers and across her hand as if it had a life of its own. Then it was moving down her hand toward her wrist, digging at the joint there.

"Damn," Rosalia muttered under her breath, reaching for the weird stone again. "Get off me."

With her broad, sharpened thumbnail, Rosalia flicked the burrowing rock off her skin, and watched as it skittered across the ground to land by the feet of the person in front of her.

"Now we are few," the speaker continued at the front of the crowd, "but soon we shall be many. Spread the word of Ullikummis and he shall come—he shall save us all."

The crowd around Rosalia began to chant, "Ullikummis, Ullikummis, Ullikummis."

As the people around her joined the chorus, Rosalia looked at her arm, wondering if the weird, burrowing rock had damaged her, if it had already infected her blood or something. Were all these people already—what was the word—hosts? Were they all carriers for this strange rock thing?

"You!" the speaker shouted. "Woman, what is your name?"

Rosalia looked up from where she crouched at her dog's side, seeing the speaker and his team standing over her. The crowd had parted to give them space.

"Who, me?" Rosalia asked, automatically offering her most enticing and flirtatious smile.

"What is your name?" the man asked, ignoring her efforts to charm him with a look.

"Rose," Rosalia told him. It was close enough, a name she would answer to without thinking. The nuns had taught her that in situations dealing with the unknown, it was best to keep a little in reserve, and to offer the truth only by slight degrees.

"Are you a believer, Rose?" the lead speaker asked, and his tone seemed fierce. "A believer in Ullikummis?"

At her side, the mutt started to whine, shuffling away from the robed men, clearly uncomfortable in their presence. Rosalia grabbed the dog by the scruff if its neck, holding the animal still.

"Are you a believer, Rose?" the lead speaker asked again, his tone demanding.

"I would like to be one," Rosalia began. "I need convincing." Once again, an element of truth in the lie was always the way to go in these situations, she knew.

"Heaven is coming," the man said. "Utopia. And you, Rose, shall be a part of it. You shall be an apostle in the order of Ullikummis."

Then, with a swift glance, the speaker instructed his colleagues. "Hold her down," he said.

Rosalia's keen eyes flashed, assessing the situation in an instant. Six men—that was all. Rosalia could take six men. She could challenge them and beat them in combat, even trained fighters, even ones who were armed. She smiled, revelling in the challenge as the first two strode toward her, the crowd watching in fascination, still chanting the name of their imaginary savior.

From her position on the ground, Rosalia moved her leg in a swift sweep, judged to a height of just above her opponents' ankles, designed to knock them off their feet. But when the blow connected with the first, instead of knocking the man over, Rosalia's leg stopped as if it had hit something made of brick.

She cried out in her surprise, and leaped backward to escape the men's grasping hands. The crowd there pushed her back at the approaching group, as Belly-on-legs barked this way and that, not knowing which way to turn, which enemy to berate.

Less than three minutes later, the crowd had dissipated and the group had left, leaving no real indications that they had ever been there.

And Rosalia and her dog?

They were gone, too, and so was the sound of her awful, strained screaming.

WHEN DOMI FOUND EDWARDS, he was lying facedown in the scrubland of the empty block, the crashing sound of the waves drifting up from the nearby ocean.

"Edwards?" she asked, prodding him with her finger. "Edwards, you with us?"

Edwards moved slightly, grunting nonsensically as Domi prodded him again.

Crouching beside her fallen colleague, Domi peered around the empty block. They were hidden behind a low wall. Beyond that, the grass was barely there and showed a lackluster shade of yellow as if any life had been bleached away by the unrelenting sun. The ground was churned up, too, where people had been here just a short while before, perhaps less than a minute ago. Domi felt eyes watching her, but put it down to an overactive imagination.

"Come on, Edwards," Domi urged, "nap time's over."

Edwards pushed himself up, rolling over so that he could rest his head propped on one elbow. "What happened?" he asked.

Domi dipped a white finger in the congealing blood that marred her colleague's head. "Looks like you got whacked from behind," she said, showing him the smear on her finger. "You remember anything?"

Edwards pushed a hand to his forehead, rubbing at a bump there. As he did so, the bump receded at his touch, disappearing as if it had never been. "There were people," he explained, "and, like, a preacher type, calling them to mass, I guess. I..." Edwards stopped, recalling the command in his mind, encouraging him to follow, to join the figures in their hoods and robes. The call of utopia.

"What?" Domi asked, wondering at why Edwards had stopped.

"I don't think it's safe here," Edwards announced. "I think something's going on that we're not quite seeing."

"What do you mean by that?" Domi asked, peering more carefully around the now-empty lot.

Edwards pushed himself up, brushing off his clothes as he got back to a standing position. "We should leave," he decided.

Domi looked at Edwards, examining the streaks of blood that washed the left side of his shaved skull. "I know you got clobbered," she told him, "but it's just an empty lot now. Nothing's going to hurt you here."

Edwards looked around vaguely, as if a dog scenting the air. "No, it's all around us," he said. "The whole place is tainted by it. Not just here, not just this little patch of shit in the middle of nowhere, but the whole ville. Can't put my finger on what it is, but I can feel it."

Domi had never seen Edwards so agitated, he was almost like a man possessed, the devil inside. "Okay," she said calmly, "we can go. We'll wrap up what we're doing down in the campsite and interphase out of here before evening. That suit you?"

Edwards rubbed at his forehead again, feeling as if he was missing something so obvious it should be right there in front of his face. "As soon as possible," he growled. "The sooner the better."

Domi agreed, promising Edwards they would clean his wound as soon as they got back to Henny at the temporary medical center before moving on their way.

"So, were you having problems with your Commtact?" Domi asked, almost in afterthought as they made their way back down the dirt steps that led them into the shanty town.

"What?" Edwards asked. "No, I could hear you and Brewster. I replied a dozen times but no one seemed to be able to hear me. I figured there was some satellite glitch."

Domi peered at Edwards in confusion. "Maybe your pickup's busted."

"Yeah," Edwards agreed. "I'll get the big brains to look it over when we get back to home base."

With that, the two Cerberus warriors made their way back through the refugee city at the outskirts of Hope. They would leave the ville and return to the Cerberus redoubt in less than three hours and whatever had been going on in the scrubland, with its talk of mysterious saviors from the skies, would be behind them.

Chapter 17

The huge stone figure of Ullikummis sat serenely in the thronelike seat at the side of the towering structure in the center of the underwater library. As Kane stepped closer, he noticed the rough sides of the reverse-funnel-like shape that towered up into the rafters, and it struck him that here was something that had been grown rather than built.

Ullikummis himself was eight feet in height, and even sitting as he was now, his immense form gave Kane a palpable sense of foreboding. Though humanoid in appearance, Ullikummis seemed to be made entirely of stone, burned charcoal plates across his chest and his thick, heavy arms and legs. Between these plates, rivulets of liquid rushed back and forth, glowing with the orange intensity of lava. The hulking creature's eyes were like lava, too, Kane knew, though they appeared now to be closed, the so-called stone god deep in sleep or concentration. Thick stone ridges emerged from the tips of his shoulders, reaching up with jagged tips and reminding Kane of the horns of a stag.

The story of Ullikummis was a tragic one. He was the princeling son of Annunaki Overlord Enlil, and his life had been guided by the whims of his father. His sole purpose had been to become an assassin, his father's hand in the darkness, and the child had been transformed from the familiar, almost beautiful reptilian appearance of an Annunaki into the stone monstrosity that now waited before the Cerberus field team. Blessed with great strength, speed and stealth that belied his tremendous form, Ullikummis was the product of many years of genetic manipulation, now as much a weapon as the lethal accessories a normal assassin would wield.

However, over four thousand years ago Ullikummis had been the victim of a greater game, and he found himself the focus of Enlil's legendary ire. Imprisoned in an asteroid and blasted into space, Ullikummis had been exiled from Earth for all time, his position in the Annunaki pantheon almost entirely forgotten.

Scant weeks ago, Ullikummis had returned during a fantastical meteor shower that had lit the skies over Saskatchewan, Canada, and he had set in motion his plan to have revenge on his father for that earlier betrayal. Kane, Brigid and Grant, along with a handful of other Cerberus personnel, had been called upon to stop the growth of a military-style training camp in the wilds of Canada, the so-called Tenth City, and their mission had ended with the apparent obliteration of the stone god himself.

And yet now, to Kane's horror, Ullikummis sat before him, intact and showing no signs of that previous fiery trauma that Kane himself had been responsible for.

"It's impossible," Kane muttered, his voice an angry growl. "We killed him. He's dead."

"Well," Clem said cheerily, "he doesn't appear to be breathing."

Automatically, Kane's eyes roved over the static form of the stone god, searching the rocky plates of his chest for signs of movement. "I don't know if he needs to breathe," Kane admitted. "What I do know is that we killed him, I saw myself as his body was blasted to atoms in a superheated furnace."

Brigid placed a reassuring hand on Kane's arm, and he turned to her, seeing the emotional turmoil in her beautiful porcelain face mirroring his own roiling feelings. "The Annunaki do have an annoying habit of escaping what appears to be certain death," she reminded him.

"But his body was—" Kane began.

"*Something* burned," Brigid agreed, "but maybe it wasn't him. Maybe we only saw what Ullikummis wanted us to see."

Brigid's words had extra meaning, Kane knew, for she had explained to him the eerie effects that the architecture of Tenth City had had on her, playing at her mind and forcing her to think in a certain, somewhat disturbing manner. From this anecdotal evidence, the theory was even now being explored that the structural layout of the other nine villes that had ruled America for approximately a century might in fact have a constraining effect on the human mind, acting as a magical sigil to direct a person's thoughts. And more, that perhaps the structural layout of every city in the history of civilization had followed this uncanny, almost supernatural pattern so as to subtly imprison and guide the human race. It had seemed incredible at first, but the past was full of the use of magical symbols that acted as focal points to power, most notoriously the swastika used by the Nazi Party in the 1930s.

While Kane and Brigid paced across the vast room, their footsteps echoing in the incredible proportions of that undersea chamber, Grant remained by the open doorway rigging up one of the powerful flashlights to illuminate the corridor they had come through. Grant could see the spiderlike creatures scuttling back and forth across the lumpy surfaces of the corridor's walls and floor as the effects of the burning flash-bangs finally faded, and he repressed a shiver that ran the length of his spine.

"Weird shit," Grant muttered as he left the flashlight poised over the doorway, setting the beam to flash at regular six-second intervals. That should be enough to keep the creatures dumbfounded, and prevent them from entering the main chamber while Grant and the crew got to work.

Like the corridor arrangement, the inside of the vast chamber had an uneven floor made of what appeared to be dried coral, its latticework intricate and obtuse, never quite repeating the same pattern twice. Grant looked around warily, checking for movements, but he couldn't detect anything living in the ridges of the flooring—no more of the spider things, at least.

Between some sections, Grant saw, in a fairly haphazard arrangement, lights glowed in a dull display of greens and blues, the colors of the ocean. Their intensity was faint, and Grant saw several flicker out as he walked past them, much as the ones in the corridor had while the Cerberus teammates had been walking its length. Peering closer, Grant saw that the lights appeared to be ridged, and he could see something moving within the body of the light itself, as if a creature trapped beneath glass. Clem had noticed this, too, and he took a knife out of the sheath he wore at his belt, just a little tool with a blade no more than two inches, and used it to pry one of the floor lights free.

"Any idea what they are, Clem?" Grant asked as the oceanographer rolled the spherical light over on the hard surface of the floor.

"Something new, but definitely alive," Clem breathed, his voice full of wonder.

Grant watched as Clem tapped at the hard covering of the glowing sphere with the edge of his blade, and the light fizzled out, its greenness winking to a lifeless black. Then the peculiar creature rolled itself across the floor on its spherical shell until it dropped into another valley in the uneven floor. A moment later it began to glow once again.

Similar lights glowed within the walls and in the struts that held the ceiling up, high above their heads. Clem looked around at everything, his eyes wide in wonder. It seemed to Grant that the poor guy was so fascinated that he couldn't look hard enough.

"Come on, Clem," Grant urged, "let's go see what the others have found."

Kane and Baptiste, meanwhile, swiftly scouted around the vast edges of the room before they made their way warily toward the majestic stone figure of Ullikummis where he waited on the thronelike outcropping of the towering structure that dominated the chamber. There were several other corridorlike structures leading off this main area, but all of them featured low doorways that barely came up to Kane's hip. It seemed that the whole undersea base had been built, if that was the right word, with visitors in mind, guiding them to this chamber while the remainder remained hidden and, presumably, formed the bulk of the Ontic Library's fearsome knowledge.

"Service tunnels maybe?" Kane suggested, indicating one of the low hatches.

Brigid leaned down, peering into the nearest of them. It was shrouded in shadow, pitch-black inside, and she became aware of a faint but unpleasant odor emanating from within, as if something had died there. "Reeks, whatever it is," she told Kane as she played the beam of the xenon flashlight over the insides. What she saw was empty, but the rough-sided, low tunnel stretched far into darkness. After a few seconds of analysis, Brigid lifted herself up from the hard floor.

Together, the two of them continued making their way toward where the mighty stone giant waited serenely beneath the colossal treelike structure dominating the vast room. As they got closer, they saw that the stone god appeared to be "wired" into the arboresque structure, tendrils snaking down from its upper levels before disappearing into the rock surface of Ullikummis's malformed skull.

"Is it feeding him?" Kane asked.

"If it is," Brigid said, keeping her voice low, "it's feeding him information."

Above them, the tendrils wound around the towering plantlike structure of the room's centerpiece, displaying a stillness that somehow spoke of their great age. Kane couldn't define it, but he felt as though he was looking at something incredibly ancient, an old oak tree planted at the bottom of the ocean, a tree of knowledge.

"What is it?" Kane asked, admiring the structure before him.

"I think that's the heart of the library," Brigid said. "Like some grand database that Ullikummis has tapped into."

"It's like something grown," Kane said in wonderment.

"It's Annunaki. Organic technology," Brigid proposed, feeling less certain than she sounded.

Close up, they could see how the towering structure had wrapped itself around the immense form of

Ullikummis. Struts appeared to have grown out of the lower regions, trapping his feet and legs like binding straps, while two branchlike limbs crisscrossed over his chest. The crossing limbs had smaller tendrils poking from them, as thin as copper wire, and the ends of these tendrils appeared to have burrowed into Ullikummis's chest, disappearing amid the cracks in the rock cladding that made up his powerful body.

Kane and Brigid were a dozen paces away from the stone god now, with Clem following a little way behind them, examining the coral weave of the floor and the unusual glowing pods set within that lit the room in a dusklike glow. This close, they could see that the limbs reaching down to Ullikummis's skull had affected a crownlike design, encircling his monstrous head in a tangle of thorny lines. Several thin tendrils appeared to have drilled into the side of his head, where the temples would be on a normal human skull, and as Kane looked around he saw more of the tendrils emerging from the back of the sleeping god's skull.

"Looks pretty full on," he remarked, and Brigid snorted.

A moment later, taking a dozen paces away from the static form of the stone-clad Annunaki, Kane raised his right hand, the retractable Sin Eater appearing there with automated precision.

"Kane," Brigid yelled, "what are you doing?"

"Offing one problem while we have the chance," he justified, aiming the fourteen-inch pistol at Ullikummis's static head.

"Fool me once," Kane growled at the unconscious, ugly form held in the sights of his gun, "shame on you. Fool me twice..."

"Wait, don't," Brigid urged.

Kane turned and glared at her. "What are you talking about, Baptiste? This asshole almost turned you into a combat zombie and you're—"

"Kane, no," Brigid said as she placed her hand over the muzzle of his weapon.

Kane had known Brigid Baptiste for a long time, and he trusted her implicitly. They had been in situations that defied a rational man's belief, had fought enemies whose description and purpose challenged even the most enlightened of thinkers. Deep in his core, Kane would always trust Brigid Baptiste's decisions. Indeed, he would trust her with his life. But now, as he looked into her beautiful emerald eyes and saw the fear burning there, he found himself questioning her sanity. She had eaten that strange mollusk, he reminded himself, and it had affected her for a while. Maybe the effects were still there somehow, still making her see things that weren't real.

"We don't get chances like this every day, Baptiste," he spat, and a familiar voice from behind him agreed.

"I see us a quick way to end a whole lot of heartache," Grant rumbled, checking the breech of his Copperhead assault rifle before he leveled it at the resting form of the stone monster on the thronelike protrusion.

"No," Brigid explained. "Whatever Ullikummis is doing here it's somehow linked to the current, rapid erosion of the structure of the library itself."

Grant cocked an eyebrow, his subgun still poised at the stone god who appeared to be asleep amid the network of organic wiring. "Want to try again in English?" he suggested.

"Right now Ullikummis is a part of the library," Brigid surmised, "and his thirst for knowledge is breaking it apart."

Kane lowered his gun a fraction of an inch, eyeing Brigid. "You're saying that in accessing the information stored here he's destroying it? I'm no archivist, but that's a pretty tough limitation on a library."

"I guess it's more like a packed storehouse," Brigid said. "Move the pieces in the wrong arrangement, and everything comes tumbling down around your ears."

"Which sounds like all the more reason to off him, right here and now," Kane reasoned.

"If you kill him now, that death could ripple through the whole structure," Brigid proposed, "destroying the library and, in turn, destroying 'the real.'"

Kane sighed heavily at the phrase, recalling how Balam had explained it just a couple of hours before. Suddenly, the gun felt like so much deadweight in Kane's hand. Beside him, Grant turned to Kane as if waiting for the kill order.

"We have to remember Balam's warning," Brigid reminded them both. "This whole place holds the very structure, the fabric *behind* reality, together. Maybe killing Ullikummis while he's hooked into this thing would be fine, but I don't want to take any unnecessary risks. Do you?"

"I suppose," Clem added from behind the main group, "that in this instance it would be best to leave sleeping gods lie."

In begrudging agreement, Kane finally lowered his pistol, and a moment later Grant followed suit.

"So what do we do, Baptiste?" Kane asked, clearly irritated at the no-win nature of the situation. "As long as this guy's still here we run the risk of the whole library breaking up, don't we?"

Brigid nodded, racking her brains for an answer.

"There's always a way, Kane," she said, "I just don't know what it is yet."

With a flinch of his wrist tendons, Kane sent his Sin Eater back into its hiding place in his sleeve holster, and he turned to Clem. "You're our resident sea expert, Bryant," he began, gesturing around the vast, dimly lit chamber. "Any ideas what all this stuff is?"

"I suspect that this material is primarily calcium carbonate," Clem stated, "which would suggest it is coral-like in nature, presumably constructed by reef builders. In essence, this means we're walking on the external skeleton of a mass of live animals."

"Nice," Grant muttered, his nose wrinkling with disgust.

"These things dangerous?" Kane asked.

Clem showed his empty hands. "Who can say?" he asked rhetorically. "While the coral itself is made up of harmless polyps, it's not unheard-of for other creatures to make their homes within its habitat, 'nesting' there, for want of a better word. The lights we can see all around us, for example," Clem said, pointing to the dimly glowing dots of green and blue, "would appear to be some kind of shelled aquatic creature, although not one I've observed before."

Brigid looked around uncomfortably, feeling a sense of unreality about the whole situation. "If they're alive, then what are they eating?"

"That's a good question," Clem assented. "Polyps reproduce by budding, so they can take over an area quite quickly. Presumably, they're getting nutrients from the ocean-facing side of the library, imbibing microscopic external creatures like plankton."

Kane gestured behind him at the towering structure

in the center of the chamber. "And what about the tower of power here? You have any insights?"

Clem took a step closer, his natural survival instinct warring with his fascination for the ocean and all its forms of life. "It appears to be a kind of shellac. Bug resin," he said in clarification after a moment.

"Which is to say it's been grown," Kane elaborated, ensuring he had understood what Clem had said.

Clem nodded. "As human beings, we can become rather entrenched in our way of seeing the world, considering constructions as purely artificial things, metal and concrete," he said. "Nature provides in vastly different ways, and that's never more clear than when you're deep in the ocean."

"I'm getting that," Kane agreed. "So, any ideas how we deal with our big, bad stone god?"

The oceanographer stepped over to where Ullikummis sat, the whole arrangement reminding him of a throne. He peered closely at the attachments around the stone figure's head, the way the tangled briars wrapped over and under one another, tangling together as they drilled into the sitter's head. "Like a crown of thorns," Clem muttered, recalling his previous Biblical reference.

After a half minute or so of silent study, Clem turned to the others, his palms wide. "Here's our Tree of Knowledge," he said. "And I suppose that the things digging into our friend here's head would effectively be the apple."

"Could we pull him free?" Kane asked.

"He looks to be a part of the system," Clem said. "He's been hard-wired into it somehow, and the two now appear to have a consensual symbiotic relationship."

"So he's feeding the system," Brigid said in realization.

"It's possible," Clem said, "though more likely the nutrients—the information—stored in the structure are using Ullikummis here to gain further knowledge and potentially access to movement."

"Incredible," Brigid breathed, her voice a whisper. "A sentient library that seeks to improve itself through shared experience."

Clenching his fists, Kane cursed in frustration. "Then what are we going to do?" he asked.

"Ullikummis came here for knowledge," Brigid reasoned, her words coming with slow deliberation, "but I wonder if there might be a way to guide the knowledge pathways that he is given. If we could somehow stream that knowledge we could, in theory, prevent him from gaining the insights he is here for."

"In which case?" Kane encouraged.

"In which case he'd depart," Clem said, following Brigid's logic. When Kane looked at Clem with confusion, the oceanographer added, "If they don't have the book you're looking for…"

"You leave the store," Kane completed.

"Stands to reason," Grant chipped in, though he was clearly as uncomfortable as Kane with the whole concept.

Both Grant and Kane were ex-Magistrates and more used to dealing with genuine physical threats such as street thieves and muties. Trying to do battle in the arena of theoretical knowledge seemed almost too obtuse a concept for them to comprehend, a battlefield neither of them could adequately envisage. But they both knew one member of their team did comprehend that battlefield and, coming to the same conclusion, they both turned their attention on Brigid.

Brigid herself looked somewhat embarrassed and bemused at the sudden attention, as if she had said something utterly inappropriate in the middle of a funeral. "What?" she asked.

"Archivist," Kane said, "meet library."

Chapter 18

As Kane's ominous words echoed through the vast undersea chamber, Brigid turned once more and admired the towering structure at the center of the colossal room, her brain whirring. It was as if she was seeing that treelike hub in a different light now, seeing it for the first time.

"You want me to…?" Brigid began, the words tumbling from her mouth without conscious thought.

Kane wrapped a friendly arm around Brigid's shoulders, smiling brightly as he looked at her. "I just wanted to shoot our visitor, remember?" he said. "You're the one who went and made things all complicated."

Brigid grimaced, shrugging out of Kane's embrace with mock irritation, but already her exceptional mind was working on the problem at hand. "If we can find an access point," she said, pacing around the uneven hub in the center of the room, "we could, theoretically, alter the protocols, feeding Ullikummis false information or convincing him that the knowledge he seeks is not contained herein."

"I don't know," Kane said. "I thought Balam said this thing contained every piece of knowledge ever. Won't it seem a bit obvious if something's not there?"

"Not really," Brigid assured him. "White light contains all seven different colors of the spectrum, and yet when we see a plain light bulb we don't wonder where the other colors have disappeared to."

"So, what," Kane asked, "you're going to lose him in the…?"

"Dazzle," Brigid said, finishing Kane's trailing sentence. "I am going to bombard him with so much false information he won't know which way is up."

Clem chuckled. "Oh, the old razzle-dazzle." He laughed. "The roar of the greasepaint, the smell of the crowd… Hmm, I'm pretty certain that's how it went, anyway."

"But I'm going to need your help, Clem," Brigid told him. "On one hand this may be an incredible computer database, but at a very basic level it's a giant undersea organism. What would we be looking for if we're to access its nervous system?"

Clem began pacing around the inverted funnel-like shape in a counterclockwise direction, rubbing at his dark beard as he started searching the towering organic monstrosity for signs of an entry port. With similar intent, Brigid took a clockwise route around the weird structure. While its appearance held some similarities to the coral floors and walls that the Cerberus warriors had seen, the structure that Brigid had identified as the library's hub seemed to have more in common with plant life. Growths poked from sections all over it, and the thick, trailing limbs that snaked across the floor reminded Brigid of the roots of a mighty tree. However, as she was about a third of the way around the base, she heard Clem calling to her.

"Found something, Clem?" Kane queried as Brigid jogged around to join them both.

Clem pointed, his finger tracing a high area on the surface of the towering structure.

Kane and Brigid looked, and they saw what appeared to be a split cone, its broken tip pointing outward from the rough coral-enshrouded surface of the hub.

"What is that?" Kane questioned. "Some kind of access valve?"

"It's a beak," Clem deadpanned, the statement sounding faintly surreal as it echoed about the chamber.

"As in a bird?" Grant asked, striding over to join the others.

"As in an octopus," Clem corrected. "This thing is most definitely alive, and it's structurally similar to an octopus. The hardened areas are probably growths that have attached themselves upon the octopus's exterior, either in a symbiosis or it may have dragged these to it to act as protection."

"Does that put us any closer to finding out how to access it?" Kane asked.

"The weak points would be at the joints where the legs meet the body, which is probably why it's covered itself with coral," Clem theorized. "An octopus can lose a limb without slowing down—it's structurally a very sound design. Of course, they are prone to psychosis, which often manifests in self-cannibalism."

Brigid and the two ex-Mags looked at Clem in baffled amusement. He was in his element here, and his frank fascination was infectious.

Realizing that everyone was staring at him, Clem coughed into his hand self-consciously and returned to the more pressing matter of how to access the weird sea creature.

"Do you think it's really alive, then?" Brigid asked as she strode with Clem to a point at the base where one of the rootlike legs met with the main bulk of the creature.

"That's hard to substantiate," Clem admitted, "without a full analysis. I suspect it is alive after a fashion, but I don't think we can truly call this beast a living creature. It's more like a—I don't know—potato. While it may continue to grow new shoots if one doesn't cook it, the thing itself is essentially dead."

"Interesting point," Brigid acknowledged.

It was hard to see exactly where the creature's leg connected to its body, there was so much armorlike shell covering the join. With practiced efficiency, Clem knelt and produced his little blade once more, using it to carefully pull away at the barklike covering. It took a little effort, but the cover snapped away with a squelchy pop, and a gummy trail of what appeared to be mucus came away as Clem wrenched a five-inch-long strip of shell from the monstrous limb. Underneath, a slimy surface was revealed, its skin oily and reptilian, shimmering blue and green as its sweat reflected the overhead spots of light. With the cover removed, it also stank, the smell like seafood, both pleasant and overpowering. Brigid winced and wrinkled her nose as she got a whiff of it, while Clem coughed lightly as he turned his head, allowing the stench to dissipate.

"It certainly smells alive," Clem observed.

Brigid watched as Clem traced his finger over the network of veins that could be faintly seen through the surface of the creature's skin.

"Do you have any idea," Clem asked, "what the stone man out there is looking for knowledge on?"

Brigid shrugged. "He's been off planet for 4500 years," the Titian-haired archivist pointed out. "He probably has one or two things to catch up on."

Warily, Brigid and Clem began peeling away at the hub organism's outer layer, seeking clues as to how to access this curious piece of organic tech. While they did so, Kane went to check on the blinking light that Grant had set up, assuring himself that it would stave off any further altercation with the foul spiderlike creatures that had attacked them in the corridor. At the same time, Grant patrolled the perimeter of the room, checking into a few nooks and crevices he found there before joining Kane at the main artery.

"You wonder how ol' stony face got down here?" Grant asked as he paced over to join with Kane, his boots crunching loudly as they crushed protrusions on the uneven coral floor.

Kane frowned, considering the question for the first time. "Ullikummis survived four millennia in space," he reasoned, "so I'd go ahead and conclude he's a tenacious dirtbag. Guess there's no reason to assume he needs to breathe. Probably just sank himself in the ocean till he got here."

"Deep sixed, huh?" Grant nodded.

"Just a guess, partner," Kane explained with a shrug. As he spoke, the ex-Mag became conscious of a noise coming from off to his left. He held up a hand to shush Grant, stepping silently toward the wall. "You hear that?" he whispered.

Grant cocked his head, listening for whatever it was that Kane had identified. Kane was renowned for his perception, employing something some had termed his point man sense—a seemingly uncanny ability to sense danger in any situation. Actually there was nothing especially supernatural about Kane's danger sense; it was merely the shrewd use of the five senses he had, for he was as human as anyone else.

It took Grant just a few seconds to analyze and separate the many different background noises in the undersea chamber—the sharp clacking noises made by the scrabbling spiders' legs as they ran along the coral corridor, the faint hissing made by the gigantic hub in the center of the room, the strangely muted nonsound created by the ocean held at bay beyond the walls. But after a moment, Grant became aware that there was definitely something else there, a near-regular sound generated by some kind of motion. It was almost familiar, yet it took him a few seconds to properly identify it. "Footsteps?" he said, his tone questioning.

Kane nodded, fixing his partner with a wary glance. "Might be we're not as alone as we thought we were," he said, and the Sin Eater reappeared in his right hand as it powered from its wrist sheath. "Let's go make friends."

Grant brought the muzzle of the Copperhead back up to the ready position and followed as Kane stalked across the room, both men's movements appreciatively silent despite the hollow, unforgiving floor. "Friends," he muttered in a surly growl. "Like *that* ever happens."

Leading the way, Kane ducked his head and to the side as he tried to identify the precise source of the strange noises. They sounded like scrabbling, the sounds a puppy's feet might make on a hard wooden floor as its unclipped claws scratched against the surface. Kane peered around him, his steely gray eyes alert to any movement. Sixty feet away and off to Kane's right, Brigid and Clem could be heard discussing the intricacies of the towering hub as they chipped away sections of its shell-like plating. He tuned out the sounds of their voices, his eyes scanning the wall to his immediate left. The wall itself was blistered with polyps, and its surface was made up of intricately intertwined cylinders that snaked and enwrapped one another with endless nuance and inspiration.

Down lower, Kane saw one of the low doorways, the things that he and Baptiste had previously presumed to be service tunnels for want of a better term. The entryway to this one came up to about the height of Kane's knee, and he eyed it warily, slowing his pace and bringing his gun to bear. There was no light around this section of the chamber; what few blue shells had been there had migrated away or winked out while Kane and Grant busily checked on their winking flashlight at the far side of the room. High in the wall, a few lackluster spots glowed green, though Kane dismissed the term *glowed* as wholly inappropriate—they seemed more to just barely exist, what light they cast doing little to illuminate the area.

A few paces behind and to Kane's right, Grant held his own blaster in a ready position, his gaze shifting from the hole in the wall to Kane and back. "Anything?" he asked, his voice barely a whisper.

Silently, Kane stroked his finger against the side of his nose, offering Grant the slightest of smiles before he proceeded toward the gap in the wall. The signal was a one-percent salute, their shared code for high-risk situations with small margins for success.

Grant smiled back, feeling reassured that despite the insanity of their current predicament, Kane still had time to make light of the situation.

This close to the hatch, Grant heard the noise, too, like the scratching of claws against wood. He watched as Kane leaned lower, crouching on his haunches and peering into the foul-smelling gap, still six feet from the gloomy opening, the nose of the Sin Eater poised ahead of him. Then, with no warning, the scrabbling noise became more frantic and something burst from the hole, leaping at Kane even as he depressed the trigger and blasted a stream of 9 mm bullets at whatever it was.

Kane's shots lit the area, and he saw the thing in a brief series of staggered bursts of light as it charged toward him. Low to the ground, it looked roughly three feet in length and was covered in glistening, dark green scales that reflected the fire of the propellant spurting from the end of his pistol. The creature appeared to have four legs—two short, flailing limbs at the front while it powered itself by two thickly corded, muscular legs at the back, each of them ending in a flipperlike fantail.

The thing's face was an ugly mess of contradiction. It seemed sharp, tailing toward a pointed muzzle at the front with two deep-set eyes, one each on the opposing sides of that fierce muzzle. The eyes were a shimmering black color, the soulless color of spiders' eyes, and they, too, glimmered with the reflections of the gunshots as Kane's stream of bullets cut through the air around it. But where the pointed muzzle finished, there was another feature, like some strange attachment hooked around the face to guide the creature's prey toward its needle-sharp teeth. These tools, for that was the only word that Kane could think of as he analyzed the hurtling creature in that split second, appeared to be something like twin shovels, top and bottom, and their shape reminded Kane a little of an old-fashioned key, with its jagged teeth and rounded end.

As the creature barrelled toward Kane across the hardpacked floor, it eerily made no noise. Kane watched in horror as his bullets banged against the side of the monstrous form, snapping against its scaled hide before bouncing off in all directions, sparks bursting across its flesh like sheet lightning. And then it was all but upon him, and Kane rolled out of its path as its feet scrabbled to seek purchase among the ridges of the floor.

The scaly creature ran several more steps before turning in what appeared to be an almost immediate right-angle turn that defied belief. It reminded Kane not so much of a mammal as something else, something he couldn't quite place.

What the hell have we found? Kane asked himself as he brought the Sin Eater to bear once more on the hideous-looking creature as it chased him.

"More company! Stay sharp," Grant shouted as Kane took aim at the hurtling creature that was rushing at him across the coral.

Kane didn't need his friend's warning; he was already aware that a second creature had emerged from the hole that now sat at his back.

"Baptiste," Kane said, keeping his voice low even as he engaged his Commtact in preference of shouting across the room.

"I heard shooting," Brigid's urgent voice came back, echoing through Kane's skull implant. Her concern was clear even through the artificial medium of the Commtact system.

"You may want to get yourself moving," Kane advised as he pumped another handful of bullets at the hurtling, green-scaled creature and watched them ricochet off in all directions. "Seems we have us some local interest."

As Kane spoke, his fearsome opponent leaped off the floor on those powerful legs, its double jaw opening as it sought to bite at his face. The jaw split large enough, Kane saw, to engulf his whole head.

"Can you keep our company busy?" Brigid urged

over the Commtact. "We're making real headway here."

Kane held the trigger down on the Sin Eater, rolling aside once more as the short, doglike creature hurtled overhead, missing him by mere inches. "Say again?"

"We're onto something over here," Brigid explained, "and I don't think it can be rushed."

As the creature landed, Grant blasted a shot from his own weapon, driving a clutch of 4.85 mm shells into its flank. The creature was forced sideways with the power of the shots, and it seemed to turn in on itself as it struggled to remain upright. There was no time to follow up the successful attack, however—the second creature had emerged from the gap in the wall and was hurtling toward Kane's supine form even as a third creature came charging out of the hole.

"Beg to differ on that one, Baptiste," Kane growled, spraying the wall with bullets as he tried desperately to find his fast-moving targets. "I think we just woke up the local guard dogs, so it's really going to have to be 'go-go' now."

ACROSS THE FAR SIDE of the chamber, hidden between two struts of the mighty funnel-like structure that formed the hub of the Ontic Library, Brigid turned to Clem, relating what she knew from the brief radio communiqué with Kane. Clem had no subdermal Commtact, relying on a portable unit with earpiece instead when out in the field.

"Seems we're even more on the clock than we initially thought, Clem," she explained.

"That's treacherously bad," Clem mused as he wrenched at another piece of the armorlike shell of the hub with his little blade. "Absolutely dreadful."

NEARBY, THE STONE FORM of Ullikummis remained resolutely immobile, eerily still amid the sounds of gunfire that echoed through the strange undersea chamber. With a body clad in stone, that utter, eerie stillness granted the rogue Annunaki the resolute appearance of a statue, something carved, created at the hands of another.

And this, too, was true, albeit after a fashion. A tool employed in the art of assassination, Ullikummis had been created like any other tool. The Annunaki were masters of genetic manipulation, and the form that Ullikummis now wore was one that had been deliberately built around the structure of his once flawless reptilian form.

Those things that had rendered Ullikummis different from his brethren had made him immune to the demands that life put upon them. Like all Annunaki, he was dismissive of man's limited concept of time, for his own lifespan was near infinite. His need for things like breath and sustenance seemed almost nonexistent, for what was the good of living forever if it demanded constant refuelling of the body?

Thus, he sat in silence, an air of such utter stillness upon him that he seemed not so much a dead thing as a thing that had never been alive, a pebble washed up on the beach. But as he sat, that air of meditative tranquillity around him in the heart of the gunfire, the information fed into him from the nerve center of the Ontic Library, information he would employ to change the world.

SKIPPING BACK FROM THE wall, Grant unleashed five devastating bursts of gunfire in quick succession at the emerging creature as it nosed out of the low gap in the wall. The shots lit the air like fireworks, smashing against the platelike scales of the thing's face and shoulders before whizzing off into the air in potentially lethal ricochets.

Unharmed and unfazed, the green-skinned creature looked at Grant with its soulless black orbs, the hard skin around them tautening as if narrowing its eyes in anger.

Grant pumped the trigger of his Copperhead, blasting another half-dozen rounds at the creature as it scented the air. It let out no noise; none of them did. Instead they appeared to be voiceless, the only noises they made coming from their strange, flat-spread feet as they scrabbled and slapped against the hard floor of the undersea base. In creating no sound, the creatures seemed that much more alien and nightmarish, like something subliminal.

A few feet from Grant, Kane had got himself back to a standing position and was warily tracking another of the green-scaled creatures as it padded across the room, sizing the ex-Mags up with grim determination.

The first dog-size creature—the one whose flank had been drilled by a flurry of bullets from Grant's gun—was prowling at a wary distance, its dark, watery eyes never leaving the two humans it had found in its undersea territory.

As Kane tracked the nearest, it flipped its large, well-muscled back legs and sprang off the ground, hurtling toward him like a rocket, its body writhing through the air. Kane squeezed the trigger of his Sin Eater, holding it down as it spit fire at the leaping, writhing monstrosity. Then, to Kane's astonishment, the green-scaled thing seemed to flip in midleap, turning around on itself and—incredibly—disappearing in front of his eyes.

"What the—?" Kane snarled as the thing winked

from sight before him. He released his finger from the Sin Eater's trigger, skipping backward hurriedly as he maneuvered out of his projected path for the leaping horror.

Ten feet away, Grant was blasting shot after shot at his own green-skinned foe as it rushed at him, leaping into the air, its curious double jaws opening like the wide mouth of a cave, spiny needlelike protrusions snapping at the air. At the last possible instant, Grant ducked and watched as the chimerical beast buzzed past him before plummeting back toward the ground. But to Grant's confusion, the thing never landed. Instead, just like Kane's foe's impossible move a few seconds before, it seemed to flip in on itself and—blink!—it was gone.

From close by, Kane was shouting an instruction to his trusted partner, his blue-gray eyes searching for the disappearing creatures. "Grant," Kane called, his voice snapping with urgency. "We have us another problem."

"Tell me about it," Grant agreed as he looked warily around for his own disappearing foe. "Seems these things have the ability to turn invisible."

Before Kane could agree, one of the green-scaled creatures reappeared right before him, just two feet from his torso, and barreled into him as it hurtled through the air.

Chapter 19

Losing his footing, Kane spun in a lopsided tangle of limbs as he tried to fend off the green-skinned monster that had reappeared before his eyes. Together the two of them fell backward, colliding with the floor with a loud crash.

Immediately Kane rolled to his left, bringing up his pistol in an automatic reaction and snapping off three quick shots as the broad-headed creature lurched at him. Its weird, key-shaped face seemed to split apart as its twin jaws yawned open, snapping at the spot where Kane had been just a fraction of a second earlier. There had been no time to aim, and Kane watched with a sense of triumph as two of his three bullets found their target, drilling into the monster's mouth and what passed for its right cheek, just below its staring, inhuman eye. The thing reared backward on its thick, muscular hind legs, shaking its head either in pain or frustration.

There was no time for jubilation, however. Even as Kane brought his gun up for another shot, another creature charged at him, its jaws snapping. Again, Kane was struck by the weird nature of these things, even as he rolled out of the way of the savage beast's charge. They were silent in their attacks. Never once had any of them let loose a cry or a howl in the usual way that wild animals would vocalize to intimidate their prey. He shoved the thought to the back of his mind as he brought the Sin Eater to bear, blasting a stream of 9 mm steel-jacketed death at his would-be devourer.

A little way behind Kane and off to his left, he could hear Grant tackling his own foe as another monster seemingly reappeared from the ether.

What the hell are we facing? Kane wondered.

BRIGID WATCHED AS Clem Bryant unpicked another small section of the towering organic construction that they had termed 'the hub,' using his short knife to score the shell-like skin before levering it away. Off in the distance, they could hear the familiar sounds of gunfire as Kane and Grant tackled the weird creatures that had emerged from the hole in the wall.

"Here," Clem said, a clear note of triumph to his tone, "this is where it links to our visiting friend."

Brigid looked at where Clem pointed, and she saw a thick veinlike tube amid an interweaving of lesser veiny threads. "What is that?" she asked.

Clem smiled. "A vein," he stated. "If this were a normal octopus, that would be running blood to the gills for oxygenation. But if you follow its path along, it links to the feeder tubes here and here—" he pointed with the tip of his knife "—that lead to the structure that surrounds Ullikummis's head."

Brigid narrowed her eyes as she followed the path of the vein, trying to imagine it in terms of an anatomical plan for the creature before her. Clem had only removed sections of the shell-like covering here and there, but there were enough pieces exposed to show that the same vein ran to the weird-looking crown atop Ullikummis's stone head.

Brigid turned back to Clem and asked anxiously, "What does it mean?"

"Anatomy of an octopus," Clem explained, counting things off on his fingers as he spoke. "Three hearts, yes? You have the main heart, then two branchial hearts that deal with pumping blood to the gills for oxygenation. It's an adaptation that allows for octopi to survive in the pressured ocean depths."

"Faster," Brigid reminded.

"Instead of blood," Clem stated, "this creature is pumping information—knowledge—which is being tapped by Ullikummis. Now, if we follow the logic of that, there must be at least one more stream that can be tapped in a similar fashion without interfering with the first."

"Go on," Brigid encouraged, trying to keep Clem's idea straight in her head.

"This would, of course, make a degree of sense," Clem said. "Rather than having a backup system for the most precious knowledge store on the planet, you have a twin system—the two branchial hearts—which can reinforce each other at any moment in time. If, as with an octopus, there's also a third heart—the main heart—then the two branchial servers would act as feeders, and were perhaps designed to be tapped while the main heart is the central processing unit, or CPU."

Brigid nodded, finally beginning to see what Clem was getting at. In terms of an archival system, something Brigid was very familiar with from her days as an archivist in Cobaltville, the main heart took the role of the master store, where everything would be kept. The branchial hearts were access points, which could relate information from the main store without requiring the physical removal of materials, like computer terminals within a reference library. "Could we jump one to the other?" Brigid asked.

"How would that work?" Clem wondered.

"If we flipped the streams over," Brigid proposed, "we could control Ullikummis's stream and potentially feed choice information to him, driving him from the system."

"Guiding the strands of knowledge," Clem said in realization, recalling Brigid's earlier, rudimentary proposition. "You'd be effectively applying computer theory to a physical being…"

"A physical being that operates as a computer," Brigid pointed out, "or more accurately, a whole bank of computers."

"One would need to have an exceptional knowledge of how to operate the system," Clem mused.

"Clem," Brigid said firmly, "I was an archivist for a long time. You get me in there and I'll make it work. Or die trying."

"That's the sort of attitude that I try to avoid," Clem said jovially, "which is probably why I haven't been assigned my own CAT team."

Brigid leaned forward for a moment, holding a steadying hand over Clem's own. "Do what you can, Clem," she said reassuringly, "but do it quick."

GRANT LEAPED BACK ON the balls of his feet as the monstrous, dog-size creature pounced at him from some impossible spot in mid-air. A moment before, the thing hadn't existed, he would swear, and yet here it was, right before his eyes, hurtling at his face with its maw wide, showing the vicious rows of teethlike spines within.

Grant analyzed in a fraction of a second that he was too close to use the Copperhead now, so he swung it up, using the stubby back end like a nightstick, striking upward with a blow that slammed against the rushing creature's jaw. The attacker's jaw snapped painfully shut with the force of Grant's unforgiving blow, and it wavered in the air for a moment before falling to the ground and sliding a few feet across the rough surface of the floor. Without hesitation, Grant turned the Copperhead on the creature once more, snapping off twin shots at its face as it turned to look at him. One shot hit the platelike armor of its scaly skin, whizzing back at Grant just a few inches over his head, while the other drilled into one of its soulless black eyes, bursting the eyeball.

For a moment, the creature stalled, lurching in place as its ruined eyeball spurted across its face like drool. Then, rotating its head, it peered at Grant with its remaining eye, feet drumming against the ground as it charged at him once again.

Meanwhile, just ten feet from his partner, Kane found himself facing off against two of the weird, scaly creatures. Both of them circled him, following a slightly erratic, almost zigzag path as they rounded on him.

Kane felt a sense of helplessness as they bided their time, preparing for another attack. It was clear they were sentries dispatched to expel unwanted visitors to the undersea base. Balam had described the Ontic Library as a living thing, and the strange shellfish should have tipped Kane off to the sort of utter weirdness he would find here. But, somehow, he found himself both fascinated and repulsed by what he was facing, his mind unable to easily label it and hence deal with it.

Suddenly one of the creatures—the one with the wound in its cheek from Kane's mouth shot—rushed him once more, its thick back legs punching against the floor as it drove furiously toward him. Behind it, the second monster was moving, too, following its charging brother, an ugly gash at its side where Grant's shots had grazed its scales.

Scales, Kane realized with a start.

And then the two monsters were upon him, and he found himself dropping back as they powered overhead.

Kane blasted a lethal stream of bullets at the first creature, the blasts popping against its underbelly as it rushed past him before it twisted and, once again, disappeared from view. Kane paid it no mind; he was too busy kicking out at the second monster as it came at him from a lower angle, its weird double-jaw arrangement open wide in terrifying promise.

Kane's boot smashed into the creature's jaw, just skirting below the needle-sharp teeth and clipping it at the point of its lower muzzle. The thing seemed to whirl in place, its momentum driving it onward as it dispelled kinetic energy in a sudden frantic waggling of its tiny forearms.

Kane snapped off another burst of bullets as the green-skinned creature flew past him before performing a strange right-angle turn and disappearing from view. "Fish," he snarled. "We're dealing with fucking fish."

CLEM AND BRIGID RUSHED hastily around the towering hub, searching for another point where they might tap in and access the organic system. Clem swiftly identified and traced the main trunk of the second vein, the one that led back to the second branchial heart of the beastlike machine.

Brigid, meantime, located a plinthlike section of the hub that seemed similar to the place where Ullikummis was wired in. This plinth seemed to almost perfectly mirror the one that Ullikummis had used as a seat, and was set at roughly the opposing side of the colossal, towering hub.

"We'll do it here," Brigid called to Clem as he continued eyeing the second vein, tracing it amid the hard covering of the octopuslike organism.

Clem looked uncomfortable at the idea, for he was clearly unhappy with the actions they were now taking. "If you'll excuse an old diving term," he said as he began working his knife into a seam in the shell-like plating, "I feel a little out of my depth, Miss Baptiste. Theory is all well and good, but have you considered how exactly you intend to hook this thing up to yourself?"

Brigid fixed him with a no-nonsense stare. "Once we get it started, Clem, I think it will find its own way into me."

Clem visibly swallowed, repulsed by the thought, but he continued working at the shell-like plates while Brigid dashed off to observe Ullikummis on the far side of the monstrous hub.

Over at the far wall of the colossal chamber, Brigid could make out the flashes of gunfire as Kane and Grant warred with the guard creatures they had found. The whole room was so gloomy, ill-lit by the phosphorescent creatures burrowed into its walls and floor, that Brigid had to strain to make out much. She watched for a few seconds as Kane leaped backward, kicking out at a dull green creature that seemed almost to swim through the air. Brigid was loathe to disturb Kane or Grant while they dealt with the interruption, but she knew that Kane would want a progress report, so she engaged her Commtact.

"We think we've found an access point, guys," Brigid explained. "Just investigating now."

Kane's voice snapped back, sounding irritated and breathless. "Investigate faster," he urged.

Brigid turned back to the towering hub, looking at the dark skin of the beastlike structure where patches of it showed from beneath its skeletal covering. Ullikummis remained unmoving in his thronelike seat, the weird crown like a series of umbilical cords reaching into his skull at the back of his head. Brigid examined the links for a moment, carefully observing how they connected to the massive bulk of the hub.

Other parts of the hub seemed to have grown, wrapping themselves around Ullikummis's still form as he sat there. They looked as if they had been there for a thousand years. This thing, Brigid realized, whatever it was, was so far beyond their field of comprehension as to be almost indecipherable. What they were about to do was tap into a construct so alien as to be nonsensical. That realization did nothing to fill her with confidence.

As blasterfire echoed through the chamber from behind her, Brigid sprinted back to join Clem on the far side of the room's centerpiece, the sense of foreboding growing heavy in her mind.

KANE CUT THE COMMTACT link to Brigid, his attention fixed on the twin attackers as they reappeared before his eyes, as if walking through a door that he simply could not see. Only now was he beginning to comprehend what it was that they were facing.

Kane blasted another stream of 9 mm bullets at the approaching creature as its wide back feet slapped against the solid floor, slamming into it with gusto as it propelled itself at its quarry.

It was a fish, Kane saw now. A weird, evolved or

genetically modified fish, but a fish all the same. The scaled hide, the dead eyes, even the strange double jaw all pointed to attributes he would associate with breeds of fish.

The first of them—the one with just one eye remaining—leaped then and Kane stood his ground, pumping the trigger of the Sin Eater and blasting a stream of shining bullets into the thing's gaping maw as it opened its mouth in utter, baffling silence. He saw, in the split second he had, his bullets ripping chunks from the inside of the creature's cheek, ripping pink shreds from the side of its tongueless mouth, disappearing down its gullet.

Then it was upon the ex-Mag and Kane's extended right arm disappeared in the double jaw grip of that hideous mouth.

Behind him, Grant was shouting something, but Kane's mind was too focused on the task at hand to care.

With all his might, Kane shoved himself forward, kicking off the ground and ramming himself sideways at the monster as if to shoulder-barge it out of his way, despite it now being a part of him. He felt the slimy interior of the thing's mouth, his hand pushing farther onward and down into its throat. At the top of Kane's arm, the creature's jaws endeavored to clamp shut, strong teethlike prongs pushing against the corded muscles at his shoulder. Lower in his arm, he knew, the fish creature could have bitten through; that was almost certainly true of his fingers or wrist. But the solid deltoid muscle at his shoulder, shrouded in the shadow suit, was tough enough to stave off this beast's attack for the few seconds it would take to finish it.

Kane's wrist went left and right as he pumped shots

down the creature's throat, feeling the kick of the Sin Eater in his hand as he peppered the beast's insides with bullets. From within, the creature started to disintegrate, wet chunks of flesh bursting from its torso and sailing across the room before slapping against the walls and floor with wet-sounding plops.

Without realizing it, Kane was slammed against the ground, his legs stumbling over each other as he absorbed the momentum generated by the fish-thing's struggle. Grant was at his side then, using the Copperhead to drill shots into the beast's side, taking huge chunks out of its flesh as they finally found a way through its armoured skin.

The teethlike spikes were pressing against Kane's shoulder now, and he growled in pain and frustration as he pumped more shots into the thing's guts. He could feel the creature struggling, finding its would-be prey a whole hell of a lot more feisty than it had bargained with. Sin Eater still blasting, Kane reached out with his free hand and plucked at his attacker's remaining eye socket, tearing its eyeball from the hole there in a loud squelch.

Finally, as its eyeball went sailing across the floor in a gummy mass, the fish creature relented, opening its jaw wide enough to allow Kane to get his arm free. He pulled his arm back swiftly, until just the end of the gun was still within the creature's nightmarish mouth. Then, aiming the Sin Eater's muzzle high, he pumped two shots into the roof of its mouth. With a loud squelch, the top of the beast's head exploded, and it lost all of its drive in a second, flopping lifelessly to the floor. Nose wrinkling in disgust, Kane removed his hand from the wreckage that had been a living thing just a moment before.

Standing over Kane, Grant looked at the squelchy mess of flesh and gunk that lay splattered across the floor like so much roadkill, even as the remaining creatures circled the two human intruders.

"Did I hear right?" Grant asked as Kane swept goo and innards from the length of his right arm. "Did you say that these things are fish?"

"Mutated," Kane said, rising to his feet, "but basically—yeah, they're fish."

"Care to elaborate?"

Instead of answering immediately, Kane whipped up the Sin Eater and blasted a stream of shots at one of the remaining creatures as it began charging at the two ex-Mags. "In a minute," he shouted. "For now, just follow my lead."

Seeing the monster barrel toward him, its jaws wide, Grant didn't need telling twice.

BRIGID TOOK A STEADYING BREATH as she sat on the jutting section at the side of the great hub. Using his short knife, Clem had uncovered enough of the inner workings of the creature that they could now see the main trunk of the second branchial vein.

"Are you absolutely certain that you want to do this?" Clem asked in a low, conspiratorial voice.

Brigid smiled tentatively. "Is anyone ever absolutely certain they want to do anything?" she asked in reply.

Clem nodded, realizing that Brigid's flippant words allowed her to draw strength as she prepared to leap into the unknown. He knew that the woman who now sat perfectly upright before him was just as terrified as he was. With a mixture of excitement and fear vying for attention in his racing mind, Clem leaned forward, reaching to a point just over Brigid's head, and he ran the sharp edge of the blade across the thick vein that pulsed there. "Stand by," he said.

Swiftly and deliberately, Clem made a small incision into the pulsing vein, pushing the knife firmly against the surface until a line of liquid oozed forth. Lacking the power of an artery, the wound did not spurt as one might have expected; it simply oozed in a line like sweat, colored white as milk, reminding Clem of pus oozing from a burst boil.

"Have you done it?" Brigid asked, trying to remain still as Clem worked the knife immediately above her.

"I've made an incision," Clem replied, "and the wound's weeping. But it doesn't seem to—" He stopped midsentence, watching in fascination as the oozing pus ran slowly down the exterior of the vein, gathering speed with its descent.

"What is it?" Brigid asked, her voice a whisper.

The milky line of liquid split, and where one drop had existed now there were three, and they hurried down behind the bright cloud of Brigid's wavy, flame-red hair. But as Clem watched he saw that the liquid wasn't simply pouring, following the path of least resistance in the way that liquid should act. No, instead it seemed to be reaching, probing, *feeling* at the air.

"Clem?" Brigid encouraged again, unsure of what was going on immediately behind her head.

Before Clem could find the words, one of those strange milk-white strands seemed to leap, like a cobra striking out at its prey, and the tip of the strand disappeared into Brigid's hair, its other end still connected to the pierced vein above her.

Brigid grunted, feeling something burning hot touch the lowest part of her scalp, just below the crown. It was incredibly hot, like the tip of a soldering iron, and for a moment Brigid's breath came with staggered rapidity through gritted teeth.

"If it does bond with the user as you've theorized," Clem told her, trying to sound reassuring, "then that's what it's doing now."

"Hurts," Brigid grunted, the word pinched between her clamped-shut teeth. And then the burning became worse, feeling like the throbbing burn of skin that had been tanned too quickly by the sun, a ceaseless ache of bad-then-worse, bad-then-worse.

Above Brigid's head, Clem watched as more strands of goo oozed from the thick vein, curling from it now like tendrils, reaching lower and lower as they grasped for Brigid's skull. A second off-white line probed out and snagged her, pushing through her mass of curling hair and pressing against her skull. As Brigid winced, yet another tendril found its way to her, and then another.

Clem watched, staggered, as twin horns seemed to emerge from the sides of the hub where he had exposed the vein, reaching around Brigid's forehead like two hands, the jagged projections interlinking like fingers to form that familiar crown around Brigid's forehead. Its surface was hard and multilayered, an intermingling of sharp briars locking together like a cage. Once again, the abstract thought came to Clem of how it looked like the crown of thorns worn by Jesus Christ in classic religious imagery, imagery long since forgotten in this future world that the twentieth-century oceanographer had woken up to.

Brigid closed her eyes as she felt the hot strings lash against her, worming their way into the back of her skull. It wasn't a piercing so much as an osmosis, a diffusion of that exceptional heat through the back of her head and on, into the receptacles of her brain. Ahead of her now, too, things were emerging from the crownlike apparatus that had surrounded her head, reaching in with a blast of hot breath against her forehead, the heat playing into her frontal lobes. Her natural instinct was to break away, to run, but she clenched her fists and told herself to endure. This was a crazy chance, the odds so long they were meaningless, and yet the whole process seemed the only possibility they might have to expel Ullikummis and save the Ontic Library from the destruction his very presence was causing.

Ahead, Brigid could see the coral-like walls of the room, the hard, lumpy floor that stretched out before her in the eerie gloom of those little pools of blue-green light. As she looked, she became conscious of something else there now, too, at the very edges of her vision. She looked left and right but it remained frustratingly beyond her ability to view.

Redness.

That was what it was. A redness as of something's blood.

All around her, across Brigid's chest and at her ankles and her wrists, things writhed, snaking around her from polyps on the exterior of the organic hub of this exceptional library. Brigid was now only vaguely aware of such things, feeling them moving along her body like a marching army of ants. Instead, her awareness was shifting as she began to see more of the world that surrounded her, the structures that underpinned that world. Above, in the ocean, Brigid could see parts of the library structure breaking off, floating away as Ullikummis's influence reigned.

I should be afraid, she told herself.

But she wasn't.

Recently, Brigid had been snared within a navigator's chair from an Annunaki starship. Organic technology, the chair had come to life in her presence, pulling her to it and clutching her close, sending sharp tendrils to pierce her skin that it might download its maps of the universe directly into her brain. At the time she had been terrified, the whole experience a perverse violation of her very being. Yet at the same time she had marveled at the star chart that played out for her eyes only, her rational mind appreciating the incredible artistry that had been brought to bear to create such a revelatory piece of equipment.

Now, it seemed to Brigid that her experience with the astrogation chair had been merely a dry run for what was happening to her here. She felt her brain begin to switch gear, shifting into a new mind-set as the burning sensation entered her thoughts.

"Here we go again," Brigid whispered as she felt herself, along with all rational sense, plummet off the precipice of normalcy.

Chapter 20

While Brigid was disappearing into the mental rabbit hole that was the data stream of the Ontic Library, Grant and Kane continued struggling with the savage, dog-size fish that had surrounded them at the far edge of the vast chamber.

"Follow my lead," Kane had instructed, though he had been less sure of himself than he had sounded in that moment of bravado. His plan was a simple one; at least in the sense that it was direct. These monstrous, air-breathing fish-things had a hard armor of near-impenetrable scales that deflected all but the luckiest of shots. But from the inside, as he had proved, they were vulnerable. All they had to do was ensure that their bullets blasted into each creature's open mouth.

Which was easier said than done, of course, particularly with the ferocity and vigor that were required to make a difference and swing the tide of the battle.

"Drill them in the mouths," Kane shouted as Grant brought his Copperhead subgun into play once more, peppering the area with a spray of bullets, countless spent shells littering the coral floor at his feet.

Even as Kane spoke, one of the two remaining creatures spun on itself and seemed to wink from existence in that baffling and utterly frustrating manner that Kane and Grant had witnessed during the earliest moments of this terrifying encounter.

"They're not disappearing," Kane insisted.

"Run that by me again?" Grant demanded as he stood at Kane's shoulder, Copperhead blazing as the fish creature he was aiming at seemed to cease to exist.

"That's what clued me in," Kane growled. "Fish move like nothing else on earth, doubling back on themselves so swiftly that they appear able to move through 180 degrees on the spot. These things are fast as hell, but they're still there—our eyes just can't follow quickly enough."

As if to reinforce Kane's observation, Grant saw the green-scaled creature reappear off to his right, turning on the spot there and leaping toward him with its mouth widening to bite.

In a blur of instinct, Grant swung the Copperhead at the monster, his finger depressed on the trigger, sending a volley of bullets wide before he finally found his fast-moving target. Bullets pinged from the creature's hide, covering it in bright sparks of lightning where they hit and filling the air with dangerous ricochets.

Then the creature was on Grant, its jaws snapping shut as it attempted to bite off his face. Grant turned away, skipping backward on his toes as the thing dived through the air at him. It didn't dive, Grant corrected—it *swam*.

A few feet away, Kane was facing his own enemy, as the last remaining fish creature prowled the surrounding area, its glassy, black eyes never leaving Kane's. The ex-Magistrate held his right arm stiff, the Sin Eater like a natural extension of the limb, as he waited for the kill shot.

"Come on, you little flounder," Kane muttered. "Let's make fish sticks for dinner."

Suddenly, the green-scaled creature turned, its tail-like back feet flapping against the uneven floor as it barreled forward, widening its vulgar double jaw as it hurried at its human prey.

Kane snapped off shot after shot from his Sin Eater, his aim never wavering as he pumped the 9 mm bullets down the beast's throat. Chunks of flesh ripped from the monster's ugly mouth as the bullets drilled past that keylike apparatus that formed its jaw.

At the last second, Kane leaped away, and the creature's mighty jaws closed shut on empty air with a loud snap.

As both Kane and the monster landed on the floor, Kane rolled away, bringing his pistol back up to bear as the hideous attacker turned to renew its savage attack. Kane blasted off another stream of deadly bullets as the monster charged at him. The green-hued fish turned then, as Kane continued to blast bullets in its direction, flitting out of his field of vision like an arrow in the air. His jaws clamped tightly together, Kane held the trigger of the Sin Eater in place and sprayed left and right in a continuous stream of fire. Incredibly—almost magically—the creature reappeared off to Kane's left as the bullets struck it, fumbling in its path before rolling over itself and crashing into the floor on its side with a noteworthy lack of grace.

Immediately, Kane leaped up and ran for the monster where it lay on the floor, its muscular, tail-like back legs flapping up and down as it tried to right itself, like a turtle rolled over on its shell. As it turned, Kane rammed his foot against the beast's side, just below the place where the fearsome double-jaw exterior met with its neckless body, the heel of his boot squelching into the fleshy triple gills that he could see opening and closing there. As the creature struggled in place, Kane brought the barrel of his pistol down and unleashed a stream of shots in the creature's face, directing bullet after bullet into the monster's gaping mouth.

Grant's attacker, meanwhile, was hurtling at the powerfully built ex-Mag like a torpedo, its body rushing through the air like some runaway train. Grant kept the Copperhead trained on the creature as he darted left and right to avoid its mind-boggling attacks, blasting 4.85 mm bullets in its direction with every opportunity.

The air-breathing fish pounced across the room like some kind of spring, bounding off the hard surfaces of coral floor and walls as it renewed its attack on the Cerberus warrior. As it rushed at him again, Grant held his ground and snapped off a single shot from the Copperhead before the trigger clicked on empty. Incredibly, the ex-Mag was out of ammunition; he had had no time to reload during the furiously rapid battle.

The fish creature lunged at Grant's torso, even as the gun jammed on empty, and with quick thinking he brought up the solid barrel of the gun like a staff, using its abbreviated length to fend off his attacker.

With a decisive thrust, Grant rammed the Copperhead into the monster's gaping mouth, shoving it in between its jaws at a near-vertical angle. Even as the creature continued at him, Grant jabbed his left elbow into the side of its face, knocking it with incredible force.

The creature reared backward, toppling to the floor as it struggled with the subgun in its mouth.

Grant did not hesitate. He brought up his right arm, tensing his wrist tendons as he did so to bring his hidden Sin Eater into play. Grant's finger was already crooked when the guardless trigger slapped against it, and a spray of bullets spit from the Sin Eater, driving through the air and drilling into the open mouth of the fish creature as it struggled on the floor.

The monster seemed to rock in place as the shots hurtled down its throat and into its gullet, ripping into its innards with gruesome finality. As Grant watched, his pistol's trigger still depressed, the shimmering green scales at the creature's side and back began to burst apart as the relentless bullets drilled through the body of the monster fish.

As his enemy flopped on its side, its body still shaking, Grant took a moment to look across to Kane. His partner was turning and walking away from a messy spray of flesh that covered the floor, all that remained of his own attacker.

Kane peered up and, seeing Grant watching him amid the wreckage of his own foe, he smiled and brushed a finger to his nose.

They had survived.

CLEM JOINED THE TWO ex-Mags over the wreckage of the strange air breathers a couple of minutes after the battle was over, checking warily to ensure that there was no chance of the creatures could renew their attack.

Grant was kneeling before the green-skinned animal he had drilled with bullets, working to free his Copperhead from the beast's now-locked jaws. "Dammit, Fido," he growled, "playtime's over."

With one final yank, Grant pulled the Copperhead free, falling on his butt as he tumbled backward. The weapon was slick with drool, and Grant bit back a curse as he wiped it down with the insides of his coat. The coat could be washed—having the weapon in working order was his more pressing concern just now.

"Well," Clem said as he peered on the floor at the

three carcasses that lay in various states of disintegration, "you gentlemen certainly know how to make your presence felt."

Self-consciously, Kane ran a hand through his dark hair before asking the oceanographer about Brigid.

"Miss Baptiste appears to be sleeping," Clem explained, "much like the stone man there. She's hooked into the library structure now, and I've crossed the two branchial veins as she proposed. By her own suggestion, we're best off not disturbing her."

Kane nodded, accepting the situation even if he did not particularly approve of it. He had been with Brigid on a recent reconnaissance mission in the Louisiana bayou. It was there that they had been introduced to what had been inaccurately described as a "voodoo chair," and was in fact a surviving navigator's seat from the Annunaki mother ship, *Tiamat*. The navigator's seat had some hidden mechanism that had ensnared Brigid when she sat in it, tendrils snaking from its arms to smother her bare flesh. In so doing, the navigator's chair had bonded with the woman, projecting highly detailed, interactive star maps directly to her frontal lobe. However, the flesh-piercing price had been disconcerting and potentially lethal. Facing an enemy who specialized in organic technology, Kane considered, was proving to be rather more involved than their initial clashes with the Annunaki had led them to expect.

"So," Clem asked, gesturing around at the scaly carcasses, "what were these things?"

"Fish," Kane said. "At least, that's what I think they are. You're the expert, Clem. Want to weigh in?"

Clem peered at the creature that Grant had killed, for it seemed the most intact of the gruesome corpses. "There are certainly instances of fish that can exist out of water for extended periods, so-called ambulatory or walking fish. The mudskipper and the African catfish eel can both snap prey from the land, and have shown the ability to live there for limited periods, in much the way of amphibians like frogs and toads. There are even reports of fish that have been seen to climb trees."

Grant looked up as he reloaded his Copperhead subgun, raising a quizzical eyebrow at Clem's words. "Must make fishing trips an experience."

"These things almost seemed to fly through the air," Kane explained. "Is that normal?"

Clem produced his little two-inch blade from his pocket and prodded gently at the lifeless corpse sprawled before him. "Haven't you ever heard of flying fish?" he asked as he scored a line along the edge of the glistening green scales.

Kane watched patiently as Clem poked at the skin of the creature before moving across to the open wreckage of the one Kane had latterly dealt with.

"They're pretty big," Clem pointed out, moving a chunk of bloody gut out of the monstrous corpse with the tip of his blade, "and they show a lot of traits one would more normally associate with mammals. This circulatory system is very unusual. It's almost as though it's been reverse engineered based on a nonaquatic design, like from a jackal or other canine."

"Well, they're dead now," Grant rumbled as he watched Clem work through the goo smeared on the floor. "The question is—can we expect any more of them?"

"No," Clem replied.

"Well, that's a rel—" Kane began, but Clem wasn't finished.

"The question," Clem said, "is what were they

eating down here?" He peered up to look at Grant and Kane. "Simple rule of survival—everything has to eat something."

"What about the spiders?" Kane proposed.

Clem nodded. "Which in turn would be eating…?"

Kane shook his head in exasperation. "Where are you going with all this, Bryant?"

"These things," Clem said, sweeping a hand at the bloody corpse next to him, "have been engineered. They've been created to live down here and protect this library construct. They're not alive. They may have taken on the properties of living creatures, but this is merely technology far in advance of anything we can create."

"So, what," Grant asked, "they're robots?"

"Even a robot needs an oil change," Clem mused. "This is something that's far beyond that."

As Clem spoke, there came a grotesque slurping sound from behind Grant, and all three men turned to see what was causing the commotion. The first creature, the one whose eye Kane had plucked out, seemed to be reconstituting itself before them, its bullet wounds sealing, the lost eyes re-forming like glistening, watery pools.

"What the—?" Kane spit. "We killed that thing."

"Inherent problem with things that aren't alive," Clem pointed out. "They can't be killed."

The Cerberus warriors backed away as the now-standing creature began to scent the air in a renewed search for prey.

Chapter 21

Down, down, down.

It wasn't like accessing knowledge, not in the sense that former archivist Brigid Baptiste understood it, anyway. It was like hearing the voice of something so immeasurably superior to her that it might truly deserve the appellation of god. And not even hearing words, more like being caught in that infinitely superior, omnipotent being's breath as it sighed.

She was swimming in a sigh.

Brigid let the breath, the sigh, wash over her, lapping at the contours of her brain.

There was a wonderful burning sensation at her temporoparietal junction, the part of the brain that processed visual and touch signals, provided for balance and the spatial information generated by the inner ear. The burning was her disconnecting from her body, at least in the sense that she understood it. One thing that temporoparietal junction was responsible for was processing information from a human's proprioceptive sensations, the sense of where one's body ended. Suddenly, as the slow, pleasing warmth filled the back of Brigid's brain, she felt as though she had disconnected from her body, as if she were floating away from it.

She was being asked something, she realized, though the question was unspecific, unclear and hidden within her own mind, like hints of a forgotten dream. She searched for the question, trying to find it, to decipher it, her sense of self seeming to spin, to invert and re-form all about her. It was like translating a foreign language, putting together the musical structure of the words until she could sense the pattern and from the pattern divine the meaning.

Of what do you seek, Brigid Baptiste?

Was that it? Is that the question resonating in my head? Brigid wondered.

She tried listening again, but it was a different kind of listening to anything that she had ever experienced before, more like working a Chinese puzzle box, sliding all the pieces this way and that until the solution was finally revealed, a listening that required logic and understanding more than any act of simple hearing.

The library was speaking to her, she realized, feeling giddy and quite, quite mad.

Her eyes roved the room, optic nerves sucking at the light around her, framing and reframing shapes to create context for her brain. Her vision, her ability to see, seemed to have altered, too, disconnected from the place where she associated her eyes, like a remote feed from a camera. The coral walls of the vast chamber had gone, and so had the floor and the wonderful, terrible room. The sounds of gunfire had also disappeared. In their place, Brigid heard bell chimes with the texture of tumbling waves on a beach, saw a wonderful, subtle miasma of everything. This was the face of the all.

Brigid blinked, using the action to recenter herself, to lift her mess of thoughts back to something coherent. As she did so, the cloudlike form took shape, and she found herself seeing things she thought that she recognized, but it was like seeing sounds or smells—familiar, yet the input felt wrong, contrary.

The Ontic Library was speaking to her, feeding her simple mammalian brain with a cloud of information. Information as an explosion, as a billion facets with no emphasis, no focus. Information that was unsorted, that had never considered sorting as an important part of the process of gathering information.

The structures that underpinned the world, Brigid realized, were laid bare before her, but she was too ignorant to comprehend what it was that she was seeing. With this information, with this knowledge, she might change the world, might rewrite everything in the world.

It was all emotion. Emotion held it all together. The sense that life had to endure because life *should* endure, because it was so deserving.

She spun through the cosmos then, seeing everything, and it felt like swimming or like poetry. The world spun around her, beneath her, turning on its axis as it held its place in the Milky Way like some gigantic gyroscope. And what she saw she didn't see, she felt. It was a new definition of seeing, a thing done with one's core, one's being, perhaps something that was only done with that thing one called the soul.

The world, the universe, was made up of so many more colors than Brigid had ever seen, so many more shapes than she had thought possible. She could look forever, as she walked there among the stars, and never have a name for everything she could see.

There were angles, too, angles that defied Brigid's understanding of mathematics. Angles that were hidden in the straightest of edges, angles that no one had ever perceived. She recalled for an instant the way the teenage girl, Pam, had described her hair as a tesseract. "That's where you hide your memories," she had told

Brigid. Brigid realized now how all those angles could exist, how they were and yet they were not, dual things occupying the same space. The angles were like music, all the notes that made up a song, the song nothing without the notes, the single notes nothing without the song.

Outside this vision, out in the immense room beneath the Pacific Ocean, Brigid's body was shaking with trauma, her physical form shuddering as it tried to absorb the vast input of the vein feed that poured into her brain. The wealth of input, all of it so unstructured, unordered, was like seeing a million faces in a second and trying to perceive every difference and every similarity, a contradiction of requirements so overwhelming it made the task impossible.

It felt like poetry. Knowledge continued to pour into her temporoparietal junction, running along the inside of her scalp like wriggling, burning fingers.

Brigid was struck by a weird sense of déjà vu, as she felt the thing scampering across her scalp. She sensed that she had been here before, done this very thing before. It was strange, and all the more so since Brigid Baptiste had an eidetic memory and the vague sense of déjà vu was, to say the least, very unusual in her because her powers of recollection were so potent.

She pushed the thought aside, blindly reaching into her hair and placing her fingers around one of the creature's limbs. In a second, she had tossed the thing to the floor, and she stamped on it as it struggled to right itself, crushing its body beneath the ball of her foot. Gloop oozed out around her boot as the creature was turned to sludgy pulp. Brigid ignored it, turning back down the corridor and shouting for Kane.

"We need a plan here, and quick," she called.

"I know," Kane growled. He looked around, playing the bright xenon beam across the corridor that they were in until it hit Brigid in the face, and she blinked so hard it was almost like waking up.

The cloud of knowledge inside her—or perhaps about her, she could no longer be sure—came back into focus and Brigid realized her sense of time had become muddled. She had been somewhere that was earlier than now, been in a place when she was just entering the Ontic Library with Kane and the others. The real was all of the rules, she knew then. The real was everything that ever was and ever could be.

Brigid Baptiste had an eidetic memory and an insatiable thirst for knowledge. These things were at the very core of her being. Suddenly, here she was holding all the knowledge of everything ever, and she didn't know what to do first, what part to deconstruct, what thing to pick up and hold and examine.

She had been shown time. How did time work? How could time work? And what was time anyway? A line, a slope, a rushing river?

From this viewpoint, with this information, she could...

Time rushed at her. Just the very action of thinking about it had brought the library's full resources to bear, filling her mind with so much information she could not begin to comprehend any of it. Having all the knowledge in the world created a time machine, Brigid realized, a thing that could be molded and changed. If she could perceive all of time in the same instant, she could pick a spot and examine it, pick a spot and stay there, outside of time's flow or caught up in the time loop, just like the one she had experienced less than a minute before.

Dammit, Brigid realized. Thinking about the time

loop made the Ontic Library show her the time loop; she could effectively trap herself in too much knowledge if she thought about the wrong stuff.

Wicked thoughts, she realized. *Wicked thoughts could kill you now; they could make you something wicked.*

But by that logic, good thoughts could generate goodness, couldn't they?

Almost without really thinking it at all, a face appeared before Brigid's eyes. A girl's face of tenderness and such innocent beauty that Brigid felt her heart break in two. It was Abigail, her niece, her surrogate daughter, her munchkin. Abigail, the girl who didn't exist.

The Ontic Library contained such supreme knowledge that Balam had insisted that its destruction could ultimately threaten reality itself. So, Brigid realized, by the same token could that supreme knowledge not be employed to reshape reality? Could she bring Abigail, her niece from a computer-simulated reality, to life?

Brigid pictured Abi in her mind's eye, a girl of five years old, with messy honey-blond hair that fell past her shoulders, and eyes the same wonderful shade of emerald as Brigid's own. She could smell her, hear her laughter, hear Abi's endless requests for ice cream in her voice that never whined, just sang like a musical instrument given life. Brigid reached for the girl, her arms outstretched to hug her close, to hold her tight.

Temptation lurks.

Those words came unbidden to Brigid's mind then, a raging inferno blasting at the heart of her brain. Perhaps it was her conscience, that one thing that separated man from the beasts, that one trait that seemed to separate humanity from the Annunaki invaders.

The beautiful girl with the honey-blond hair looked

at Brigid with wide, clear eyes in her pale face like emeralds in the snow. Brigid felt the mothering instinct welling within her, the desperate urge to hold the fruit of all that she believed in and fought for, all that she dreamed of.

"Stop!"

Brigid reared back at the sound of her own voice, seeing the girl's body form before her, feeling all those emotions she had felt for the dead thing that was just a computer program tapping into her brain, feeding her what she wanted.

Using this omnipotent knowledge, the vast power of the Ontic Library, for personal gain was wrong. Manipulating time, making unreal things into real things, into sentient things—this was not why she was here. Without focus, it was easy to lose herself in her own thoughts instead of tapping what was being presented to her, easy to become consumed by the lure of temptation.

"Sorry, munchkin," Brigid muttered, and in the real world, where her body sat at the base of the towering octopuslike core, her lips moved, forming the words.

Brigid needed to command this thing inside her head, needed to make sense of it, not let it overwhelm and tempt her. She had once been an archivist, a voice told her, whether her own or the library's she couldn't say.

Archives were storage facilities that kept things ordered, that held records of things that have happened. The Ontic Library had to surely be no different, Brigid realized; it was just an archive on a grander scale. She simply—simply, ha!—had to know what it was she was looking for.

Though Brigid was unaware of it, her lips moved once more, whispering the instructions in the way she had years ago to the mike pickup of her computer back in the Archives Division at Cobaltville. Some things, it seems, some habits, became so ingrained within us that we could never fully shake them.

"Ullikummis," was the first word that Brigid's lips formed, working slowly, like those of a drunk or a stroke victim in speech therapy.

The library did not respond. The breath or sigh or whatever it really was that Brigid felt all over her was still there, a slow, regular breathing, as of someone drifting off to sleep.

"Ullikummis," she said again, the name feeling more familiar in her head now. "The interloper." Was he an interloper? she wondered. Wasn't she the interloper, and Ullikummis the one who was here as a part of his heritage? She had come here to block his access to this incredible knowledge base because his very access was damaging the Ontic Library, but he belonged here far more than she did. The moment in the time loop had shown her how unprepared she was for this sort of archive, and her own brush with temptation just moments ago had confirmed it. She was in well over her depth.

Brigid recalled something then, a conversation she had had years ago, in her earliest days with the Cerberus operation. She had been expressing reservations about having to actually hit people during a self-defense session with Grant. It was something that had seemed so removed from her previous life as an archivist. Her trainer had explained it simply to her as he showed her how to throw a man.

"This is who you are now," Grant had said. "This is the world you've always lived in."

"No, it's not," Brigid had insisted. "You're a Magistrate. You and Kane were trained to do this."

Grant had shaken his head in disappointment. "You

have to learn to assert yourself, Brigid, or the whole world is going to knock you down."

With that, he had insisted that she try again, despite her protestations. "I don't want to throw you," she told him. "You're my friend."

"You won't hurt me," Grant assured her, showing her once again where best to place her hands to throw an opponent twice her weight.

Under Grant's tutelage, Brigid had thrown him to the mats that lined the floor of the training room, 250 pounds of solid muscle launched over her shoulder in defiant proof that she could be the person she needed to be to face this new world.

It was strange to think that archiving required her to assert herself just as much as that throw had. But she began to see now how to get the information that she required from this alien library so that she was not tempted or distracted, so that she could make it bend to her will.

"Show me the entry path," Brigid said, forming the instruction in her mind. "Show me *his* entry path."

With brief acknowledgment, the library acceded to the request.

Chapter 22

One by one, the three mutant fish creatures rose from the ground before the eyes of Kane, Grant and Bryant. They were wounded, messy things now, no longer truly alive—if they ever had been.

The one that Kane had ripped into struggled to stand, gristle and bone sagging from the ruins of its head, colorless ooze spurting from the bullet wounds in its torso. Yet still it endured.

With a long-practiced flinch of his wrist tendons, Kane called the Sin Eater back into his palm, its familiar form unfolding to just under fourteen inches of blaster in his hand. Beside Kane, Grant held his Copperhead—now reloaded—in a two-handed grip, the weapon low to his body as he eyed the stalking fish creatures.

"We killed them once," Grant growled. "This time we'll just make sure of it, right?"

"You remember when we were Magistrates, partner?" Kane asked. "Well, I always did hate dealing with repeat offenders."

As the words left Kane's mouth, the first of the monstrous beasts decided to make its move, and its tail-like back feet slapped against the floor as it began to charge.

"Oh, my," Clem yelped as he saw the things in action for the first time, stunned by their speed.

"Stay behind us, Clem," Kane ordered as he tracked the onrushing creature with the nose of his pistol.

Whatever Clem said in response was lost amid the sounds of fierce gunfire as Kane and Grant peppered the hurtling form of the undersea guardian with bullets, their shots lighting up that corner of the vast chamber amid the gloomy blue-green illuminations.

The hideous monster ran at Kane, its dead eyes glaring at him, pus oozing from both orbs where the creature was now rotting inside. His bullets having little effect, Kane watched in horror as the creature leaped from the floor, powering itself with a flick of huge legs that looked like a split tail. The thing was in the air now, its double jaw opening as it hurtled toward him, swimming through the air with continuous motions of those powerful legs. As the monster barreled at him, Kane reacted with exceptional speed, rolling to his side as the beast clamped its awful jaw around the place where his head had been, that weird keylike arrangement instead snapping closed on empty air.

Kane took that opportunity to reel off another burst from his Sin Eater at just a few feet away from the monster, and he watched in growing frustration as the beast seemingly flipped in on itself and disappeared from view once more. Even dead, these things were relentless and gifted with exceptional speed.

"Dammit, they're—" Kane never finished his sentence. Even as he uttered those words, the second of those awful, undead creatures rushed toward him like a green blur, its heavy back feet slapping loudly against the hardpacked coral floor.

Kane turned at the sound of the beast's approach, saw immediately that it was the monster with the ruined head, the one he had physically ripped apart. If ever a creature was going to bear a grudge against him, this would be the one.

Beside Kane, just eight feet away, Grant was tangling with the third monster. This one had leaped into the air at a dead run, slamming against the nearest wall with its powerful left hind leg and using that momentum to hurtle toward the dark-skinned ex-Mag as he struggled to keep it within the firing arc of his Copperhead. As the monster powered from the wall, it turned itself over so that it came at Grant with those muscular hind legs first, kicking out as it approached like a missile.

Grant tried to sidestep, but one of the attacker's back legs crashed into his shoulder, knocking him so hard to the floor that he rolled backward over himself before he came to a stop. Grant's shoulder scized with sudden pain, and his whole chest heaved as he recovered from the impact—it had been like taking a cannonball to the body.

Still clutching the double grip of the subgun, Grant turned, scrambling across the floor and unleashing a burst of fire at the fish creature as it landed. He watched in increasing irritation as his shots were deflected from the creature's hard, armorlike scales. And then there was no more time to think; the hideous monster was charging him again.

As Kane and Grant wrestled with their relentless foes, Clem worked at one of the handy pouches he wore at his belt, pulling free a tape measure that he carried as a matter of course during diving expeditions. Coated with plastic, the tape measure was a half-inch wide and as floppy as a piece of string, much like the kind of tape measure used by a seamstress.

His hands working with urgent precision, Clem swiftly unraveled the tape measure until its full six feet of length trailed across the floor at his feet. Then, with the urgency born of necessity, Clem took one end of the unraveled tape measure and tied it on itself, creating a loop in its length that operated on a slip knot. As he worked, six bullets drilled across the wall just to the side of him, and Clem stepped away as the coral there erupted into clouds of dust.

"These ricochets will be the death of me," he remarked as he went into battle with the loop in his hands.

THE ANNUNAKI CALLED it the cascade. Like a cardsharp fanning out the deck out in his hand, all the options of knowledge ran before Brigid's senses, whirling in place, waiting to be digested by the library user.

It was a maze, too, a minotaur's habitat, a labyrinth in pitch blackness. Brigid fell, or so it seemed, a trick perhaps played on her inner ear, losing her sense of balance. So much new had been forced upon her that she had lost all sense of direction, and whatever depth perception her eyes once had seemed to be inverted, the close and the faraway intermingling.

Down, down into the gloom.

Brigid looked around her, trying to anchor to something so that she might stop the incessant movement, the crazed unrealness of the real.

She refused to be overwhelmed. Instead, Brigid Baptiste, ex-archivist from Cobaltville, began to regiment everything she saw, to structure it and hold it and lock it in place, a million memory tricks dividing the whirl over and over. Until it started to make sense.

To Brigid, locked within the nonscape of the Ontic Library, it was a gleaming row of bookcases that stretched on forever. The floor was lined with tiles of such rich and intricate mosaic that they seemed to contain every color of the spectrum. The whole incredible room was lit by the rays of the morning sun, giving the scene such purity that it made her just want to dance in place.

She turned, delighting in the solid world that now surrounded her, after so much whirling and madness. Here was something she understood.

She reached for a book, her left hand stretching out to pluck it from the shelf before her eyes. The book was bound in imitation leather, and it was colored the pink of a girl's blush. As Brigid's hand grasped at it, she noticed for the first time the motes of dust that danced within the beam of sunlight lighting the bookcase. Big things and little things—the fundamental nature of the real.

The book felt heavy in her hands, and Brigid flicked through the pages, seeing the solid black type there, in the way of books of yore. Though she didn't read the whole book, from what she skimmed Brigid saw that it was a story about a house with a thousand rooms, each one different and yet utterly interchangeable.

She stopped for a moment, reading the words imprinted on the page: "Namu amida butsu."

She closed the book, its heavy leaves slamming against one another with a sound like clapping hands. A moment before she had been able to read words, and yet now there was just nonsense there. What it meant, perhaps, was that her hold on this interpretation—for that was all that it was, she realized—of the Ontic Library was slipping, that it was losing definition like a radio tuning away from a specified station.

Brigid looked up, seeing the library of books within the sunlight once more, seeing the way the light played against the towering windows, a hundred tiny panes of glass in every one.

Intrigued, Brigid paced to the end of the aisle, one foot in front of the other, heels clip-clopping on the multicolored tiles beneath her feet.

When she reached the end of the third bookcase, each one as long as a city block, she found a tidy row of desks laid out in a familiar line. It was like the Historical Division at Cobaltville, from back when she had been an archivist by trade. Each desk was neat, regimented, its paperwork filed carefully in In trays and Out trays and trays marked Pending. But there was no one around.

Brigid walked the row of desks, looking at the mishmash of stuff that had been placed in the trays, wondering how much information was being stored here, how it could even be possible for a library to hold the foundation keystone on which all reality was constructed. If this library were to break apart, would that really spell the end of the laws of reality? And if so, would a new reality take its place, just as the Mayans had speculated with their Long Count calendar belief? Perhaps each version of reality was superseded by the next, not through cataclysm but through the destruction of its structural rules, as contained in a metaphysical library just like this one.

Strangely, as Brigid walked the seemingly endless line of empty desks, she noticed a vase made from delicate porcelain and shaped in imitation of the stem of a rose, a gracefully curved line. She picked it up, saw the picture of the dog on its surface, and her brow wrinkled in a frown. She knew this vase, it had been something in another life she had led.

The girl Abigail came back to her then, Brigid's niece from the virtual reality trap that never was—the Janus Trap. This vase had been in her apartment and it had been smashed, the visage of the dog split into three.

And in so doing, those three parts had split the dog's face into three, and that had told her something about Cerberus and the world where she had truly belonged. It had been a clue then and it was a clue once more.

"I am controlling this illusion," Brigid whispered in realization. "I am conjuring whatever I require to comprehend it."

Whatever the true nature of the Ontic Library, it generated in the minds of its users in a manner with which they could interface. Suddenly, Brigid began to understand how she had created this place, how its look had been designed to set her at her ease, how the towering bookshelves existed only as props in her own mind, and that anyone else who entered would see it as something else, perhaps even something utterly alien to her.

"I am standing in reality's most malleable interface with the human mind," Brigid realized, "and I have no idea how to get it to do what I want."

She walked farther, leaving the aisle of desks behind and pacing past another mountainous bookcase, walking its colossal length, marveling at its breathtaking majesty. Idly, wary of the power of her thoughts now, she wondered where the design for the library had been drawn from. Was it something within her? Something she had seen in her years working through the archives of the times before the Program of Unification? It was all so bright and joyful, the sun playing across immense windows that dwarfed Brigid's frame.

Her nose wrinkled then as she smelled a waft of something, drifting over from another aisle of the massive library. It was the smell of paper burning.

Brigid trotted down the bookcase aisle, turning at the junction between the towering bookshelves, following her nose, faster and faster. A moment later, she was jogging, looking left and right as she searched for the source of the burning, her heels clattering hollowly against the colorful tiles that lined the floor. The clattering sounds of her own feet urged her to go faster, almost as though the noise was not herself but someone chasing her.

There was a noise then—a voice coming from a little way ahead of Brigid. It was the voice of a child, of that young age where it is difficult to tell if a child was male or female. And the voice said, "I know. I know. I know." Repeated like a mantra, the words came with such regularity that it was almost like the ticking second hand of a clock, a constant sound that was relegated into the background by the very familiarity of its repetition.

Brigid turned a corner, her hand brushing against the wooden bookcase as she passed it. There, sitting before her in a clump of books, was a boy of no more than eight years, with a soup-bowl cut of brown hair, tossing books into the flames of a raging fire. He was reading them before he threw them aside, Brigid noticed, checking their title page and their index, before adding their pages to the billowing black smoke that poured from the inferno he was feeding.

Each time the child discarded a book, he would murmur that phrase once again: "I know."

Brigid had stopped running, and she watched for a moment more as the child threw another of the heavy leather-bound tomes into the flames. Then, striding confidently forward, Brigid addressed the boy.

"What are you...?" Brigid began, but her words ceased in her suddenly dry throat as the child looked up at her.

The boy's eyes were the flowing orange of lava, and

those magma pools seemed almost to rage in accusation as they looked at Brigid.

It was Ullikummis, she realized, shaped in a way that she might understand him, but the stone god all the same.

Remarkably, the boy just looked at her, not saying a word.

"What are you doing, Ullikummis?" Brigid asked, addressing the boy by name.

"Power demands facts," the boy replied, his voice suddenly duotonal, both that of a child and also the familiar bone-shaking rumble of the stone god.

Brigid realized with a start that the duopoly of the child's voice was cognitive dissonance in effect again, that very thing that Clem had spoken about before they had embarked on this quest. Her own knowledge seemed at odds with what she saw, and her brain was trying to meld both things together, to hold both thoughts at once. It was like trying to turn fast enough to see one's own face.

"Facts about what?" Brigid asked, taking another step closer as his latest book tumbled from the child's hands and was engulfed in a whoosh of flames.

"My father hurt me, Enia," the child replied, and Brigid wondered at the name he had called her. "Tricked me and then discarded me, as if I had never been. My attachment to the Annunaki is broken. I have lost the collective memories."

The Annunaki were an ancient and almost immortal race, who were said to hold all of the memories of their ancestors, Brigid recalled. It was this very shared existence that had engendered the stultifying boredom within them that in turn had caused them to come to Earth many millennia ago and begin tinkering in the affairs of the primitive race that they had found there, the childlike race known as humanity.

The boy child was still speaking, his voice two separate things. "I need to learn where Enlil is, what it is he does. I need to know about my father," he said.

Brigid clenched her fists as another book slipped from the child's fingers and fell into the flames, sparking and spitting as the pages curled up and burned away as cinders, sparkling in the air like a cloud of fireflies over swampland. In his actions, Ullikummis was destroying the Ontic Library, without even seeming to notice. How could she stop this, the destruction of all knowledge? How could a human archivist turn a god prince away?

GRANT DUCKED AS THE green-scaled fish creature rushed at him, its jaws clacking as they opened wide in their attempt to consume him. The monstrous fish flipped upon itself once more, just as he lined up another shot from his Copperhead, and Grant's blast went wild as his target literally disappeared.

The broad-shouldered ex-Mag took that moment to refocus himself, bringing his rapid breathing down to a more reasonable level, calming his racing heart. The eerie, undead creature could reappear at any moment, he knew; he just had to wait it out.

Just twenty feet away, the monstrous fish with the shattered head rushed at Kane, leaving wet, pus-filled footprints on the coral floor of the Ontic Library as its many wounds wept across the surface of its hideous frame. Kane took careful aim, struggling to decide what part of the ruined, devastated creature he should shoot to halt its progress. It was relentless, a dead thing come back from the grave to attack again and again and again, an abomination made flesh.

Kane drilled a 9 mm bullet into the gaping wound where the creature's head had been, another into its flipperlike forepaw, and yet still it lumbered onward, picking up speed as its feet splattered against the floor spurting clouds of pus.

From nearby, Kane could hear the sounds of Grant's own blaster cease, as his partner struggled with an undead fish creature of his own.

Just then, from the corner of his eye, Kane saw a chartreuse shimmer in the air, like a falling leaf catching the sunlight, and another monster reappeared, slipping back into his field of vision as it swam relentlessly through the air toward him. Kane was knocked flat on his back, the breath bursting from his lungs as the reappearing creature crashed into his left knee, butting the ex-Magistrate off his feet.

Kane scampered backward as quickly as he could as he saw the other headless monster rushing toward him, its bare feet slapping at the coral floor. Just to his left, the first creature snapped its hideous double jaw, clamping down on empty air as Kane moved swiftly to keep himself out of its path.

The headless one lunged, but as Kane tried to avoid it, it found itself brought up short as one of its muscular hind limbs was pulled away from under it. The fish creature slammed against the hard floor with an almighty crack that reverberated loudly in the vastness of the colossal undersea chamber.

Standing behind the headless monster, Clem pulled back on the length of his homemade lasso as it snagged the creature's hind leg, yanking it backward. "No good going fishing without a line," the oceanographer stated as he reeled in his catch, pulling at the tape measure with a brisk hand-over-hand action.

The creature's short forelimbs pawed at the floor as Clem reeled it in, struggling to stop its backward progress. Clem shoved the heel of his shoe against the slimy, putrescent surface of the thing's writhing back as it flipped and flopped, pressing all his weight there as it tried desperately to escape.

Kane had no time to consider what was happening to his other foe, meanwhile; instead, he turned his attention to the other creature as it charged for him across the six feet that now separated them. With a swiftness that seemed almost inhuman, Kane brought up his Sin Eater and rammed it at the thing's open jaw, smashing the creature with such force that one of its protruding spines snapped in its mouth. Then the beast clamped that incredible jaw around the barrel of Kane's gun, the second pair of jaws shutting around the weapon like a set of double doors.

Heart pounding, Kane held down the pistol's trigger, unleashing a stream of bullets into the deadly creature's mouth. At the end of the barrel of the gun, the fearsome fish shook and rocked as the volley of bullets drilled into its innards.

"Take it and love it," Kane growled at the creature, "'cause it's all you're getting from me."

Nearby, Grant saw a sliver of scales reappear in midair as his own foe emerged from nothingness, darting through the air with a graceless wriggle of its tail-like hind legs. But now the beast was hurtling away from him, heading toward the hub that dominated the room.

"Good riddance," Grant muttered as he watched the

thing scamper away, touching the floor in little bounding leaps as it scuttled from him.

Then something occurred to Grant, and he began sprinting after the creature as it surged away. It could be after Brigid—or even Ullikummis—where they were hooked into the weird organic library. If it managed to somehow disrupt either one of them, there was every chance that Brigid would be hurt or, worse, this whole "real" thing would be damaged.

"Here, Fido," Grant growled as he chased the retreating form of the fish creature. "Grant's got a bone for you. Your own!"

As he spit out his threat, Grant unleashed another deadly volley of gunfire from his Copperhead, spraying the floor at the monster's feet. Miraculously, the green-skinned beast halted, skidding to a stop and leaping from the path of the bullets as they carpeted the coral floor before it.

Grant watched in increasing irritation as the beast turned back to him, piercing him with its swollen-eyed glare.

"Here we go again," Grant muttered as the ugly mutant fish began to charge.

Chapter 23

Inside the mental environment of the Ontic Library, Brigid Baptiste wrestled with her options, trying desperately to come up with a way to eject Ullikummis. Clem had crossed their knowledge streams so that they could interact, but the rest was up to her.

"My mother's still alive," the child said in its young-old voice that sounded like the grating of stone on stone.

Ninlil, Brigid realized, the image brought to her own mind by the Ontic Library within which she was immersed.

And Brigid knew that Ninlil was now Balam's child, Little Quav, hidden but still vulnerable to this monster. Without wishing it, without any conscious will, a book dropped from the shelf beside Brigid, its pages open. She looked down, idly brushing her hair back from her face. There, in bold black lines, was an illustration of a scoop that could reach through the quantum ether, a time-trawling device that might be employed—Brigid felt sick—to snatch the child straight out of her hiding place in Agartha. As if, in thinking of Little Quav, the exceptional library had provided all of the answers.

And if she could call up that knowledge so easily, without even meaning to, what was to stop Ullikummis doing the same? What was to say he had not already done so?

I have to distract him, Brigid realized. *And not just distract him—eject him.*

Even as the thought came into her mind, the library began to offer her distractions heaped upon distractions, opening before her like the petals of a flower.

A hundred thousand diversions raced past her mind's eye, as Brigid struggled to retain the focus of what it was she was doing. Music and speed and bodies and blood, distractions of the flesh and of the spirit and the mind, distractions of simple chat and complex logic puzzles, distractions of sound and light, a flickering box in the corner of a room, people watching it as if they had no will of their own. Brigid saw a lone disk, as bright as the sun, swinging back and forth, captivating her mind before she could turn away.

"Stop!" she cried out, and the image ceased, disappearing from her head. She was returned then to the tableau of the library as she understood it, with its towering shelves and its desks and its pile of burning books, never increasing in size but never diminishing, black smoke charring the ceiling high above.

"So," Brigid said, trying urgently to clear her mind, "you require information on your father…"

SMOKE BEGAN TO POUR from the green-scaled creature's mouth where it was still clamped to the end of Kane's Sin Eater handgun, and the bitter stench of cordite filled the air. Finally, the undead thing let go, its wicked twin jaws opening and its ruined head pulling away, smoke billowing from its gaping maw.

Despite the damage it had taken, the creature was not dead. Kane watched in amazement as it continued to move, in a slumping, rolling gait as if stunned.

Then, incredibly, the fish beast picked up speed and

spun over on itself once more, disappearing from view like a light bulb winking off. It wasn't so clean this time, seeming to flicker in afterimage for a few swishes of its tail before it had finally gone.

A short way across from Kane, Clem was struggling to hold the headless fish creature down, and was being bounced and jostled as the beast flipped beneath his foot. "Any chance of a little help?" he cried as he saw Kane scanning the room for his foe.

Kane held up his free hand in silent reply as he waited for the other mutant fish to reappear. Suddenly Clem was tossed free of the monster he had trapped with his homemade lasso, and Kane watched as the oceanographer toppled backward and cracked his skull against the ground with a loud clap.

"Dammit, Clem," Kane growled to himself, "couldn't you just stick to admiring the shells?"

Kane took to a brisk run as the headless monstrosity struggled to pull off the lasso encircling its leg. As it worked at the tape measure, nosing at it though it no longer had anything resembling a nose, Kane kicked it in the side so that it rolled over, feet in the air.

"One…" Kane snarled, unleashing a burst of fire into the open wound of the beast.

"And two," he continued as the other weird fish creature reappeared a little way across the room.

The headless thing finally keeled over, the energy leaving it at last. Its body had been so punished that it barely resembled anything now, just a mess of gore and body parts, black holes where bullets had sprayed it and the glistening metal ends of several bullets visible among the sickening, bloody debris of its torso and head.

Kane sprinted across the room, chasing after the other genetically modified fish.

GRANT'S SHOTS WERE BLASTING wildly as the fish rushed toward him once more, leaping into the air and flipping over itself to disappear. Grant continued shooting, hoping against hope that he could fell this abomination when it reappeared. Then it was upon him, and there was nothing else he could do but lumber back with the weight of the beast and the impact of its driving body as it slammed into him, seemingly from nowhere.

Retaining his balance, Grant hoisted the hefty creature over his shoulder, slamming it to the floor as its vicious-looking jaws snapped shut.

The Copperhead in his hand blasted three rounds at point-blank range as Grant slammed the weapon against the ugly beast's torso. Its body jerked as it took the bullets, each one piercing its armorlike plating at the same spot.

Blood spurted then from its jaws, bursting forth in a sickening gush of crimson.

"Nobody likes a guest who won't take a hint," Grant growled at it as he saw Kane rushing past, chasing his own quarry. "Now, get your coat and leave."

The fish at Grant's side shuddered, its tail-like legs flapping as it struggled to right itself. Standing over it, Grant blasted another burst of bullets in its face, watching as it rocked under their impact, the stench of cordite heavy in the air now.

Finally the creature spurted out a slimy trail from its side and, despite flinching in staggered, spastic motions, seemed to finally cease its attempts to attack. It wasn't dead, Grant knew, but then—if Clem was right—it had never really been alive. Perhaps the best way to think of it was that now, like a machine, it was out of commission.

Grant took to his heels as he chased after Kane, who raced toward the looming inverted-funnel shape of the hub in pursuit of the last of the fish creatures. Grant peered behind him for a split second, saw Clem lying unconscious beside the bloody corpse of the third fish, but at least nothing new was emerging from the dark access hatches. If there had been more, perhaps these savage things had already killed them, turning on one another in the millennia that they had remained down here unguarded. Or perhaps Ullikummis had killed them, disposing of their corpses before the Cerberus warriors had arrived.

"This has to be the worst fishing trip I've ever been on," Grant growled as he chased after Kane and his quarry.

"Go around," Kane instructed, seeing his partner rushing after him. "Stop it getting to the hub."

Grant didn't need telling twice. With adrenaline pumping through his veins, he urged more speed from his legs, sprinting toward the towering, octopuslike thing that dominated the vast chamber while Kane continued to drill shot after shot in the retreating beast's path. The fish creature reared back at Kane's shots, leaping away as the coral around its feet splintered apart with the relentless impact of each 9 mm slug.

Head down, Grant ran onward, his breath coming harder now as he forced his aching muscles to keep going. The tails of his coat whipped out behind him as he ran at an angle, coming around on the far side of the creature as Kane closed in on it.

Kane ejected an empty clip from his Sin Eater and, as the fish creature watched him warily, brought another from the ammo pouch at his belt and slapped it in place. The whole reloading process took less than three seconds, a practiced move so natural it was nothing more than muscle memory at work now. Years before, both Kane and Grant had found themselves in potentially lethal situations when they had been Magistrates in Cobaltville; there, a Mag's ability to reload quickly could mean the difference between life and death.

Kane raised his pistol, trigger already locked, blasting a stream of steel jackets at the gruesome, blood-smeared thing before him. The bullets cut through the air, driving against the fish creature's natural body armor, many of them flying off at all angles in bursts of light amid the gloom. Still, some were having an effect, finding chinks now in that awful solid skin that the creature wore.

The wounded creature looked nonplussed, rearing away from Kane as bullets dug into its flesh. It turned, feet pounding against the floor as if to run. Once it leaped, Kane knew, it could double on itself and disappear from vision. Somehow he needed to keep the thing grounded.

At that instant, Grant was across from Kane, circling around to trap the monstrous fish, ensuring that it had nowhere else to go. "You about ready to finish this thing?" Grant shouted over the echoing sounds of gunfire.

"More than ready," Kane assured his partner as Grant raised the Copperhead and unleashed its full destructive power at the wounded monster flipping in the air, the bullets driving at the incredible rate of 700 rounds per minute, riddling the air above so that it could not jump.

As bullets lashed at the decaying creature's body

from all sides, Kane and Grant watched emotionlessly as it flopped to the floor, staggered and slumped, sinking on the floor amid chunks of its own flesh.

An instant later, Grant and Kane ceased fire.

The weird creature appeared—finally—to be dead.

Gradually, the Copperhead still held ready in case the creature so much as flinched, Grant made his way around to Kane's side.

"You okay?" Kane asked, his own weapon still poised in his hand.

"Remind me never to piss off any more undead fish," Grant rumbled.

WITHIN THE MIND-BOMB of knowledge that was the Ontic Library, Brigid struggled as she tried to come up with a way to stop Ullikummis from destroying everything, find how to turn him away.

He trusted her, she realized. Whatever it was he saw there, it wasn't Brigid Baptiste. He had called her Enia—a code? A name from his past, perhaps?

Brigid held out her hand to the little boy, smiling benignly as she encouraged him to join her. "This is a big place, little man. You're in the wrong section," she said.

Ullikummis, the strange boy with the volcanic eyes, reached for her hand and grasped it in his. Though his hand looked small, like a child's, it felt like rock, cold and lifeless. Cognitive dissonance, once again, Brigid realized—the act of simultaneously holding two opposing beliefs about a thing.

The boy followed as Brigid led the way away from the fire, letting it burn as it would.

There had been the time loop, and there had been

Abi, and even this library didn't really exist, not in the way that Brigid perceived it right now at least. If she could use the power of the Ontic Library to shape things, then she could use it to make things; new things that never were, things like her niece Abi and the vase with the dog on its side.

She willed it then. Brigid dug deep in her own thoughts as she followed the length of the bookcases, the boy's hand in hers, and she thought about the outside of the library, and how it would look and smell and feel, how the wind would play across its bricks and gutters and vast windowpanes. She walked toward the sunlight that rippled on the windows, and she imagined a thing beyond them, a door into the garden that surrounded the library in her mind, a door into summer.

"Almost there now, little man," Brigid promised as she felt the child tugging away from her. "Just a little farther."

The boy looked up at her hopefully, his inhuman eyes glowing like twin pools of lava.

"Just a little farther," Brigid repeated, a friendly, motherly smile on her lips.

When they reached it, the door was there, just as Brigid had imagined it. A double doorway of glass, French doors leading out onto the paving of a patio.

"Where are we?" Ullikummis the child asked.

"There's the best book out here," Brigid assured him, and she led the way into the garden, where bees buzzed and the scent of orchids lay heavy in the air.

She knew then, just for a second, that he didn't want to go. Ullikummis was resisting her suggestion; he was looking around frantically, wondering at where he was.

For the briefest instant, she saw the library as he

perceived it, a dead rock pyramid spinning in space, the books like ancient tablets of stone. And, for just a second, she saw her hand as he saw it, shimmering scales of crimson flushed with pink.

"All the information is right here," Brigid said, and when Ullikummis turned to where she indicated, he saw the lone book that rested on a picnic blanket laid out on the grass by the roses, the book that Brigid had generated from everything she knew, forcing it to manifest as a physical thing. Had the library helped her to do this, guided her hand somehow, in its need for self-preservation? Was she, in fact, the library's hand in darkness? She couldn't say.

Ullikummis let go of her hand and ran for the book, his short legs skipping through the bright green grass.

Brigid stepped back into the archive building and gently closed the doors, turning the lock once to seal the Annunaki prince outside. And as he opened the book, she saw the look of horror snap across his child's face, and Brigid Baptiste, willing tool of the Ontic Library, knew that she had to turn away.

Chapter 24

And then god woke up.

Kane and Grant still had their guns trained on the twitching corpse that had once been a fish when, from the corner of his eye, Kane saw Ullikummis begin to stir.

Something in Kane's body language altered, and Grant began to ask what it was, but the corpse of the fish creature saw the change, too, and it took its chance to pounce. The muscular tail-like back legs of the green-scaled corpse propelled it into the air—alive once more—even as Kane realized his mistake.

In a fraction of a second, something slammed Kane in the chest with such a solid impact that he was knocked from his feet. As he tumbled, Kane saw the leaping fish creature spring through the space where he had been standing an instant before; Grant had pushed him out of its path with one single, frantic shove.

"Head in the game, partner," Grant reminded Kane as he turned his Copperhead on where the beast had landed.

The corpse opened what was left of its ruined jaw, that ugly, broken hinge flopping out at a wretched angle as it chewed at the air. Grant blasted one, two, three bursts of fire at it, stepping forward with each blast and forcing the wounded creature back.

As he scrambled up from the floor, Kane's steely-gray eyes went back to the stone giant rising from his seat at the hub of the library, pushing the thornlike crown from his ugly, misshapen skull.

"Deal with the fish," Kane instructed his partner as he began to sprint away toward the towering hub that dominated the room's center. "I've got me a god to kill."

Grant spit a curse as he watched Kane retreat, before turning back to the deformed, moving corpse of the mutant fish that prowled on the floor, the broken stubs of its ruined limbs clicking against the hard coral. With its one remaining eye, the creature glared at Grant as he leveled the nose of the Copperhead at it.

"Come on, you ugly son of a bitch," Grant urged. "Let's you and me finish this."

A second later, the creature leaped, its bottom jaw hanging wide as it rocketed toward Grant's chest.

BRIGID WAS STILL STANDING in the palatial library, gazing about her at the wonders on show there. She wanted to read everything, to take the beautiful leather-bound books from the shelves and leaf through each one like a child opening birthday presents, delighting in new wonders. But she knew now that she must not. However the interface worked between the Ontic Library and its users, she had no comprehension of its nature. Perhaps merely by being here, she threatened to destroy it in some fundamental manner that she could not comprehend, just as Ullikummis's fury had poisoned the things he had touched, the data he had accessed.

For a prolonged instant, Brigid gazed longingly around the tall shelves of that impossibly huge room, watching as the motes of dust danced in the sunlight that lashed through the windows, the heat radiating on her skin.

Given enough time, given instruction, Brigid could make this place work for humanity, make this exceptional database alter the course of history, repel the Annunaki alien invaders once and for all.

But then, there was no time. Potentially, her being here would generate a Heisenberg effect, her existence here irrevocably altering the very things she set out to study.

Brigid shook her head sadly as the sun played in her hair.

It was time to go.

SLOWLY, ULLIKUMMIS ROSE from his thronelike position at the side of the symbiotic library hub. He seemed confused, unwieldy, and his movements were staggered and graceless.

At full height, Ullikummis stood eight feet tall, a towering stone creature with hornlike protrusions sweeping out from his shoulders, thick legs that widened at the bottom like a tree's trunk. The single record that did exist of his previous time on Earth, an ancient Hurrian tablet, had described him as a sentient stone pillar, towering up from the underworld to kill the god Teshub. Seeing him stand now, Kane could well believe that this ghastly, hideous rock thing could be mistaken for a pillar of stone.

There was information to digest, the stone god knew, facts that needed full appraisal before they could be employed. He had seen a way to use his abilities to create the thing he would require, a magnificent life camp. The final file had been corrupted; it had forced him from the library even as he absorbed its rogue contents.

Something had gone wrong in the downloading procedure, and Ullikummis realized he had been here for too long.

The crown of wires lay on the floor between his immense stumplike feet, and Ullikummis bowed his head, staring at it as he recovered himself. The passage to and from the Ontic Library was not a sharp, simple thing, not in the way of human technology. No, this was more akin to the acquisition and shaking of a viral infection, like the common cold or influenza. It came upon the user with a strange kind of suddenness that one tried almost to deny until one was surely within its grip. And when one tried to recover from using the Ontic Library, it was like trying to shake a disease, the traces of it still in one's system, gradually diminishing during recovery.

Ullikummis peered up then, hearing the footsteps rushing toward him across the coral floor, and he saw the familiar figure of Kane running at him, the pistol in his hand. He knew Kane from Tenth City, where the Cerberus warrior had tried to kill him. To Ullikummis at that moment, there seemed to be two or three figures, each of them the same man, blurred and shimmering like a mirage.

"Time to finish this, you worthless piece of lizard spit," Kane snarled as he raised the barrel of the Sin Eater and began firing.

ACROSS THE VAST CHAMBER, the dead fish monster leaped at Grant through the open air, and the ex-Mag drilled a stream of shots into its undead body. The shots seemed to have no effect; it was just a war of attrition now, the dead beast unable to feel pain as great gobs of its flesh broke off and speckled the floor and walls in red.

Then the monster was on Grant, and he batted at it with the breech of the assault rifle, knocking it away through the air.

The thing didn't land but just spun about itself, flipping on its tail-like appendages, and then it had disappeared from Grant's sight once more.

"Fuck it," Grant snarled as he saw the creature wink from view, his breath coming hard and fast.

Almost instantaneously, the dead creature reappeared, swimming through the air and slamming into Grant's left bicep so hard that he was shunted sideways across the hard floor. For a moment, Grant found himself struggling to stay upright, and what remained of the horrible creature's double jaw clamped on his left shoulder as he toppled.

Without conscious thought, Grant swung the Copperhead one-handed—one of the advantages of its bullpup design—and dug the end of its barrel into the side of the creature's head where its eye socket peered with horrific emptiness. Then Grant pulled the trigger, driving a handful of steel-jacketed bullets into its skull.

Grant felt the beast shake beneath the impact of the bullets as it struggled to stay clamped to his arm. Then suddenly the monstrous fish had let go, and Grant watched as it sailed across the room, his bullets chasing it as the eye socket smoldered with gun smoke. Grant felt the trigger click on empty as the creature shook beneath the impact of his bullets.

Eerily voiceless, the creature recovered, its blood-drenched feet pawing at the rough floor as it prepared to charge for Grant. His head down, eyes fixed on the fishlike abomination, Grant let the empty Copperhead drop from his hands as he stalked toward it.

The monster began to charge and, twenty feet away, Grant did, too, a mirror image to the hideous creature he faced. Head low, shoulders pumping, Grant ran at the beast, the hard-impact soles of his booted feet slamming against the coral with such intensity that chunks went flying and sharp protrusions were pounded into dust. A blue light winked off beneath Grant's tread as he rushed past.

His attacker's wounded feet slapped wetly against the coral floor, the two hind limbs driving it like a racehorse while the shorter forepaws struck the floor to pull it onward, affirming its direction. Then it leaped, and Grant leaped, too, his right fist pumping through the air toward the bloody wreckage that had once been the thing's face.

As the monster's jaws opened wide in readiness for its prey, Grant punched it across its lower jaw, hitting the thing with such force that its head snapped back and it began to flip on itself in midair.

As Grant landed, his knees folding in a recovery crouch, he called the Sin Eater to his hand from the recess of its wrist holster, unleashing a stream of high-caliber death at the monster as it flopped to the ground. A dozen rounds blasted through its ruined skull from a distance of less than three feet, rendering it nothing more than a bloody pulp atop the neckless torso. Still it sagged, struggling to find and kill its objective, the bloody remnants of its head swaying like some nightmare pendulum carved of flesh.

Grant pushed himself up off the floor, stalking toward the creature as its misshapen lump of head swayed back and forth. Then, with a savage boot, Grant punted the creature's spoiled head from its torso, the toe of his boot ripping the last remaining vestiges of muscle away with finality.

The beast finally slumped to the floor, gunk pouring from the ruined gap where its head had once been, the viscous liquid oozing into the gaps in the coral and draining from sight. Grant ignored it, turning his attention to the far side of the central hub where Kane continued to battle with the stone god Ullikummis.

BULLETS RATTLED AGAINST the rock plates of Ullikummis's chest with the noise of some hideous drum solo. Sparks flew up from the stone, bursting before the Annunaki prince's vision. His eyes and his mind were beginning to recover now, taking in the world around him once more.

Fifteen feet away, the human he had met with in Saskatchewan was blasting at him with a hand pistol, in the race's indelicate way of waging battle. Ullikummis's burning eyes smoldered, pools of magma in his craggy face, focusing on this pathetic human. When they had met before, the human—Kane—had used some manner of explosive to force Ullikummis back, cause him to topple toward an open furnace. But Ullikummis had abilities that the human did not suspect. The genetic engineer, Lord Ningishzidda of the Annunaki, had bonded the exceptional mind powers of the child to a telekinesis program, allowing him control over rock. To some it had seemed magic.

Kane continued to blast shots at his towering stone foe, the Sin Eater kicking in his hands as he steadied it with a two-handed grip. The last time they had fought, Ullikummis had been covered in flames, and the fire had licked across his rock shell with willful glee, as if it could kill a thing made of stone. His city—the City of Ten—had been destroyed, however, and there had been nothing left but rubble, all thanks to Kane and his team.

As the bullets batted harmlessly against his rock skin, Ullikummis strode forward, his great tree-trunk legs crashing determinedly against the floor as the sounds of gunfire filled the air.

Kane watched in growing irritation as his bullets had no effect on the stone thing that towered before him. Last time he had used explosives to fell Ullikummis, but he could not do that here for fear of damaging this precious archive of facts. The stone god raised one of his jagged hands, the fingers like escarpments carved by the sea, and the bullets rattled ineffectively against the palm of his hand.

Kane had forgotten how quick Ullikummis was. In an instant, the stone monster closed the gap between himself and the ex-Mag, moving ten feet in the blink of an eye. His stone hand powered forward, batting Kane's Sin Eater aside as bullets continued to rattle against it.

"Submit," the stone god instructed, his fierce eyes glowing with the red liquid flames of magma.

"Never," Kane spit back, ducking as the stone god swept a mighty arm at his head.

Kane was trained in many different arts of combat, his body geared to endless adaptation in the heat of battle. Even a stone god, he reasoned, was subject to the laws of gravity. Even here, twelve miles beneath the surface of the ocean, a stone god would fall if pushed.

Kane's outstretched leg swept out, knocking against Ullikummis's monstrous shin in a blow that felt for all the world like kicking the trunk of a solid oak tree.

And then—remarkably—the stone god fell. Ullikummis was still disoriented from his trip through the Ontic Library and his sudden ejection. What advantage that gave Kane, no one could truly say, but for one incredible instant, the combat prowess of one man proved enough to topple an ancient god.

The sound that Ullikummis's heavy body made as it crashed to the floor of the Ontic Library was like a mighty redwood being felled in a forest. The whole undersea base itself seemed to shake, and the strange, living blue-and-green lights flickered and dimmed for several seconds, winking on and off as if in sympathy to the felled giant.

Kane looked across to where his foe had fallen, feeling the reverberations of that savage blow run through his leg, stinging the muscles at his groin.

Grant was rushing over then, his own Sin Eater held ready, skipping lightly on the balls of his feet as he kept Ullikummis's fallen form in his sights. "Everything okay?" Grant asked, not really knowing what else he could say.

Kane began to reply, struggling to lift himself to his feet. Suddenly Ullikummis moved, one of those mighty arms lashing out with incredible swiftness. The stone arm met with Kane's side as he stood, slapping the ex-Mag back down with an almighty blow. Kane unleashed a pained growl as he was tossed across the bumpy, uneven floor.

When he looked up again, Kane saw that Ullikummis was standing, his impressive stone form looming majestically over his partner. Grant pointed his Sin Eater at the godlike creature, but Kane could see the hesitation there—Grant didn't believe his blaster could have any effect on this incredible figure. He was most probably right, Kane realized. They had been foolish to challenge the stone god, needed far superior weaponry and planning to take on such an exceptional specimen of power. And meantime, Brigid Baptiste was wired into this ghastly library, her whole body at risk from a stray shot, her mind caught in its grip.

Reluctantly, Kane issued the order as he struggled up from the floor. "Let him go," he said. "We can only lose here."

Slowly, the irritation clear on his puckered brow, Grant lowered his pistol. Ullikummis continued to watch him, with all the calm fascination of a man watching an animal in a cage at the zoo, knowing that animal could never break through the bars to reach him.

Then, without a word, the stone god turned, and his fiery eyes looked at Kane as if to assess him.

"Go," Kane said, "before I change my mind."

Ullikummis looked at the human whom he dwarfed, and his stony expression showed no change. Yet, for just a moment, Kane sensed something in those flaming eyes of lava—and it looked like pity. For all his talk, for all his bravado and his determination to put his people before the destruction of this false god, Kane knew in that moment that it was nothing more than evasion. He was no more important to this magnificent, towering being than an insect was to a man.

As that thought began to sink in, Kane watched Ullikummis stride from the chamber, his huge, lumbering form stalking toward the sole exit of the undersea structure. Kane listened for an awful moment as the stone behemoth's heavy steps echoed down the corridor of spiders, like the sounds of heavy construction. And then the stone Annunaki prince was gone.

It didn't matter. Maybe they had lost; Kane wasn't

sure. Only Brigid Baptiste could tell them if their plan had been successful.

"Baptiste," Kane whispered, making his way past Grant and over to where Brigid was still sitting, wired into the Ontic hub, "you had damn well better be all right."

Chapter 25

Disengage.

Suddenly, with a snap like fire on the skin, Brigid found herself ejected from the Ontic Library, thrown from the vastness of its infallible knowledge base, with all the force of a cork firing from a champagne bottle.

Around her, strands of knowledge, buds and growths of new ideas and theorems raced past, hurtling at a million miles a picosecond, buzzing past her ears and her eyes and her nostrils, the smell of facts so strong she could taste them at the back of her throat.

Brigid thought she might be sick. Worse, her heart was pounding so hard in her chest that she thought it might explode. It felt like a hammer pounding against a wall, threatening to burst through in a blast of ruined flesh and bone.

Her head, by contrast, sang. It sang with a hundred thousand ideas; it sang with all the possibilities of the things she had seen, the briefest of things that she had learned here in the Ontic Library. For an archivist to immerse herself in a pool of ultimate knowledge was an incredible thing, and a part of Brigid never wanted to leave.

Tell me more, she heard herself yearn. *Show me more.*

But no. Just as the presence of Ullikummis had threatened to destabilize this exceptional library and, in turn, the whole of the real, so, too, Brigid realized, could her presence here. It had seemed, in the idealized and dreamlike way in which she had witnessed it, that Ullikummis had caused the library to decay by his rapid movement through knowledge. In discarding a fact, an idea, he threatened to destroy it. Was this, then, the flaw in the library? Was it possible that the Ontic Library had been set up never to be accessed, that the knowledge of the gods was a dangerous thing? Every religious text in the history of man held that very warning, did it not?

Or perhaps it was an attitudinal factor. That Ullikummis had come here seeking a specific branch of knowledge, and had sought it for a specific and malicious usage—might that have caused the library itself to rebel? Had her ejecting his presence been Brigid fulfilling the work of the library where all of its other defenses had failed? Could it be, in fact, that the library had been waiting for a protector in the form of an archivist, someone who comprehended things in the long-forgotten terms of shelf reference and cataloging classes? Had she been the library's strong right arm?

Brigid's thoughts were so hurried they seemed almost beyond her own ability to interpret. Whatever it was that the library had done, it had engendered in her a thought process like hyperspeed.

Hyperthought.

Brigid clung to that as she sent the disengage signal to the library and felt it eject her through the different classifications and subclassifications that housed all knowledge to the rules that underpinned the universe. For a brief second she wondered if she might turn back, might look for some way to defeat the Annunaki and eject them from her world.

To turn back would be a simple thing, the matter

of less than a second, Brigid told herself. To look for something that might help the Cerberus exiles win in their terrible war against superior beings would surely be reason enough to stay, to risk the destruction of the real by her own hand, her own interference.

To save Kane and Grant and Lakesh and countless others, all she need do was to swim against the tide, turn and create a path back into the rushing whirl of all knowledge.

And then I could save Abigail, too.

The thought struck Brigid like a slap. She was contemplating threatening all of reality simply in the hope she might be able to find a shortcut, a cheat, to destroying their foes and getting what she wanted. Even as she came to that conclusion, the redness in her vision turned to solid black once more, the background effect of the bleed fading away, and she sat upon the protruding arm of the towering, octopuslike hub in the center of the undersea complex, tasting the air around her like a newborn taking its first breath.

Immediately, Brigid began coughing, the constriction of her lungs making her want to weep in pain. She doubled over, dragging at the air with such loud breaths that she sounded like a wounded animal caught in a trap.

"Baptiste?" the voice came from nearby, but Brigid was doubled over and in such pain that she didn't look up to see who it was. She knew; of course she knew. It was Kane. Always Kane. Her *anam chara,* ever at her side when she needed his protection and his support, just as she was ever at his.

Brigid's whole body shook as she struggled for another breath, breathing in through her mouth to get as much air as she could into lungs that burned like fire.

It felt as if there was blood at the back of her head, and something sharp was jabbing against her forehead like the thorns of a rose. She reached forward blindly, her hand finding the thing that had attached itself to her head, ripping it away in a moment of mindless agony, tossing it aside. Vaguely she heard the thorn crown land upon the hard floor, sounding like an insect's feet as it skittered across the coral.

"Baptiste?" Kane asked again, and she saw his shadow at her feet as she sat there, her head on her knees. "Are you going to say something or aren't you?"

Slowly, the weight of movement feeling strange and faintly unreal, Brigid looked up and saw Kane standing over her, his face etched with concern.

"Temptation lurks," Brigid whispered, her voice hoarse.

Irrationally, Kane smiled at her, looking almost as though he was holding back laughter. "I'll take your word for it," he said as he reached for something behind her. "You stay still, I'll get you disentangled from this nightmare machine in a moment."

Brigid watched Kane as he fiddled with the stuff that had connected to her, pulling at threadlike creepers and spiny protrusions, all of which had submerged themselves beneath her skin. It was like removing a splinter, only it was a thousand splinters, and each one was magnified a thousand times. Brigid ignored it, concentrating on the things she had seen within the complex of the Ontic Library, trying desperately to cling to the richness of knowledge she had seen there.

To process everything required hyperthought. It was all so tangled, so clear yet obtuse, separate and interlinked all at once. And her ability to perform hyperthought was leaving her—had left her. Now she was only Brigid Baptiste, an ex-archivist from Cobaltville with the remarkable talent of a photographic memory, but with nothing left to remember, a camera trying to take pictures of the dark.

And so, Brigid Baptiste—the ex-archivist from Cobaltville with the remarkable talent of a photographic memory—forgot.

As Kane pulled away the last of the tangled threads that had reached into her, Brigid looked up at him with those beautiful green eyes and said, "I'm so sorry."

"For what?" Kane began, but the reason for Brigid's apology became clear before he had finished the query.

Having lost all the mental knowledge she had gained from her involvement with the Ontic Library, her whole system rebelled, and she vomited over Kane's boots where he stood in front of her, purging her body as the library had her mind. With infinite care, Kane reached for the dangling strands of Brigid's sunset hair and pulled them away from her face. And then he held her while she disgorged everything she had eaten for the past twenty-four hours until only saliva and stomach acid remained, dribbling from her mouth in a bitter-tasting stream.

When he was certain that she had finally finished, Kane placed a comforting arm around her shaking form, and laughed. "Boy, Baptiste, when you lose it you really lose it."

"Thank you, I think," Brigid replied.

"Reckon it's about time we got you home?" Kane asked his companion.

Brigid looked around her, feeling washed out and

slightly unreal. "Where is Ullikummis?" she asked, struggling to stand.

"He's gone," Kane said. "You did it. He left the library."

"And you didn't…" Brigid began, the implication clear.

"I tried," Kane told her. "But then something came up and I had to prioritize one thing over another."

Brigid frowned as she tried to work out what Kane meant, why he, the most relentless man she had ever met, would ever allow an enemy to escape when he had him dead to rights. Then sudden realization dawned. "You mean me, don't you?"

Kane smiled enigmatically in response. "You have to ask?"

"No," Brigid agreed. "I guess I don't."

ULLIKUMMIS MADE HIS way out through the tunnel, uninterested in the wants and the needs of the few humans he had seen in the body of the Ontic Library. The humans were more like vermin than ever, spreading across the globe like a virus, infecting every inch with their prattling and their meaningless excuses for anger.

He had recognized the one who had pushed him in the furnace, and he had seen the other, the one with dark skin—the man-bull—on more than one occasion. Ullikummis's memory was long; he would not forget such foes.

The Ontic Library itself had rejected him after five days immersed in its glorious data flow. He had all that he needed now, the rest did not matter. It had been sheer tenacity that had caused him to seek additional data on his father, drawn in by the seductive, velvety nature of hyperthought.

The construction would come first, the camp where he could reeducate humankind, remind them of who their masters were. His father and the other overlords had been pathetic in their second reign on Earth, he had learned, establishing nothing but their own ability to squabble among themselves. When he left Tenth City, Ullikummis had created one dozen followers, each of them strong and loyal, each one gifted with the stone of his own body. Even now, those loyal followers were out there, recruiting others, new blood for his devotion, to do with as he willed.

Utopia was coming, and all it would take would be the utter reeducation of humankind. His father had been a fool.

WHILE GRANT TENDED TO Clem's wounds, Kane helped Brigid stand and walk.

"I feel dizzy," Brigid said, her voice lacking its usual strength.

Kane looked at her, that roguish grin playing across his lips. "Maybe the world just sped up," he told her.

"Must be it," Brigid agreed, leaning against him.

Apart from nursing a headache, Clem proved to be otherwise okay. "That fish packed quite a punch," he observed, feeling foolish. "You wouldn't want to meet him on a dark beach," he added, looking around nervously.

"We pretty much eviscerated them, Clem," Grant assured the oceanographer as he helped him to his feet. "Though, based on previous experience, might be wise to get ourselves the hell out of Dodge before they re-constitute themselves all over again."

Clem nodded, wincing as the pain reignited in his skull. He saw Kane helping Brigid walk, and she looked like a woman who had just given birth, weak and stumbling, having given everything she could, no strength left in her muscles. Then he noticed the empty place where Ullikummis had been perched at the edge of the towering, alien hub.

"Where's Ullikummis?" he asked.

"He woke up," Grant said. "The rest—that's a story for the ride home."

Clem smiled, gazing about the magnificent undersea chamber one last time. "You know, friends," he said, encompassing Kane and Brigid as they neared, "we should consider ourselves very much honored to have been here, in this amazing facility. It's doubtlessly the chance in, well, 'a lifetime' doesn't cover it. The chance in generations, perhaps?"

"It's a big bad world out there, Bryant," Kane told him, "and you'll get plenty of chances to see the craziest of crazy. But let's do that another day, okay?"

Clem nodded slowly in agreement, his head pounding once more. Kane was right; one exceptional, once-in-countless-generations opportunity like this was more than enough for one day.

Chapter 26

A different ocean. A different day.

Ullikummis stood at the deserted shore, staring out across the swirling blue of the Atlantic as night fell. He had paced across the land for three days since leaving the Ontic Library, the knowledge of what he had to do next clear in his calculating mind.

Out there, as seagulls cawed their ugly cries and dipped at the ocean's waves, there was nothing but sea. A nothingness so absolute that it reminded the Annunaki prince of the bleak solitude that he had called home for four and a half thousand years as he had spiraled through the outermost reaches of the galaxy. He needed no one, craved for no affection, no company. Even now, his loyal followers were dedicating themselves to his cause, and recruiting more and more to do his will when the time came.

Thus, it was time to begin the second phase. When an individual, be he man or god, raised an army he had to have somewhere to teach it, to train it in the ways of combat and to instruct it in the nature of the new reality it was destined to create.

Beneath the starry night sky, Ullikummis raised his thick right arm, the scars in the rock there where he had once lost the limb only to have it regrow thanks to the work of the Annunaki genesplicers. He was the master of the rock, and his will would be done. His lava eyes burned fiercely, twin coals amid the gloom, as he set to concentrating on his task.

There, beneath the waves, lay silt and rocks, masses of debris that made up the bed of the ocean. He felt them in his mind, as a normal man might feel a cool breeze against his skin, felt them rumble as he touched them with his thoughts.

One by one, the rocks began to hurry to the surface, bubbling through the waves in a rush of water. The first popped out of the ocean with such speed that it almost clipped a seagull's white wing, the bird cawing in anger as the stone brushed its feathers before plummeting back to rest upon the surface of the sea. One by one, the rocks came, one by one then two by two. And then it was a cascade, a reversed waterfall, except where there should be water there was only stone, and where it should be falling it rose.

Whatever it was that passed for a smile on Ullikummis's ugly, misshapen stone-clad face appeared then, just for an instant, jagged and lopsided like his abused body.

Out in the ocean, the island was beginning to form. The island of Bensalem, the training camp that would be his home.

SOMEWHERE IN THE OLD province of Mandeville, Dylan, the first priest of the new order, stood before his congregation in what had once been a massive sports venue. The football field had been bombed out and never rebuilt, but its basic oval shape remained, with towering struts marking it out where even the nuclear ravages of two hundred years before had not quite been enough to utterly destroy it. Like so much in this brave new world, once you got outside of the protective walls of the villes themselves, all you found were skeletal monuments to a past long ago forgotten.

Before Dylan, standing in what had once been the sports field itself, almost seven hundred people waited in patient silence. Some had been blessed with full ascension into the new order, while some merely craved to join, seeking something to save them now that the villes had fallen.

"People," Dylan greeted them, his voice amplified by a jury-rigged PA system that was running off a chemical battery. As he spoke, the lights around the vast, open-air auditorium sparked to life, illuminating the field and the people within it. "You are the new utopia. You are the future of the world. Ullikummis will save us all, if we but let him into our hearts."

As one, the crowd repeated the name: "Ullikummis, Ullikummis, Ullikummis."

Chanting it with one voice.

"If it ain't Ullikummis," Dylan announced, making up the speech as best he could, "I won't be buying it. He's our future. Not some clown baron—yes, clown— who never took the time to care about us, to look at how we live and what we need. To try to understand how we talk, how we act. Ullikummis is our future, as he has always been our future. He came from the heavens to bring heaven to Earth, and all you need to do is agree to let that happen."

Dylan took a breath, surveying the congregation before him. He had never played to such an audience— hell, a simple sodbuster from Canada, Dylan had never seen so many people in one place. "Do you agree to let heaven rule on Earth?" Dylan shouted, his voice doubling over the PA speakers.

"Ullikummis, Ullikummis, Ullikummis," the crowd replied.

"Show us heaven, god," Dylan shouted, caught up in the fervor of the crowd. "We are ready."

"Ullikummis, Ullikummis, Ullikummis," the crowed replied once more.

Everyone that was, except for one lone woman, with long dark hair, olive skin and brown, flashing eyes. She stood among the crowd, working at a cut she had made on her inner forearm, using a needle from her sewing kit to prize free the lump there. The obedience stone had budded again, Rosalia knew, another one flourishing in her system, trying to dull her mind.

This one was free now, but there would be more yet until she removed every last insidious one. Beside her, her pale-eyed dog barked as he chased his tail, caught up in the excitement of the chanting crowd.

"Ullikummis, Ullikummis, Ullikummis," they cried in time with the priest who stood beneath the spotlights, struggling to turn his words into something that crowds would listen to.

Later, she told herself, when the moment was ripe, she could stop this pretense and get away from these blathering madmen. That was if the multiplying stone beneath her skin didn't get her first. But for now at least, she had to fit in with these simpleminded fools as they spoke of utopias and heavens and saviors, as they chanted the name of their idol and dragged her along on their crusade.

Amid seven hundred others, Rosalia raised her fist in the air, the thin line of her cut all but invisible. Let them think she was one of them. "Ullikummis, Ullikummis, Ullikummis," she shouted in time with the crowd.

AT THE CERBERUS REDOUBT, high in the Bitterroot mountain range in Montana, Brigid Baptiste was just getting out of recovery, having spent three days under observation following her mental ordeal at the hands of the sentient library. It had not meant to hurt her, she knew; it had merely overwhelmed her, like a kid who played too rough. Shortly after they had left the ocean bed, Brigid had fallen into a deep, trancelike sleep and it was only now that she was able to keep her eyes open for more than twenty minutes at a time.

"She isn't really tired," Kane said jokingly. "She's just missing my scintillating company. Can't stay awake without it." But he was worried, probably more so than anyone else.

Eventually, when Brigid was up and about, she went to locate Kane, finding him at his usual evening haunt outside the rollback doors of the redoubt, gazing out across the plateau at the darkening sky overhead. The Cerberus facility was at the top of a mountain, and its location afforded some breathtaking views when the skies were clear. This night, however, a few heavy clouds marred that view, doing little to disguise the threat of rain in their intentions.

"Kane?" Brigid said, knowing better than to sneak up on the ex-Mag.

Kane turned, visibly admiring his trusted partner for a few seconds. She was dressed in one of the standard-issue jumpsuits, a white one-piece with a blue zipper running a vertical line up its center. Though the tight-fitting suit did much to accentuate the curves of Brigid's athletic frame, she looked disheveled to Kane's knowing eye, her hair a wild mess pulled hastily back in a ponytail.

"How are you?" Kane asked, the concern clear in his voice.

Brigid thought for a moment before finally answering her colleague's question. "Forgetful," she said.

Kane held up his empty hand with the palm flat, and rocked it as though it were a teeter-totter. "Good thing—bad thing?" he asked.

"He who fights monsters must take care lest he become a monster," Brigid said with good humor. "I gazed too long into the library and found that the library gazed back into me."

When she saw Kane's bemused expression, Brigid added, "Nietzsche, by way of Baptiste."

Kane smiled. "'By way of Baptiste' is always my favorite way," he assured her, pulling the red-haired woman to him and holding her close for a moment. "I'm glad you're okay. That stone monster is a whole heap of trouble. I think we're in for some dark times ahead."

Brigid reached her arm around Kane's, pulling herself closer to him. "It's never that dark," she assured Kane. "Not if you know where to look."

In silence, Kane nodded his agreement, pulling Brigid closer still as the night winds played across the plateau. For now, at least, the dark times could wait.

* * * * *

JAMES AXLER

DEATH LANDS®

JAMES AXLER

DEATH LANDS

Downrigger Drift

A new breed of hero walks tomorrow's hellish frontier...

Downrigger Drift

A new breed of hero walks tomorrow's hellish frontier...

In the nuke-altered region of the Great Lakes, Ryan and his group face the spectrum—from the idyllic to the horrific—of a world reborn. Against the battered shoreline of Lake Michigan, an encounter with an old friend leads to a battle to save Milwaukee from a force of deadly mutant interlopers—and to liberate one of their own.

Available January 2011 wherever books are sold.

TAKE 'EM FREE

2 action-packed novels plus a mystery bonus

NO RISK
NO OBLIGATION TO BUY

GE10

AleX Archer
RESTLESS SOUL

The relics of the dead are irresistible to the living…

A vacation spot picked at random, Thailand ought to provide relaxation time for globe-trotting archaeologist Annja Creed. Yet the irresistible pull of the country's legendary Spirit Cave lures Annja and her companions deep within a network of underground chambers— nearly to their deaths.

Available January 2011 wherever books are sold.

www.readgoldeagle.blogspot.com

GRA28